MURDERS LIKE PYRAMIDS

BY

GILLIAN OGILVIE

Published by Anvil Authors (UK)
LA14 3AT

ISBN 978-1-291-58032-7

Also by Gillian Ogilvie
Murders like Buses
Lost in France
Broken Wings
Living without Lucy
Dragonfly Crossroads

Cover
Artwork by Gillian Ogilvie
Graphics by Graham Troth

Another one for Felicity FF with my love

To Lynn

with very best wishes

Gillian Epdne

WALNEY
25: XLS 13

Wednesday

Footsteps approaching. Mike's stomach muscles clenched against remembered pain when he heard the sound.

He winced as the metal door scraped open against the rough concrete flooring. The harsh sound emphasised his personal acquaintance with that floor – the floor on which he lay.

The voice he hated and feared greeted him cheerfully.

'Good morning, Michael. So glad to see you're back with us again.'

Through slitted eyes he could barely open Mike made out a shape against the dim light. He tried to speak through his cut and swollen lips but his tongue was as hard and dry as a piece of wood, unwieldy in his mouth. Unrecognisable sounds came out. He couldn't articulate. He had swallowed nothing but his own blood for . . . how long?

'What's that you say, old chap? Top of the morning to me?'

Then came the manic giggle that shrivelled all Mike's courage.

'Perhaps not,' the hated voice went on. 'Let me see what else could it be? I have it. You want to know what day it is. It is Wednesday, Michael. Wednesday. The day you are going to die.'

Thursday Ridminster

'What are yer doin'? said Lenny. He was squashed into the front seat of the van between the two of them. He knew them both by sight but why would they want him to go with them . . . anywhere?

'Just taking you for a little ride, Lenny,' sniggered the bloke on his left. 'That's good innit, Jake?' he went on. 'A little ride. Just like in the flicks.'

'Shut up,' said Jake, the driver. 'You talk too much. Always did.'

Not bothered, the other went on, laughing senselessly, 'Well, our guest,' he emphasised the word, 'asked me a question. It would be rude not to answer now, wouldn't it?'

Jake grunted and kept his eyes on the road.

Lenny could see they were heading out of Ridminster, not to the new by-pass but onto the seldom-used old road. He frowned. If they kept on this way they would eventually be out in the country and then could link up with the Bristol road. But why? He tried again. 'I've seen you blokes around, haven't I? By the bookie's?'

At this the driver glanced at him. 'That's your problem, mate. You've seen altogether too much round the bookie's.'

Lenny swallowed the lump that had suddenly appeared in his throat. He thought of the packet that had slipped out of his hands, slipped out of his hands and into a deep puddle, disintegrating the envelope and revealing its contents. 'I never touched, nothing,' he said. 'S'welp me, I never.'

Jake, the driver, shrugged. 'Don't worry me, one way or t'other, mate. Not my problem.'

'But it sure is yours,' sniggered the other one.

No one spoke while the van left buildings and people behind. It was teatime. Kids would be coming home from school. Mothers, finished the shopping, waiting for them. Lenny thought of his old Ma. If she was still here she'd be getting him a nice bit of steak and chips. It was a quiet time of day and the road was empty. They'd seen no other traffic for at least a mile. Ahead there was a long straight stretch. The van stopped.

'What you got in your pockets then, Lenny?' said Jake.

Lenny frowned. 'Nothin', nothin' at all,' he said.

The driver sighed. 'Come on. Empty them.'

Lenny wanted to say no. But with a grinning idiot on one side of him and the hard eyes of the driver drilling into him from the other, the small amount of courage he possessed deserted him. What did they want? 'I'm not worth robbin',' he whined.

'Shut up and empty your pockets,' said Jake.

As Lenny obeyed, the other bloke snatched the items one by one, giving a running commentary while he examined them. Lenny couldn't take his eyes off the gold ring in the bloke's ear. What kind of a fella wore gold earrings?

'One handkerchief,' said Gold Earring. 'You can have that back then. One lighter,' he flicked it experimentally with his thumb, 'in working order,' he grinned and pocketed it. 'One packet of fags with . . . three left.' Those went the way of the lighter.

Lenny didn't protest. It was two against one after all.

'One used cinema ticket,' the voice went on. Lenny was beginning to hate the sound of it, taunting, gloating. 'Like going to the pictures do we, Lenny? Two betting slips. Come on, Lenny. Dig deep.' As he spoke, Gold Earring shoved his hands into Lenny's pockets, turning him roughly to reach both outside pockets of Lenny's jacket, the one on the inside and his nearest trouser pocket. 'You do his trousers your side, Jake,' he said. 'Make it good.'

When all pockets had been turned inside out and were truly empty, Gold Earring pawed the contents. The loose change amounted to just four pounds and thirty five pence. Jake leaned over and took the four pounds. Gold Earring gave Lenny back the pennies, together with two used tissues and the handkerchief. 'Now out you hop,' he said.

'You what?' said Lenny.

'Time for a little exercise,' said Gold Earring.

Lenny looked across at Jake but the driver was watching up and down the road. 'Get on with it,' he said.

Gold Earring jumped down from the van and pulled Lenny with him. 'End of the road for you, chum,' he said.

Lenny felt his knees give way with fear. But the other bloke grinned at him and pointed back down the road. 'Home's in that direction, boy,' he said. 'It's only a few miles. You're a runner aren't you, Lenny? If you step on it you could be home for bedtime. Sweet dreams,' he sniggered again and swung himself back up into the cab of the van.

Lenny stood and stared as the engine started and the van moved slowly off up the road. With a gasp he filled his lungs. He hadn't realised he'd been holding his breath ever since his feet touched the tarmac. He didn't have the foggiest idea what was happening but here he was and in one piece. He turned his back and started walking down the road towards the outskirts of Ridminster.

He hadn't gone far when he heard a motor engine behind him. He stopped and looked back. It was the van. It slowed as it reached him. Gold Earring looked out of the open window. 'Hello, Lenny,' he said. 'Fancy seeing you here. Want a lift?'

Lenny stepped forward, hand outstretched to the door handle. The van moved off.

'Perhaps next time,' chortled Gold Earring.

Lenny dropped his hand and started walking again following the disappearing van. It continued until he lost sight of it at the bend. He plodded on. He had no idea what that was all about. Just the blokes having a laugh? But why him? Hello! There was the van again. He'd stop them playing silly buggers this time. Lenny stepped out into the road and waited for the van to reach him. He held up his hand like a policeman stopping traffic. He was fed up with this game. He wasn't going to play any longer.

When the van was a few feet from Lenny the engine note changed. The van surged forward and carried

Lenny quite a distance before his body slid down the front of it. There were two distinct bumps as the wheels twice passed over Lenny, but he didn't feel a thing.

Lenny the Hare, they called him. A bookie's runner. He was slightly built. His eyes were never still and he had the habit of walking with his head tucked into hunched shoulders like a wary tortoise. As a boy he'd won medals for running.

But when the time came he just couldn't run fast enough.

Tuesday Glasgow

'What's that you've got?' said Andy Fraser to the top of his wife's head. The rest of her face was hidden by the newspaper she was obviously enjoying to judge by the chuckles he could hear.

'It's the local paper Mum sent.'

'Your Mum sent? Heavens, Flick, we only left home on Friday afternoon.'

'I know and we missed the kids' concert. There's a terrific write-up in the paper and Mum knew I'd like to see it. Apparently they brought the house down as Bill and Ben, complete with "flobbolop-plop" language. I do wish we hadn't missed it,' she sighed.

'There'll be other concerts,' Andy comforted. 'I'd like to have seen them too. Sounds a riot, but we'd have missed my Mam and Dad's Golden Wedding if we hadn't taken the Friday evening flight.'

'I know. We couldn't miss that. It was worth the rush from work just to see their faces when we walked in. Your sister, Jessie'd managed to keep the whole thing secret. I was glad we could make it and there will be other concerts. Not to worry, love.'

'At least we've got our wee break as a bonus. Might as well make as much as we can of your Mum while we've got her.'

'Yes.' There was silence for a while as Flick thought exactly what Andy meant. Their twins, Jude and Natalie, had been born at a time when Sergeant Andy was a hot-pursuit driver for the Metropolitan Police Traffic Division and Flick was a Detective Sergeant with the Vice Squad. She had used her maternity leave to study for her Inspector's exams. They couldn't have managed at all without Mum moving in to be on hand to help out. Eventually she had sold her house and they had sold theirs. With the proceeds they had bought a larger family home with a garden for the twins in a quiet road in Lewisham. The set up had worked wonderfully, until Andy's accident.

'Penny for them?' Flick's thoughts were interrupted by Andy's voice. 'You looked quite fierce just then,' he laughed. 'Whatever were you thinking of?'

'Nothing much. Must be just my face,' smiled Flick. No way was she going to remind Andy of the reckless, thoughtless idiot responsible for the loss of his right arm, the months of mental and physical agony and painful rehabilitation. Now he used his fantastic prosthetic arm with ease but, with a passion, Flick still hated the reason for it and the person who caused it.

'So what are we going to do today? Our time's our own now we've done all the duty visits round the "rellies",' went on Andy.

Flick smiled. 'You can't blame your aunts and uncles etcetera wanting to see you and make sure your English wife is still looking after you as well as a Scots lassie would have done,' she teased. 'We haven't seen some of them since our wedding. I'm glad I thought to bring so many photos of the twins. I've got a huge list of e:mail addresses now to send all the latest news and photos as things happen.'

'You'll have to do a regular Round Robin.'

'Good idea. But I'm going to have my hands fuller than usual once we get rid of Tubby Jackson. Apparently the Super says they're not replacing him. Not that it will matter that much,' she added. 'I never knew anyone so capable of wriggling out of doing anything requiring effort. Thank God he's going.'

Andy grinned. 'You really like the guy don't you?'

Flick shook her head. 'You don't know the half of it. Seriously And, I've never told you just how much he's hindered me at every turn. I knew you'd blow your top or do something stupid, man to man, and he's not worth you getting into hot water for.'

Andy frowned. 'What do you mean? He didn't try it on did he?'

Flick laughed. 'No. He's not that stupid. He could see very clearly he'd have no joy there. But I do believe he's tried using his rank in the past to lean on younger female staff. Civvies from what I've heard, but no-one would come right out and accuse him.' She twisted her mouth in distaste. 'He's a nasty, devious, idle piece of work and I shall shout Hallelujah when he walks out of the Station door for the last time.'

Andy wasn't prepared to let things go. 'So what did he do to you?'

'Be as obstructive as possible. Not pass on messages; and then blame me when things didn't get done. I know that sounds petty, but when I was the new girl, he made me out to be incompetent at the very time I was trying to establish myself and become a valued part of the team. How could the DC's and DS's respect me and my judgement if he, the established older DI, was constantly putting me down behind my back, making me a joke and undermining every idea or request I made. It was lucky for me he was unpopular before I arrived. It made some of them give me the benefit of the doubt when it was him or me. And then when I twigged what he was up to I made sure I checked and double-checked every last step we had to take.'

'I had no idea. You didn't say.'

Flick smiled. 'See previous answer. I know you, love. You'd have been furious at the thought of me being treated so unfairly. But I'm a big girl. I knew I could handle it, and I did. I'm not the only one who will heave a sigh of relief once Tubby is gone for good.'

'Right. Work is a no-go subject as from now. We've got three more glorious free days alone together - if you know what I mean - before we get on that plane on Friday morning. I want to show you my Glasgow. It's a great place. Your Mum said she'd like to stay over the weekend to hear about our trip and then go back to London on Monday. The twins won't want her to go away again but she's got her own life to lead and I've tried to explain that to them. After all they're twelve now; they should be understanding.'

'I know. But she was a constant in their lives from the first. It's only been a year since she moved back home to join Aunty Flo. From what I gather they have a ball. If it's not the Old Tyme dancing, it's the pub quiz, or the Senior Citizens' Club outings. Not to mention the Bingo. I don't think a day passes but they're out somewhere.'

'Good for them. I hope they enjoy it. Your Mum certainly deserves to after all the years she's given to us.

Now put that paper away and let's start following her example.'

As Flick folded the newspaper she saw a small Stop Press paragraph.

Hit and Run

The body of an unknown man
was found on the old Bristol
road in the early hours of Friday
morning. He appears to have
been the victim of a Hit and
Run incident. Police are pursing
their enquiries.

Thursday Marylands Ridminster

As Major Edward Carver brought his Jaguar to a halt at
the foot of the two shallow steps leading to the entrance
to his home the front door opened. Carver smiled. On
the button as usual. What would he do without Manners?
He got out of the car and stretched. The gravel of the
drive had been evenly raked; the grass of the lawns
surrounding his large detached house was smoothly cut;
the flowerbed edges neatly trimmed but no flowers were
allowed to grow there. Shades of green shrubs were
acceptable but flowers brought on his allergy and even
the sight of them reminded him of a condition he looked
on as a weakness. Inside the luxurious house his life ran
with silent, seemingly effortless, efficiency. Nothing
disturbed his routines, his peace, and the enjoyment of
his retirement from the Army.

Ten years they had lived here now. He was
recognised as someone to be respected in the town. He
belonged to Toc H and could be counted on to support
any worthwhile charitable cause. He played off a
handicap of 11 at the local Golf Club, thereby making
him a useful team member. He was gallant with the
Ladies but never overstepped the mark and was known to
one and all as a thoroughly nice chap, a good egg in fact.

'A satisfactory meeting, sir?' queried Manners as he
took the Major's overcoat. Despite the Spring sunshine

there had been quite a keen wind this morning when he had set out.

'Quite,' replied Carver. 'A cup of tea in the study I think, Manners,' he smiled.

'Certainly, sir. And I have some beautifully fresh crumpets.'

Carver's eyes brightened. 'Oozing with butter, Manners?'

'Of course, sir. Just as you like them.'

Once Carver had demolished his first crumpet from the tray on the table beside his armchair, Manners placed two more logs on the generous fire, moved to the window and glanced out. He twitched one of the curtains into place, then turned and inclined his head towards the Major. 'The meeting, sir?' he said.

'Yes, the meeting. Superintendent Sutton was there. Unusual for one of our monthly "Police meets the Public" committees. It evened up the numbers on the platform, three police and three of us. There was no great reason he was there, as far as I could see, apart from marking the retirement of Detective Inspector George Jackson.'

'Ah,' said Manners.

'Quite so. He leaves us at the end of the week. Tomorrow in fact will be his send-off. He didn't say much. Just thanked the Super for his kind words, the usual guff, you know. Said he hoped his contribution had left his department in better health than he had found it so many years ago. Polite laughter there. Some of us went on to the pub for lunch as usual. The Super didn't stay but I had quite a chat with Jackson over coffee and the three brandies I bought him – as he was retiring.' Carver paused to take another bite of crumpet. He wiped the final piece round the butter lying in the bottom of the hot plate while he chewed, then popped the last morsel into his mouth. He cleaned his fingers on the linen napkin Manners had provided, swallowed and continued. 'He did confide in me as the brandies did their stuff. Said he feared for the future of the Force when they allowed chits of girls to have authority that went to their heads.'

'That will be Detective Inspector Fraser.'

'Of course. According to Jackson she is so far up herself she can't see the wood for the trees, has no idea how to conduct a case and should be at home looking after her children instead of trying to do a man's job.'

'Still, she was with the Met.'

'Was, being the operative word. Had she been the high-flyer Jackson said they had promised him, she wouldn't be burying herself here in sleepy Ridminster. She could hardly have an ulterior motive for such a demotion. No, I think Jackson must be right. You know what happens. They can't get rid of people. The Federation wouldn't wear that. So they sideline them. I can't see her rocking any boats.'

'Anything else of interest?'

'The Superintendent congratulated the members of the various Neighbourhood Watch Schemes on their vigilance. Apparently there are regular reports telephoned into the Station of ne'er-do-wells in respectable neighbourhoods.' Carver grinned. 'You should have heard Jackson on that topic afterwards. Bloody time-wasters, spooked old virgins, and lily-livered nosey parkers were some of the names he had for the conscientious citizenry.' Carver paused, gazing into the fire, then looked across at Manners still standing by the window. 'He mentioned he hadn't found the identity of the hit and run victim mentioned in the local paper. I asked him if he thought it was anyone local, or possibly a vagrant. Apparently no-one local has been reported missing so he was quite happy to agree there was nothing to get too concerned over. After all a tramp's identity would be very difficult and time consuming to establish, not to mention costly in manpower and money. I suggested to him he must be very satisfied to be leaving his post with no loose ends for anyone else to worry over. He agreed it was a great comfort to him.'

Manners smiled. 'You are always so considerate of others feelings, sir. May I clear now?' He crossed to where Carver sat, but before lifting the tray he brushed his hand across the shoulder of the Major's jacket then let it lie for a moment. 'A speck of dust, sir, just a speck of dust. Nothing for you to worry about.'

.

Friday

Detective Inspector George Jackson, ("Tubby" to those he had known as a young PC and those too senior for him to object), looked round his office - all his for the moment as DI Felicity Fraser was away – thank God. For the last week he had been able to do things his way, the proper way, the way that had never let him down, without her looking over his shoulder. On the otherwise empty desk top stood the last of the three cardboard boxes holding his possessions.

Not a lot to show for so many years. Of course he had the house. He'd been able to hang onto that through the divorce because Marge had gone off with that plonker, Pillings, from the garage on the Bristol road. Plonker he might be, but he had the money. Tubby would love to have been able to pin something, anything, on the bastard who had stolen his wife. God knows he'd tried. He'd had the garage watched until ordered to leave it alone. He'd stopped cars without number, always looking for something dodgy, but without success. He'd even dropped hints about Pillings, until the DCI had hauled him in and had a quiet but very uncomfortable word in his lug. It left a bitter taste in the mouth that James Pillings and Marge, now Mrs Pillings, had the neck to still swan around Ridminster right under Tubby's nose and seem not to care. It made him feel slighted. They were having a laugh.

Well, the last laugh was on them. At least that was what he told himself and repeated to anyone who would listen, as he boasted of never again having to toe the line, agree with "the brass" no matter how bloody stupid their ideas were, or hang around, bored and cold, keeping some low-life under observation. Loudly he proclaimed how he welcomed his retirement and how he would enjoy his pension. Perhaps if he said it often enough and loudly enough he might start believing it. In truth he was buggered if he knew what on earth he was going to do with himself day after day without the friendly, or at least familiar, faces around him.

Tubby kicked the desk, then bent and opened a drawer. He pulled out three very thin files, placed them on the desk and tapped the top cover with his fingernail. Bloody idiots. Why did they have to die on his last watch? The vagrant wouldn't be missed. And nor it seemed would the other two. Just his luck the suicide was found by chance and the other one had to snuff it after a punch up. No joy there. It could have been any or all of the fifty youths involved outside the Phoenix nightclub. Phoenix. That was a laugh. Wasn't that supposed to be a guy, or was it a bird, who rose from the dead? Well, this corpse wouldn't rise again that was for sure. Probably some gang-related argument. No-one seemed to know or care that he was missing. No MISPER report anyway so least said soonest mended? And he had been assured there would be no comeback.

Trouble was that interfering know-it-all girl would be back on Monday, poking her nose into anything outstanding, trying to make him, George, look bad. He scowled down at the folders.

23

She couldn't snoop into something that didn't exist though, could she? And who was going to tell her? There was enough self-preservation at work here that no-one was going to offer up extra unnecessary cases, meaning endless hours of questioning, interminable dead-ends, and abuse from the public who didn't want to know anyway.

Come to that who did know of their existence? Well, the original calls about the gang fight, the Fail to Stop RTA and the suicide would have been logged. But they had been passed on and, no doubt, forgotten about. Who read old logs? By now those small entries would be buried under possibly hundreds more. As luck would have it he had fielded all three. DS Booth had accompanied him on each case but, like the morgue, Booth wasn't about to argue when Tubby had decided further investigation would be a waste of time and money. Junior officers didn't argue with Tubby. It just didn't pay to do so. And God knows the "brass" were always banging on about lack of resources. He'd been following the Party line, hadn't he? Well, hadn't he? Time and money saved. He'd buried Booth under the mountain of daily and accumulated paperwork that, until yesterday morning had permanently covered Tubby's desk top. That would keep the younger man well and truly occupied long after Madam Fancypants had returned. He wouldn't be running to anyone with tales of dead cases.

Tubby raised his head. Footsteps were coming down the corridor. He didn't bloody believe it. Was he going potty? Was she haunting him? Quickly he shoved the three folders deep into one of the cardboard boxes on his

24

desk and picked it up just as DI Felicity Fraser walked into the office.

'What the f . . ? What are *you* doing here? You're supposed to be on leave?' Tubby spluttered.

She smiled. 'I heard it was your last day today. Obviously we'll have to do a handover/takeover so I thought if I popped in now we could get it over with. Then you can enjoy your farewell bash and not have to worry about coming back in on Monday to deal with it.'

'Wasted journey, little girl,' sneered Tubby. He was leaving. He no longer had to hide his contempt or dislike. 'Nothing to hand over. Clean desk, see? Clean slate. Nothing for you to worry your pretty little head about.' He could see how difficult she found it not to give him a mouthful for that remark. 'But delighted you're here. You must come to my farewell do. Fill your boots. Bring Handy Andy too. Get a drink inside you and perhaps you could come down off that high horse and mix with the ordinary mortals,' he sniggered. 'See you later, darling.' He clasped the cardboard boxes tighter to his chest, pushed past Fraser and hurried through the door. That would teach her.

Monday

Spring was in the air and in Flick's step when she arrived at the Station on Monday morning. She had a cheery greeting for everyone she met on the way up to her office on the first floor. Blissfully, it was empty. No scowling Tubby Jackson. Glorious freedom from his louring, miserable, undermining presence. Flick laughed. She should have been able to let his antics ride over her, like water off the proverbial duck. But he was so "in your face" - used to be - she corrected herself. Like the elephant in the room he couldn't be ignored. Well not any more. From today this would be a Tubby-free zone. Out of sight and definitely out of mind.

She buzzed a number on her desk phone. 'Can you give me a minute, Dave?' she said.

When DS Dave Booth filled her doorway she looked up and smiled. 'Stop blocking the light and take the weight off your feet,' she said.

Booth grinned and came to sit on the chair opposite her desk. He was exactly what he looked like, a very fit, very large young rugby player. He was also a very new Detective Sergeant having only passed his exams and been upgraded three months ago. Happily for him he had been slotted into the space left by a retiring Sergeant and so had been able to stay on his home patch without changing the Station statistics.

'So what mischief have you been getting up to in my absence?' queried Flick. As she watched for an answer she saw an uneasy expression cross Booth's face. Was it alarm? Or guilt? Certainly there was discomfort there. 'Hey!' she said. 'It was just a general remark. I'm not accusing you of anything. Unless,' she paused 'there is something you would like to tell me?'

Booth hesitated. 'No, boss. I've kept my nose clean. Just done everything I've been told.'

Flick frowned. Funny way to put things, but after all the boy had been working with Tubby for the last week. Perhaps some of Tubby's misogyny had rubbed off on him? Well, neither Booth nor anyone else would get away with disrespecting the female DI, or any other female staff member come to that. Damn! There was Tubby in her thoughts again. She pushed his unwelcome image away and turned her attention back to the large young man on the other side of her desk.

'DI Jackson seems to have left me the unusual luxury of a clean desk,' she said. 'So is there anything to report? I see nothing of interest to us has come in over the weekend but you can fill me in on anything ongoing.'

'Nothing much really, ma'am. The MISPER reported last Thursday has been found fit and well. Forensics from the two burglaries you know about are still at the lab. They're backed up there, as usual. Harry Whiteman and a guy from Traffic are beginning the rounds of the local Primary schools. That was set up before you went away. Did you have a good leave, ma'am?'

'Very good and very welcome, thank you. I feel as fresh as if I've been gone a month. That reminds me. What happened about the Fail to Stop RTA?'

Booth's mouth dropped open. Was the boy blushing? 'How did you know about that?' he said.

Flicks eyebrows rose. 'Why? Was it a secret?'

'Er, no, of course not. But you were away when it happened.'

'Yes. And now I'm back and in charge and I want to know what it was all about. Who was he?'

Booth shook his head. 'I don't know.'

'What do you mean? You don't know. Was someone else working the case with Inspector Jackson? I assume he handled it? Traffic would have passed it on after deciding it was a fatal accident – or murder.'

'Murder?'

'Possibly. Don't rule out anything until you have all the facts, Sergeant. Always work on the ABC. Assume nothing, Believe nothing, Check everything. Now, who was he, why was he there on that road at that time and how did he come to die?'

'He was run over – we think,' said Booth.

'I got that impression from the newspaper report I read,' said Flick watching understanding dawn on Booth's face. Pity. She could have traded on a gift of second-sight or superior omnipotence, even for a day or so, but there was a job to be done. 'What I don't know and am still waiting to find out,' she emphasised, 'is the answers to my other questions.'

Booth shook his head. 'I don't know either, boss,' he said.

Flick took a deep breath feeling her former happy mood slipping away. Give me patience. 'Let's go back to the beginning. A body was found. A report was filed. Did you attend the scene?'

28

'Yes.'

'With DI Jackson?'

'Yes.'

'And?'

'And what, ma'am?'

'Sergeant, I know you are newly qualified, but you've been with CID long enough to know the drill. What did you, and Inspector Jackson, find?'

'Deceased was a vagrant male about forty to fifty years of age. Multiple contusions and position of the body indicated death caused by a moving vehicle. Discovered by a driver taking the old road on his way into Ridminster.'

'ID?'

'Nothing on the body to say who he was.'

Flick frowned. 'Nothing?'

'No, ma'am. No letters, bills, nothing with a name on. Just a few coins and a handkerchief.'

'Where was his kit?'

'Kit?'

Flick sighed. 'You're beginning to sound like a parrot. Even a vagrant has possessions; a carrier bag with a blanket or warmer clothes; some souvenir from the past; a copy of War and Peace, even.'

'Really?'

'It has been known. Vagrants do have past lives you know. But our particular vagrant had nothing you say. So how do we know he was a vagrant?'

'Inspector Jackson said so, ma'am.'

'Ah. And did he share with you on what grounds he based his assumption?'

'No, ma'am.'

'What was done to try and trace the man?'

'No MISPER was filed for him. And I think the Inspector asked around.' Booth looked distinctly uncomfortable.

'Give me strength. So, because no Missing Persons Report was filed for someone answering to this description we conclude he is an unknown?'

Booth wriggled in his seat. 'I wasn't in charge ma'am,' he burst out. 'I did ask the Inspector if we should get a mug shot from the morgue, perhaps show it around the pubs at least, but he said . . . he told me . . .' Booth's voice dwindled into silence.

'Yes. Go on. What exactly did the Inspector say?'

The young Sergeant took a deep breath, seemingly bracing himself for the wrath to come. 'He said, "who the hell do you think you are? Don't set yourself up to tell me how to do my job. You're as wet behind the ears as that snotty-nosed girl and about as much use" . . . ma'am. You did ask.'

Flick couldn't make up her mind whether to laugh at the expression of anguish on the face of her young Sergeant or give vent to some very unprofessional language with regard to her former colleague. Damn and blast the man. What had he been playing at? Sloppy procedure in the past, yes, and lazy, almost certainly, but this was negligence at its worst. Why?

'So nothing more was done at all to identify this man?'

'Not as far as I know. No, ma'am.'

'But there was an initial report filed?'

'Yes, ma'am.'

'Well, bring it to me, please.'

'I haven't got it. The last time I saw it, it was lying on Inspector Jackson's desk.'

'Well, it's not there now. Look through the drawers and see if he's left it in one of them. If not go to Records and request it. He may have sent it down.'

But although every possible place was searched, no report on the Fail to Stop RTA came to light.

After an hour Flick's body sat behind her desk but her thoughts were on the old Bristol road. How long ago had the incident taken place? Was anything to be gained by visiting the scene? Suddenly she got up, unhooked her outdoor coat from the back of the door, glanced in the small mirror she kept on the wall there – a source of constant sarcasm from Tubby over the seven years they had worked together – then walked into the main office. 'You're with me, Booth,' she called and strode on. Let him run to keep up with her. She needed to sharpen this boy up, the whole team in fact. From now on things were going to be done her way.

When Dave Booth eventually caught up with her at ground level he turned towards the front door, but Flick continued across the hall and out to the car park behind the station. She threw him her car keys. 'You can drive,' she said. 'It's the Vauxhall over there, the green one.'

While Booth settled himself into the car, adjusting the seat to accommodate his long legs, Flick opened her mobile and dialled. 'Martin?' she queried when a voice answered the summons. 'Flick Fraser in Ridminster. Would you be free to meet us at the mortuary in about an hour?'

Dave Booth's eyebrows rose in surprise.

'That's fine. Many thanks. See you then.' Flick closed her phone and did up her seatbelt. 'Okay. Make yourself useful and take us to Flax Bourton. I presume you know the way?'

Dave kept his mouth shut as he drove the DI's car with the greatest care towards Bristol. These days all the area post mortems were done in one place. It meant a trek for miles to reach there and if the pathologists were busy cases could be backed up for days. But the PM on the Fail to Stop had been done over a week ago. As the Crime Scene Investigator, Tubby had attended. Dave couldn't think why they were coming back. Surely the DI wasn't a ghoul who took delight in seeing dead bodies? He almost smiled at the thought, then remembered she was sitting beside him and no way could he give her an answer if asked why he was grinning like an idiot.

Once arrived outside the mortuary Flick left Booth to park the car. He joined her at the doorway but, beyond sending a questioning glance towards her serious face, he kept his thoughts to himself.

Flick peered through the glass porthole into the business section of the mortuary. Steel tables shone clean under lights dimmed now. Each table was empty. No-one was there. She turned to her right, knocked on the door marked Office, and pushed it open.

Martin Barnes, the pathologist, looked up from the form he held. He pushed his glasses up onto the top of his head and walked across to where a counter held the usual paraphernalia for tea and coffee making. 'Hi, Flick,' he said. 'Which?'

Flick smiled. 'I am awake thanks, Martin, and I don't want to be bouncing off the walls so I'll stick to tea, your coffee being lethal to ordinary mortals. The same will go for my Sergeant, Dave Booth. I don't know if you two have met before?'

'No,' said Barnes, with a nod in Booth's direction. 'Welcome. Don't be frightened. We don't bite and neither do our visitors. And we're very quiet today.'

Booth looked around for anyone else in the office.

'He means the cases,' explained Flick. 'And that's why we've come, Martin.'

'I didn't think it was for the pleasure of my company. But, like I said, we've no-one new in.'

'I'm going back to last Thursday week. Fail to Stop RTA on the old Bristol road. I was away. DI Jackson handled it. I wonder what you found? What did you tell him?'

'Nothing. I sent up my report and am still waiting for follow-up.'

'Why? What did it say, and where did you send it?'

'Why don't you ask Tubby? Oh, no . . . you can't can you? He's off. But you should still be able to read the report. Isn't that why you're here?'

'No. I'm new to the case. I want to start from scratch. Just humour me, please.'

Barnes pulled open a filing cabinet and fingered through the sheets of paper in a folder. 'Here we are. Well nourished male although probably existing on junk food. Heavy smoker, probably nervous type, bit his nails. Own teeth and hair. Clean and tidy under the surface dirt and abrasions from the collision. Age anywhere from forty to fifty. Not manual labourer, hands too soft. Last meal was fish and chips about four to five hours before death. I'll make a copy and have it sent to you. No-one's come forward to claim him then?'

'Not as far as I know. Would you think he was a vagrant?'

'No way. Reasonable clothes, shoes not worn down, slip-on's not trainers or boots so beloved of our wandering homeless. Had a handkerchief in his pocket fairly recently laundered and ironed even. Clean socks. Vagrant? Whoever put that idea in your head?'

In reply Flick asked another question. 'This car that ran him over. Any idea of make?'

Barnes tutted. 'It would be far better if you read the report. No mention of a car there. No sign of one on the body.'

'Why?'

'In cases of collision with a car there is plain evidence of the bumper hitting the victim's legs - below the knee in an adult. No such thing here. The first impact would have been about chest height.'

'So what are we looking for?'

'Some kind of lorry or maybe a van,' offered Barnes. 'Flat fronted. From the height of the victim and the injuries received I would say it may be one of those delivery vans, a panel van perhaps.'

'So we're looking for a white van man?'

Barnes grinned. 'Possibly. I'm not going to commit myself to that but it seems likely. And he was hit full frontal. Quite deliberate.'

'No possibility of it being an accident?'

'No way. You've got a murder on your hands, young Flick.'

Flick sipped her mug of tea. This was beyond even what she had thought Tubby Jackson capable of. Supposing he had read the report - and why wouldn't he have done - the facts screamed out to be followed up. But he had done nothing, had even, it would appear, deliberately concealed the incident from her and everyone else. Why? Surely he wasn't the one who had run the victim down? No. As far as she knew he had no van. Could he have hired one? Possible, but why? Moving house on his retirement? That would fit, but hang on just because she couldn't stand the man she had no reason to think he had committed a murder. She crossed over and rinsed her cup under the hot tap. 'Thanks Martin. I'll be in touch. Come on, Booth.'

When they left the mortuary Flick was in thoughtful mood. She said little on the way to Ridminster. Back at the station Dave followed her into the basement. 'Next stop Records,' she said.

'What exactly are we looking for?' asked Booth as Flick opened the large Evidence Bag she had signed out from the Detained Property Store.

She shook out the contents onto the table below the overhead strip lighting that cast a harsh cold light onto the pathetic collection of the dead man's belongings. She sorted through them as she spoke.

'I want to know who this man is. These objects are the last things to have contact with him. What can they tell us? Lay them out in order. Start with his shoes.'

She handed one to Booth and examined the other. 'Not expensive but not shabby. Leather. Could be unusual these days. And they have been recently polished. Socks. No holes, clean. Pants, vest. Not new but not worn out. Both from Messrs M&S, so not cheap but hard wearing. Shirt ditto. Jeans more worn but still respectable. Jacket. Waterproof or at least showerproof. This man was no vagrant. When did you last hear of a tramp cleaning his shoes? And look, you can still see the creases where this handkerchief was ironed. Who the hell has time to iron hankies?' She shook her head. Then she had a thought. 'Unless he has a doting wife or mother? No wedding ring but a lot of men don't wear them. But why hasn't the woman in his life reported his absence? Does that mean he isn't local and hasn't been missed yet? What about the contents of his pockets?'

Booth tipped up a brown envelope and consulted the list of contents. 'Not much here; in fact practically nothing. Apart from the handkerchief which I think should be in here too, there are two used tissues. Possibly useful for DNA?'

Flick nodded. 'Well spotted. What else?'

'That's it except for these coins, thirty five pence worth.'

Flick frowned. 'It doesn't make sense. What do you make of it?'

Booth pushed the coins around with his gloved fingers as he spoke. 'No vagrant. Well cared for, fed and clothed, but no ID on him at all and only a few pennies in his pocket. Either he was robbed or no-one wants us to know who he is.'

'Exactly,' said Flick. 'And why?'

'Because his death would cause a stink? If he's very important. Or because we could link him to someone else? Or perhaps he grassed someone up?'

'All possible; but if he was that important I think we would have heard he was missing by now, no matter how far away he might live. It's been more than a week. You can check the MISPER reports and see if anyone fits. Likewise if he ratted on someone I think it would have been talked about by now. 'Specially if it got a result. And if it was a punishment killing, surely the killer would want it known, as an example to anyone else who might think of crossing him. As to a link, let's get a mug shot and show it round. If he's local someone must know him. Ask Martin for the photo. And, while you're there, ask him if there was any sign of nicotine patches. Martin said he was a heavy smoker but there are no fags or matches here, no lighter, or papers for roll-ups.' Flick bent and sniffed the jacket. 'Still stinks of smoke so I don't believe he'd given up smoking. So where's his gear?'

Monday

Tubby Jackson greeted Monday morning with a bleary eye and a jaundiced expression. With an unsteady hand he fumbled the last two Alka Seltzers into a glass and groaned as he drank the mixture down. Why couldn't he have stayed in blessed oblivion? Heaven knows he had tried hard enough. As long as he was spending freely there had been cronies to join him in the mammoth pub crawl he had called a continuation of his "leaving do". But by Sunday evening his forced bonhomie had worn thin. He had descended by way of self pity, through maudlin regret, followed by morose behaviour towards his companions, thus hastening their departure. Finally he resorted to physical violence resulting in him being ejected into the street by a landlord fed-up with biting his tongue whenever the "filth" deigned to patronise his less than delightful establishment.

Head in hands Tubby considered his future. What to do? He'd been an idiot to take those files. No-one knew better than he did that if you don't keep on top of your indiscretions, they will creep out of the woodwork when least expected or welcomed. So he must face the fact that Nosey-parker Fraser would one day find out about the three cases he had "buried". As to the other business, well he must have been mad.

It was her fault. She always rubbed him up the wrong way. Always undermining him, showing him up, trying to bring her big-city ways into *his* nick. Ridminster'd plodded on quite well before she came. No-one rocked the boat and everyone knew their place. If any, of what he liked to call, his "clientele" stepped out of line they got squashed. If something more serious happened, like a visitor trying it on in Tubby's patch, his snouts were quick enough to let him know. He had a few nice little arrests under his belt and everyone on the home front was happy.

Respect. That's what he'd had. He was a good copper with a good record. And then she'd arrived. It was no use him telling people things were out of his hands. Although he was older and had warmed his seat for years in Ridminster, she was also a DI and seemed to have the guv'nor's ear. Arrests and disturbances in his comfortable arrangements began to worry certain people. Tubby was the one who was supposed to make all this go away. God knows, he'd tried, but first she wouldn't listen and then he'd realised if he wasn't careful he could lose his job, his pension, the lot. So he'd dropped a word here and there to be more cautious and stepped softly himself.

Seven years he'd put up with her. The result was an ulcer and chronic indigestion, but he'd won, he told himself. He'd won. He'd retired victorious and she was left to cope when the shit hit the fan.

Tubby blinked. No, that wasn't quite right. If he was around he would still be in the firing line of blame. Some of said shit would land on him. Quite a lot if Mrs Smartypants had her way. Could they take away his pension? Even after he'd retired? A holiday was in order. A long holiday. Who was it who had said that to him, only the other day, that he deserved a decent break? He shook his head. He couldn't remember and anyway it wasn't important. But where? Somewhere they served decent beer, that's for sure. Where was his passport?

After a shower and shave, thanking God for the invention of electric razors so he didn't cut his throat, Tubby drank a strong coffee and munched a piece of toast. The holiday idea deserved serious thought. He dug out a large suitcase and packed most of his clothes before he even considered where he was going. Would he really need all four of his jumpers in Spain? No, not Spain. Gibraltar - where they knew about English beer. Gib always sounded warm but maybe it wasn't that hot in the winter?

At this point Tubby realised he was contemplating flight not holiday. In April one did not pack for a winter abroad if return in the foreseeable future was on the cards. What was he doing? He couldn't just up sticks and go – could he?

The door knocker made him jump. Tubby peered round the front room curtain and relaxed. It was only the post. He opened the front door, took his mail with a grunt of acknowledgement then walked from the hall through to the kitchen, sorting as he went. Several brightly coloured flyers advertising fast-food takeaways; a letter offering him Life Insurance – that was a laugh. Did he want to change his motor insurance? They all went in the bin. The thick brown envelope left was typewritten. Tubby frowned. He hadn't ordered anything, but this was too bulky to be simply folded paper. It was one of the larger padded envelopes. He slit the end with a knife, tipped the contents out onto the table and stared. A British passport lay on top of what looked like tickets. Spooked, Tubby looked over his shoulder. Had someone been listening to his thoughts? Had he spoken aloud? But how had anyone got hold of his passport?

First he picked up the tickets. One way flight to Amsterdam in his name, attached to a pre-paid booking for one night in the Hilton Hotel. The flight left this evening. The other ticket was one way to Praia, the capital city of Santiago, the largest island in the Cape Verde group. He vaguely remembered the telly talking about the temperate climate of the islands. But this wasn't for him. It was made out to an Albert Henderson and attached to a piece of paper with an address printed on it. Who the hell was Henderson? And why was his ticket sent to Tubby? Was he coming here to pick it up? Tubby opened the passport. This was Henderson's too but - hang on. Tubby's face looked back at him from the usual appalling photo that made the most virtuous citizen look like a fugitive from a Wanted poster. Suddenly Tubby was afraid.

He was even more afraid when he counted the wad of banknotes that made up the rest of the envelope's contents. Ten thousand quid. Ten thousand bleeding quid. Who would want to give him that kind of dosh?

Tubby sat down heavily on a sturdy kitchen chair and searched his memory. Sure, in the past he had done favours for certain people. But not ten thousand quid's worth, surely? A parking ticket here, a small fine there. He could, and had, made them go away. He'd closed his eyes once or twice, and for one person had made sure neither he, Tubby, nor any other copper had been in a certain area at a certain time when requested. He didn't know who those favours had been for. Just a voice over the telephone. But the voice had known things about Tubby, so he'd done it. On each occasion an envelope had arrived to swell his pension fund. No robberies or muggings had been reported so no harm done. But this was not good news. Same kind of envelope so possibly the same person? And that person wanted Tubby to disappear, that was obvious. But what about his pension? His legitimate pension? He could draw that if he lived abroad, but not if his name was Albert Henderson. And ten grand wouldn't last forever. Would there be more once he reached Cape Verde?

Tubby started to sweat. What had he got himself into?

For the next hour Tubby wracked his brains trying to figure it out. All the "favours" he'd done put together were nothing, nothing at all in the great scheme of things. So why was he being rewarded like this? Rewarded or threatened? What would happen if he didn't use the tickets and passport? That was the real question and the one that worried him most.

Finally he made up his mind, finished his packing and closed up his house for a long absence. It would have been good if he could've sold the car to make a few extra quid but there was no time. The only quick sale he could have made was at Pillings Garage and he was buggered if he would ask that plonker for any favours. Anyway the car wasn't worth that much and he might want it when –

if – he came back. Because he could always change his mind and come back – couldn't he – after a decently long interval. He still had his own passport. He'd hang on to that. Finally he took a mobile phone out of his pocket and gazed at it, a frown on his face. He had been lugging it about for weeks now. By rights, he should have given it to Fraser, but it had never rung and it wouldn't now – would it? He hesitated, then shrugged and shoved it to the back of the kitchen drawer hidden behind the odds and ends that had collected there since his wife had left. Carefully he pushed the drawer closed and left the house.

At the airport that evening Tubby's eyes were never still. He scanned the crowd. At any moment he expected to feel a hand on his shoulder – the long arm of the law. He paid excess baggage for his two heavy suitcases and waited in Departures. His ulcer was playing up. He swallowed three antacid tablets and longed for a drink, a proper drink. There were no known faces around him, in Duty-Free, or in the Boarding queue. But it wasn't until he felt the aircraft leave the ground and then heard the thunk of the undercarriage being retracted that Tubby at last relaxed. He'd made it.

Tuesday

Dave Booth burst through the door of Flick's office on Tuesday morning. 'We've got a result, boss,' he cried.

Flick looked up from her desk. 'Well that sounds promising. Now sit down and tell me the what, where, how, and when.'

'The Fail to Stop, the vagrant,' said Booth. 'At least, of course he isn't. You were spot on there. Seems he's quite well-known in town, if you know where to look.'

'Calm down and start from the beginning.'

'I did like you said. Got the mug shot from Barnes and had several copies made. I thought we might as well get started right away so I made sure the night shift guys had copies. I thought they could show them round the pubs, you know.'

Flick hid a smile. 'Seems you've been doing a lot of thinking. Well done.'

Booth grinned. 'It worked. The landlord at The Crown and Sceptre, you know, boss, down by the station, he recognised the face right away, even though it looked as though he was asleep.'

Flick nodded. Martin Barnes was known for being able to prepare his "clients" for mug shots with an expertise that made it possible for the pictures to be shown to the general public without turning stomachs or giving any indication of how the subject had died. 'Go on,' she said.

'Well it appears this fellow is a bookie's runner. Works regularly, if you can call it that, for Global, the bookmaker near the station. I gather he used to be in the pub most days - probably waiting for the races to start.'

'And his name?'

'Yes. Sorry, boss. He's called Lenny. Lenny the Hare, they call him. Runner? Hare? Not difficult to see the connection, but no-one as yet seems to know his surname.'

'Right. That's next then. Get your coat, Booth. We're off to the pub. We'll get the landlord before he opens. In the meantime get someone to collate any other info on this character that might have been brought in overnight.'

'Yeah,' said the landlord of The Crown and Sceptre, having taken another look at the photo. 'That's Lenny, poor little sod.'

'Why?' asked Flick.

The man shrugged massive shoulders. 'He always seemed a bit lost, if you know what I mean. Never really joined in, or was one of the crowd, like. He just supped his beer and smoked his fag. Quiet, well-behaved, never give me no trouble.'

Flick could well believe it. To match the shoulders the landlord had huge hands. "A bunch of bananas" sprang to Flick's mind. At some point his knuckles had been split. Old scars and calluses bore witness to work other than pulling pints of beer. 'Boxer, were you?' she said.

The landlord grinned. 'Yeah. Twenty years in the ring, and out of it too, but you didn't hear that from me and I'd deny it if you repeated it. When you can't make top class, bare knuckle can tuck a bit away for the old age.'

'But it takes its toll,' suggested Flick.

'That it does. That it does. If me old lady hadn't made me give it up, the arthritis would have. But I still have a bit of a rep in these parts, so no problems in the pub, see?'

Flick nodded. 'Not that Lenny could have been trouble.'

'You'd be surprised, missus. Some fellows can start an argument then just step back when all hell breaks loose. I think they do it for devilment, but not if I catch on first they don't, not in my pub.'

'Lenny,' prompted Flick.

'Yeah. In here regular. Didn't mix much. Like I said, no mates, no trouble.'

'Do you know his last name?'

The landlord shook his head. 'Never heard it. Always just Lenny. Maybe some of the punters would know. I'll ask around.'

'Thank you,' said Flick. 'Here's my card. If you hear anything, I'd appreciate a call.'

The landlord took the small card in his big hand and studied it. He looked up at Flick with renewed respect. 'Right, Inspector,' he said.

As Flick and Booth turned away he called after them. 'His old Mum died a little while back,' he said, 'Lenny's Mum. Very cut up about it he was.'

'When was that? Do you remember?'

'Must ha' been about two months ago. I remember him saying he'd broke his promise. On her birthday and that was Valentine's he'd promised to give up the fags and he hadn't done it right away. Then it was too late.'

'And he didn't give up afterwards?'

'Nah. Said there didn't seem no point. And he wouldn't be parted from his Dad's old lighter.'

Flick's ears pricked up. 'Lighter? Was it a special one then?'

'Yeah. Real old. Second World War. Funny looking thing. He showed me it once. Round it was, like a tube and there was a bit at the top you could slide up and down to stop the draught blowing out the flame. Clever idea if you was outdoors a lot. Said his Dad got it in the Army. Very proud of that lighter, Lenny was.'

'But he didn't have it on him when he died,' said Flick as she and Booth sat in the car outside the pub.

'Perhaps he did and whoever "offed" him took it?'

Flick nodded. 'I think you're probably right and hopefully that will help us find his killer. The Global bookmaker next stop, I think. Global sounds very impressive, like a worldwide chain.'

Booth grinned.

Stan Hatcher, the proprietor of the Global Bookmaker's, was helpful but not forthcoming. On presenting her name and Warrant Card Flick thought she had caught a flicker of something in his eyes before his face took on a bland, questioning expression. Had it been alarm? Unease, definitely. What secrets had this man to hide? But then everyone had secrets, didn't they? It didn't mean to say he was involved in Lenny's murder. Flick was more and more certain Lenny had been murdered.

She looked around the inside of the betting shop. It was a good match for the exterior. Both could have been smartened up. Flick was no businesswoman but even she could see, with a small outlay the premises could have attracted more business. These days gambling at a bookie's was legal, big business, attracting both men and women. She knew the old saying "there are no poor bookies". Betting was a popular pastime. Business should be good, probably was. So why hadn't the owner made more of it? The whole set up was . . . Flick searched for a word . . . innocuous. Yes, that was it. Innocuous. As if not wanting to attract attention. She felt a tingle between her shoulder blades. It was a sensation she knew she would ignore at her cost, but for the life of her she couldn't think why it had happened just then.

'Lenny?' said Hatcher, 'yeah, I employ him sometimes. Just as a handyman, you know, sweeping up and all that.'

'Running errands?' suggested Flick. Again that flicker of unease behind Hatcher's eyes.

He nodded. 'All that sort of thing. Charity, really. Hasn't got much up top and not very reliable. Sometimes doesn't turn up for days. Like now. No word, no message, just hasn't come in to work.'

'Possibly because he's dead,' said Booth.

Stan Hatcher was no actor. The expected expressions of shock and sorrow wouldn't have fooled a baby.

'But you knew that didn't you, Mr Hatcher?' said Flick.

'Me? No. How, why?'

'It was in the papers wasn't it?

'Oh yes. But it didn't say his name. I mean, how was I to know it was Lenny?'

So he had seen the article about the hit and run. In spite of his protestations Flick had seen first the look of alarm when he had been accused of knowing about Lenny's death, and then the relief when the newspaper article was mentioned. So he thought that let him off the hook, did he?

Booth cut in. 'It didn't occur to you, Mr Hatcher, to wonder if it might be Lenny, with him missing from work at the time?'

'No. I told you. He would often not turn up. No warning. Nothing.'

'I'm surprised you still employed him then, as he was so unreliable,' said Flick.

'Well, he was no trouble and it's not as though it was a proper job.'

'No,' said Booth. 'Bookie's runner doesn't really fit the bill down at the Job Centre.'

'This employment,' went on Flick. 'I don't suppose you kept any records, for tax purposes, National Insurance and all that legal stuff, did you?'

The man was starting to sweat. Could she find an excuse to look at his books? They'd probably make interesting reading. But she had to stick to the subject.

'Come on, Inspector. I told you. It wasn't a proper job. I gave him the odd bit of beer and fag money, that's all.'

'But you do know his surname and address?'

'Of course. He lives with his Mum, Mrs Strickland, at number 47 Hyacinth Terrace, down off the factory road. Lived there all his life, he has.'

'But not any more,' said Booth.

'Er, no. I suppose not,' said Hatcher.

Tuesday

Back at the nick Flick set the wheels in motion to obtain authority to break into Lenny's house, if necessary. She called together a small team in a Briefing Room and laid out what was known so far.

'From the injuries on the body it seems pretty certain the victim was facing the vehicle that hit him. Not just facing but standing in front.' She watched puzzled frowns appear and glances being exchanged. A hand shot up. 'Yes, Constable Jarvis?'

'Is it possible he was trying to commit suicide?'

'Not trying,' someone offered. 'He bloody well succeeded, didn't he?'

A ripple of amusement greeted this truism. Flick allowed herself a small smile. She ran a fairly relaxed team. All too well she knew how excessive discipline could produce tension in junior officers causing reactions varying from anxiety to please, to truculence and inattention to detail. Heaven knew the job itself produced enough tension and emotional battering without adding to it. She was confident, when the time came, her team would work to the best of their ability and go that extra mile to achieve a result.

'Good thinking, Jarvis,' she said. 'It is, of course, a possibility and bearing in mind his mother is supposed to have died not long ago we can't rule it out. But I want to proceed as if it is murder simply so we don't miss any pertinent fact. Dave Booth will come with me into the house. If it turns out to be a crime scene we will call in the CSI, but the mother probably died of natural causes and we know Lenny died on the old Bristol road.'

Dave Booth looked up from the notes he was taking. 'His boss didn't seem to know the old lady was dead,' he said.

'I can't be certain,' said Flick, 'but I imagine Lenny was not encouraged to chat to, or confide in, Mr Hatcher. And I can't actually see Lenny or anyone offering up such news in the expectation of sympathy or understanding. Can you?'

Booth grinned. 'No, boss.'

'Right. While Booth and I are in the house I want you, Jarvis, and Barry Spencer to take the photos and go house to house in the immediate area. There's been no mention of a car so presumably Lenny walked to and from his work. Some of the neighbours must have seen him and know him by sight. I want the usual stuff. Last sightings; anything unusual; anyone strange hanging around. Get everything you can on him, and his mother. He seems such an ordinary little runt. Why would anyone want to get rid of him?'

She asked Booth the same question later that day as they went through Number 47 Hyacinth Terrace. Both wore gloves. DS Booth's were the regulation latex but Flick had been diagnosed with latex allergy not long after Andy's accident. The specialist was of the opinion the worry and stress of that awful time had been a factor, but who could say? Flick had been offered vinyl as an alternative but when she found the nitrile ones she heaved a sigh of relief. Now there was always a stock on hand at the nick for her use. That had been another factor Tubby Jackson had used to belittle her whenever possible. Tales of "special treatment" and "poor little housewife hands" had set Flick's teeth on edge on several occasions. But no more.

The little house was spotless. Lenny had probably eaten cereal and toast for his last breakfast. The bowl and side plate, together with a mug, had been washed up and left on a rack to drain dry. The dishcloth had been rinsed out and hung over the tap. The table and surfaces were wiped clean.

Upstairs were two bedrooms and a bathroom. One held evidence of female occupation. Dresses, coats and skirts still hung in the wardrobe. A hairbrush on the dressing table clung onto one or two grey hairs, and a bottle of Devon Violets scent took pride of place.

The other room was obviously Lenny's. Again everything was neat and tidy, the bed made and dirty laundry put into a hamper awaiting attention. The chest of drawers held piles of neatly ironed clothes, but those in the airing cupboard showed signs of a less competent operator. Flick felt an unaccustomed tightening of the throat as she thought of poor Lenny trying to keep up the standards his mother had instilled in him. How long had he carried around the handkerchief so lovingly ironed for him?

Back downstairs the furniture was dust–free. In pride of place in the centre of the mantelpiece was a large birthday card to The World's Best Mum. Beside it a smaller card brought greetings from someone called Patrick.

'Nothing for us here, boss?' said Booth from the doorway.

Flick agreed. 'It appears our Lenny led a blameless life as a devoted son and non-aggressive member of the public,' she mused. 'In fact he seemed to go out of his way not to be noticed. Anything significant in that do you reckon?'

Booth shook his head. 'No. Plenty like that around, 'specially in a rough area like by the station and along the factory road itself. Bit better here, mind, but he had to run the gauntlet every day. He was only a little chap; wouldn't want to get in anyone's eyeline who was out of sorts. And you know, boss, when gamblers lose their money they like to blame someone else, not their own folly. No, nothing sinister with our Lenny. Reckon he just wanted to keep his nose clean and out of trouble. Probably dinned into him by his Ma.'

'Right. We'd better close up the house and see if there are any next of kin to inform. Hopefully the neighbours will let us know that.'

'There's Patrick, of course,' said Booth.

'Yes. Brother, cousin, old boyfriend, new boyfriend come to that? We don't know how old Mrs Strickland was, although the framed photos Lenny kept so well dusted show a woman who looked after herself. We'll leave Lenny's but bring Patrick's, in a bag. You never know if we might need his prints.'

While Booth carefully placed the birthday card into an evidence bag Flick poked through the contents of a wastepaper basket. 'How long has Lenny been dead?' she said.

Dave Booth stopped and considered. 'You must have just missed it, boss. First report of the body came in on Friday so we reckoned he died on the Thursday. Thursday to Thursday, then the weekend and now it's Tuesday that makes twelve days. Why?'

'For someone so meticulous it seems strange he wouldn't have emptied the waste baskets. I wonder what day the binmen come round?'

'Mondays here, I think, boss. Fortnightly that is.'

'That would probably explain it,' murmured Flick. 'Oh, no!'

'What is it?'

'Patrick. Or at least I think it is. Let's see his card.' She smoothed out an envelope she had taken from the wastepaper basket. 'Yes. I'm pretty sure that's it. Better bag it with the card.'

'But that's good isn't it? It will give us a postmark. Makes him easier to trace.'

'Yes,' agreed Flick, 'easier to trace Down Under in the large city of Melbourne.'

Booth shook his head. 'You can't win 'em all,' he said.

Back at her desk Flick dealt with the paperwork and messages that had come in during her absence. She wanted to get on top of routine things before her afternoon briefing so she could concentrate on Lenny's death.

Her phone rang. It was Chief Inspector William Westcott who summoned her up to his office. Flick heaved a sigh. With a glance in the mirror behind her

55

door she made sure she was neat and tidy then walked up the stairs.

DCI William Westcott was the kind of man whose summons made even innocent parties check their consciences. He was a big man with beautifully barbered stone grey hair giving him an air of distinction. His strong face sported bushy eyebrows that shaded eyes which could make strong men tremble. But Flick could think of no reason he would be displeased with her. The only problem was what Tubby Jackson had, or rather had not, done.

In the soft burr of his West Country accent he welcomed her back from leave and asked after her family. Then he frowned.

'You've not got much on at the moment have you, Inspector?'

'Not a great deal, sir, just one suspected murder.'

Westcott's frown deepened. 'Murder? What murder? There was nothing on my desk about it this morning.'

'No, sir. It happened while I was away. Fail to Stop RTA on the old Bristol road.' Flick felt she ought to get all the details in while she had the chance.

Westcott searched his memory. 'But that happened two weeks ago, just before I went off to the Area Conference. Always one damn conference after another,' he grumbled. 'Tramp wasn't it? Tubby Jackson assured me it was all taken care of.' His sharp blue eyes bored into Flick. 'I know you two didn't always see eye to eye, Inspector. Clash of the old and new, probably, but he's gone now. I hope you're not trying to start a witch hunt to discredit a brother officer?'

Flick was shocked and indignant. 'Certainly not, sir. I would hope you know me better than that by now and I resent the insinuation.'

Her obvious outrage got through to her boss. He muttered an apology. 'Of course, of course, sorry about that, but I need you to have a clear mind now on our latest problem.'

Flick was still seething but managed to answer reasonably. 'Problem, sir?'

'Yes. You'll know by now we have drugs on our patch, Inspector. Of course there have always been a low level of what they like to call "social" drug taking. As soon as we catch one pusher another pops up, but by and large we've been able to contain it. Now, however things are getting out of hand. It would seem we have not only drugs being sold, but possibly manufactured and passed from our area into the adjoining patches and to heaven knows where.'

'What kind of drugs, sir?'

'The usual E's, upper and downers, but now we have a refined version they are calling F's - stands for Fantasy Fun, so you can imagine the effect it has on the users. In powder form you can sniff it like cocaine, and it also comes in tablets. It has been found in other parts of the country before now, as you should know, but now we seem to have it here. Two kids in hospital this morning. The Drug Squad are interviewing them and will keep us in the loop. But I want you and your people with your specialised knowledge of our area to be exceptionally vigilant.' He paused, as though waiting for a response.

'Of course, sir,' said Flick. 'That goes without saying.'

'Naturally,' Westcott paused again. 'But you, personally – I don't suppose you've heard anything?'

Flick was baffled. Why would she have any special knowledge of drug movements? 'No, sir,' she said. 'Of course I'm just back from leave.'

'I know that,' said Westcott sharply. 'I just thought, hoped, there might have been something to go on. But of course, there wouldn't be.' He said the last few words as he turned away. Flick wasn't sure she'd heard them properly. She waited for further enlightenment but Westcott stared out of his office window. When he turned back it was almost as if he had forgotten she was there. 'Dismissed, Inspector,' he said. 'But if you have any contact at all, let me know immediately, day or night. Is that understood?'

'Yes, sir,' said Flick, but as she went down the stairs she had to admit she'd been lying. How could she understand when she hadn't a clue what the Old Man was on about?

Tuesday

The man leaned on the ship's rail and watched the choppy waves of the English Channel so far below. No-one noticed him. No-one would remember having seen him on board. He was that sort of person, inconspicuous, invisible almost. He had no distinguishing features, nothing remarkable in his appearance. The few who had seen him would have said he was a very ordinary chap with nothing notable about him. Had they looked into his eyes they would have thought differently.

He was quietly satisfied. The last loose end had been tied up. A manic giggle escaped as he thought about that. Now, if the police kept their noses out, his timetable should run smoothly. Then things could settle back into their proper calm routine.

The ship's wake stretched away behind the ferry that carried him back to England.

Tuesday evening

Honey, I'm home,' called Flick as she opened her front door. It was the private joke and signal between her and Andy that all was well. Although this evening it wasn't quite true. She was still smarting from the DCI's remarks and puzzled by his behaviour. But that wouldn't affect the kids who now came hurtling down the hall to greet her.

'Mum. It's not fair,' cried Natalie who was usually able to beat her twin to the draw. 'We're not babies. Why can't we come home?'

'Hello, Nat, hello, Jude. How nice to see you. Yes, thank you I'm very well and I've had a good day.'

Natalie giggled. Jude grinned. 'Hello, Mum,' they chorused and waited while she put down her heavy briefcase and took off her coat.

'And I see you are home,' said Flick, 'so what's the problem?' As if she didn't know.

'Nat's right, Mum,' said Jude, usually the quieter of the two. 'Why do we have to go to Mrs Baker's after school?'

As arranged, their grandmother had returned to London on Monday to the home she shared with her sister. The household routine had reverted to the twins staying at the next door neighbour's after school until Flick or Andy got home.

With the twins hanging onto an arm each Flick crossed the hall into the big family kitchen that was the heart of their home. Hello, love,' she said to Andy who was lifting a casserole out of the oven. A delicious smell reminded Flick she had eaten no lunch – apart from a Mars bar. Her tummy rumbled.

'Mum!' squealed Natalie. 'That's gross.'

'No, darling child. That's hunger,' said Flick and leaned forward to give Andy a kiss. 'Everyone wash their hands and let's eat. No more questions until my tummy is happy.'

While they ate their meal Flick watched her children. She exchanged knowing looks with Andy as the twins reverted to whatever long-running argument they had been pursuing before her arrival. They were a constant source of joy and amusement to both parents. Once Flick's mother, Amanda Faucherand, had decided to return to London, Flick and Andy had had to work out an arrangement that would allow both of them to keep on their jobs and yet safeguard the children. Happily, while living with them for so many years, Mrs Faucherand had become friendly with the next door neighbour, Elaine Baker. When Amanda returned to London, Elaine had offered to watch the twins on those days when shift patterns or Flick's crazy hours meant neither she nor Andy could be home when the twins arrived from school.

At twelve years old they were allowed to walk home without adult supervision. It was not far and, provided they were at least together or with some of their friends, Andy and Flick had decided to give them this amount of responsibility and freedom. So far it had worked well, but the arrival of their beloved grandmother who had met them from school each day and taken them out for some treat had disrupted the routine. They hated the fact she had left again and it was showing in this rebellion against the rules.

'Now then,' said Flick as she pushed aside her empty pudding bowl. 'What's your problem?'

Both twins spoke at once. Flick didn't interrupt. She was used to it and could easily make out what each was saying. This time it amounted to the same thing. When they had finally run out of steam she waited until she had their attention.

'While I agree with you.' Both twins sat up straighter and looked pleased. 'That, at twelve, you are really ancient,' Flick went on, to giggles from the children. 'For some strange reason Dad and I are happy to have you still around. The day will come I'm sure when we shall kick you out to have places of your own and give us a bit of peace, but not yet.

'Seriously . . . you know what Dad and I do for a living and you are both old enough to realise there are some very unpleasant people around. Some are evil and some are sick but the results are the same. They do bad things. Do you really think Dad and I would be able to concentrate on our jobs if we knew you two were here in the house on your own? That is if we even knew you had arrived safely from school?'

'But we'd lock the door,' said Jude.

'And we'd text you we were home,' added Natalie.

'And you'd always remember to do that, would you?'

'Yes, of course,' they replied.

Flick looked thoughtful. 'Now let me see. Who was it who left the gas on after heating up the soup on Saturday?'

Natalie was mortified. The twins had only just been trusted to use the cooker hob and she was the guilty party. Before Jude could crow over his twin, Flick went on. 'And who left the back door wide open and went off to play with his mates for an hour?'

Jude bit his lip. He'd asked permission to go out and, that being granted, had flown out of the house, the only thought in his head being the promised game of football.

'So,' continued Flick, 'I rest my case. I think we'll leave the arrangement as it is shall we? I thought you liked Mrs Baker?'

'We do. It's just that it's nicer to be home.'

'I know pet, but let's face it. It's not so very often either Dad or I can't be here for you is it?'

When eight years earlier a hopped-up kid in a stolen car had caused the smash that had taken Andy's right arm he had thought his career was over. And of course as a Hot Pursuit Driver it had been. But he'd opted to accept the offer to do desk and promotional work. He was a popular choice to give Crime Prevention talks, especially with elderly ladies. His pleasant looks and the charming Scottish accent he had never lost made him a great favourite.

When he first realised he had lost his arm there were dark days. The daft thing was his car hadn't even been moving at the time. All those occasions when Flick had worried about him being involved in a high-speed accident chasing some maniac joy-rider or fleeing thief, and there he was, sitting in a parked car waiting for his oppo to come back with the coffees. The crash had come out of nowhere. A lorry had swerved to avoid a stolen car roaring along on the wrong side of the road and slammed a transit van, shoving it into the driver's side of Andy's Mondeo. The metalwork had crumpled as if it had been cardboard, and that was that. At first he wished the crash had finished him off completely, but gradually he came out of his depression and began to put his life back together.

Nowadays he appreciated he was lucky to be alive, to be able to continue in a job he loved and contribute to the wellbeing of his family. He'd learned to cook to a reasonable standard and now NanaManda wasn't here the twins helped more round the house. The system worked well. Life was good and Andy was grateful.

When the children were in bed, Flick and Andy relaxed. Andy poured his wife a glass of wine and helped himself to a lager. 'Now then,' he said, 'what's bothering you?'

Flick smiled and raised her glass in a silent toast. 'No fooling you, is there, mister?' she said.

'Do you want to? Fool me, that is?'

'No. Of course not but it's nice to feel you know me so well - comforting really.'

'Do you need comfort?'

Flick thought for a moment. 'Do you know I think I do.'

Andy grinned. 'Always ready to oblige,' he said.

Flick laughed. 'Not that kind, mister. Although, maybe later. I just have that helpless feeling you had as a child when someone had treated you unfairly and you didn't know what to do about it.'

'Sorry, love. You've lost me.'

Flick told him about her interview with DCI Westcott. 'I just couldn't believe he'd said that. How dare he?' she cried as indignation rushed in again. 'And then all that cryptic guff about me having heard something and if contact was made. I had no idea what the hell he was talking about. I still don't know.'

'Hey, easy on. You're quite right to resent that kind of inference but don't let it get you in a tizzy. And it's not really like the Old Man is it? He must have a bee in his bonnet about something. What was he saying about drugs here?'

'Some serious new stuff about apparently. I would have thought if it was that bad we'd have got wind of it. And surely it's not that recent, like overnight or during the last week while we were away. That's not how it happens. It builds up until the whispers get noticed. A snout will say something or the users are more likely to give it away. But I've heard nothing. What about you?'

'Not really. I did hear about the kids in hospital but thought it was probably E's or drink. If the Drug Squad is waiting to interview them, how come Westcott already knew what kind of drugs they'd taken?'

'I've no idea. Perhaps he was guessing. But I really don't like the look of this. The riddles he was talking made me feel as though I was missing something - something he thought I should know. What's going on, Andy?'

Wednesday

Wednesday was dustbin day in Flick's street. As she manoeuvred her wheelie bin into place on the pavement, Elaine Baker was doing the same.

'I hope the kids haven't been playing you up, Elaine,' said Flick after greeting her neighbour.

'No, of course not, dear,' said Elaine. 'I know they would like to go straight home, but they never give me any trouble. I love having them and you and Amanda have brought them up to be polite and considerate. I appreciate that.'

Flick laughed. 'Well I appreciate the fact they remember to behave when they are in someone else's house. It doesn't always happen at home, believe me.'

Elaine smiled. 'You couldn't expect it to could you? They're normal children, not angels.'

'No,' agreed Flick. She hesitated and then plunged on. 'I might be asking you to have them more often for a while, or I might even ask Mum to come back again.'

Elaine looked concerned. 'Isn't our arrangement working, Felicity?' Apart from Mum, Elaine was about the only person who used Flick's full name. When she had been christened Felicity, representing affirmation of the joy she had brought to her parents, no-one thought of the teasing such a name might inspire among insensitive schoolmates and colleagues. She had been Flick to practically everyone since secondary school. 'I told you

I love having the twins,' went on Elaine. 'I wouldn't mind in the least them coming for longer or more often, provided I have a little notice, that is.'

'That's just the problem. I think I'm going to be working some daft hours at short notice for a while.'

'Ah, yes, that murder on the old Bristol road. I suppose you're involved with that aren't you dear?'

Flick knew her mouth had dropped open. Hastily she closed it. 'How did you know about that? I only found out myself yesterday.'

'Yes, dear, it was on the local radio this morning. Poor little Lenny.'

Flick's antennae came alive. 'You knew him did you? Lenny Strickland.'

'Not really knew him.' Elaine smiled. 'Brian, my late husband, was a bit of a gambler. Nothing serious, of course, but he liked a flutter now and then, the Grand National; the Ashes; and the big rugby matches. I suppose he went often enough to be looked on as a regular customer. I know he had an account with Global, I think they're called, down by the station. One day he wasn't very well and had telephoned in his bets. He won – he used to do that quite often. I suppose that's why he kept going.'

Flick waited, but nothing else seemed forthcoming. 'Lenny?' she prompted.

'Oh, yes, dear. Little Lenny. Well, he came round with Brian's winnings that day. And as my Brian's health deteriorated Lenny became a frequent visitor. Quiet chap, very unassuming, but neat and tidy. Later on, he sometimes stopped for a chat with Brian, which was good of him.' Elaine's eyes took on that look people

67

have when remembering times long past. Flick fished her car keys out of her pocket and turned to walk up the drive.

'I saw him you know,' said Elaine. 'Quite recently.'

'Who?' said Flick, her mind still on Brian Baker.

'Lenny.'

'Lenny? When was that exactly?'

'Let me see. It was about two weeks ago. Amanda and I were in town and I meant to change my library book. Silly me,' Elaine laughed, 'I'd forgotten the library closes on Thursdays.'

'Thursday. It was definitely Thursday when you saw Lenny?'

'Yes. Not last Thursday because that was the day Amanda was getting ready for you coming home from Scotland . So it must have been the week before.'

Yes it had to be the week before. Thursday. The very day Lenny died. Flick couldn't believe her luck. An eye witness.

'Where did you see Lenny, Elaine? Can you remember and what time it was?'

'It was after lunch. Amanda and I had been into that nice little cafe on the High Street. They do lovely open sandwiches there, really delicious and plenty of filling.'

Flick clenched her hand in the pocket of her jacket. 'And where was it you saw Lenny, Elaine?'

'Let me see. We'd sat chatting for a while over lunch and Amanda was watching the time for picking up the twins so we cut through Marks and were heading for home along Mafeking Street. If you go that way it cuts out a huge loop. You can't drive it because you need to cross the railway on the footbridge, but walking is quite quick.'

'Lenny?'

'Yes. It was after we'd crossed over the railway onto the factory road. He was with two friends. One of them was laughing. It was nice to see him with someone his own age. Poor Lenny. Just listen to me chattering on. I mustn't keep you back, dear. I know how busy you are. Goodbye.'

Elaine turned away and started up her drive. For a moment Flick thought of calling out to her but there was no rush. First she had to find out where this latest information fitted in with what had been gathered overnight.

'Nothing at all to add, really, boss,' concluded Dave Booth in the Briefing Room after Constables Jarvis and Spence had made their reports. 'He was just a quiet little guy who kept himself to himself. A loner who didn't rock the boat.'

'He rocked someone's boat enough for them to kill him,' reminded Flick. 'And he wasn't a total loner. He did have friends.' She told them of the two people seen with Lenny on the day he died. 'I want you to go back out and revisit everyone you've spoken to. I want these friends identified. Perhaps they can tell us what Lenny might have done to get himself killed. When you are doing your interviews, just remind yourselves of the common motives for murder. Desire, Power, Control, Hate, Revenge and of course Money.' She shook her head. 'Lenny doesn't spring to mind as being associated with any of those but you never know. Back here this evening. And I want some results.'

Flick was frustrated. This enquiry was going nowhere. She'd see if Elaine could tell her anything more. 'With me, Dave,' she said. 'You can drive. I want to think. But first I want to see Fred Updike.'

After a tap on his office door, Flick pushed it open and greeted the grey-haired Crime Scene Investigator.

'Hi, Fred,' she said. 'Just a courtesy call to let you know you and Martin were quite right. Victim was not a vagrant but a chap by the name of Lenny Strickland, bookie's runner and apparently led a blameless existence so dear knows who would want to murder him. But that's my headache so we'll leave you in peace.'

'Thanks for letting me know, Flick, but what about the other two? Martin's complaining they're filling up his trays and he's becoming *my* headache.'

Flick was on her way to the door. She swung round and frowned at Fred Updike. 'What other two? What are you on about?'

'The other two who came in in the same week.'

Flick looked at Dave Booth. 'Well, Sergeant? Have you anything to tell me?'

Booth opened his mouth, shut it, then tried again. 'It was like the tramp, boss. DI Jackson dealt with it and I was sent to my desk to do paperwork. I have no idea what happened and I didn't know that you didn't know – if you see what I mean?'

'No. I don't see. How could I know? I asked you what had been going on in my absence. You realised when the Lenny affair turned up that I knew nothing. I told you DI Jackson said everything was tidied up. It obviously wasn't but you didn't think to let me know what had been going on. I expect common sense and loyalty from my officers, Sergeant. You would do well to remember that.'

It was the measure of Flick's upset that she tore Dave Booth off a strip in front of Fred Updike. She was usually totally loyal to her own team and would wait to reprimand a wrongdoer until there was no-one else present. But she was filled with a sick anger. Not at Booth but at Tubby Jackson. Was the idiot so consumed with his dislike of Flick as to hide cases? And why? To get her into trouble? But small victory for him if he wasn't here to see it.

Fred had turned away and busied himself with some task. While sympathetic to Flick and despising Tubby Jackson he had no desire to get involved in departmental politics.

Flick turned back to him. 'Sorry about that Fred. You will have realised I haven't any notes on either of these deaths, so no clue about the circumstances. I would be really grateful if you could let me have duplicate copies of the notes you sent up to DI Jackson asap. I know how busy you are and I'll owe you. I'll ring Martin and ask for a copy of his too.' She managed to give Fred a smile before turning on her heel and stalking out of his office. A chastened Sergeant Booth hurried after her.

Flick led the way across the main hall towards the rear entrance giving onto the car park behind the station. As she arrived at the door it opened to let DCI Westcott enter. Flick stood aside to let him pass. He paused,

71

inclined his head towards her and raised his eyebrows in query.

'Sir?' she said .

He frowned. 'No news then?'

'No, sir. You'll be the first to know.'

'Right. Carry on, Inspector,' he said and went on his way.

What the hell am I doing, thought Flick? Am I dreaming or in *Alice through the Looking Glass*? The Chief is talking in riddles and now I am answering him as though I know what he's on about. I'm going potty. I can't go and see Elaine in this mood. She'll have to wait.

She retraced her steps and, still followed by a silent Booth went upstairs. As they walked through the big outer office the buzz of conversation stopped. Flick stalked straight ahead. Dave Booth followed her. People sitting at their desks took one look at her face, exchanged worried and puzzled glances then, with heads down, became extremely busy.

Once in her own office, Flick hung up her coat and sat behind her desk. She looked at Dave Booth with cold eyes. 'Shut the door, then sit and speak,' she said. 'From the beginning and don't leave anything out. Start with Lenny. I was clearing my desk on Friday and left sharpish to catch the plane north. So DI Jackson got the shout and took you with him and found Lenny. Then what?'

'It was just as I told you. He took over and told me to get on with the paperwork. That was Friday. On Monday morning by chance I heard a body had been found on the Sunday behind the Phoenix nightclub. You know, the one that used to be a cinema. Seems there was a disturbance on the Saturday night – not really unusual after kicking-out time these days. There'd been an almighty ruckus, sore heads, a couple needing hospital stitches and a few arrests for disturbance of the peace, just the usual. But a couple on their way to church the next morning took a short cut through the alley leading to the car park and found the body of a white male about six foot. He had been very beaten up apparently, not a pretty sight. The woman passed out when her husband turned him over to see if he was drunk or in need of help.'

'So we have a Good Samaritan. I assume he was interviewed?'

'Yes, boss, but he couldn't tell us anything. Didn't know the chap, or couldn't recognise him if he did after what had been done to him.'

'Then, after the CSI had finished at the scene the body was taken to the morgue and what further action took place?' said Flick.'

'I don't know. I just had to check on any MISPERs and then it was back to the filing. No-one reported missing answered even the brief description we had.'

'Go on. What's next?'

Booth swallowed. 'Pretty much the same, boss. The shout came from a postman. He was delivering mail to one of the big houses on Waterloo Road and heard a car engine in the garage. He thought that was strange because the family were supposed to be away for another fortnight. He'd been warned to make sure the post went right through and dropped down so no-one would know the house was empty. He went to listen and smelled gas at the side of the door. He dialled 999 and set things in motion. That was on Tuesday morning. I went with DI Jackson but the fellow was long dead according to Fred Updike. We left the CSI team to it and DI Jackson said suicides were more trouble than they were worth. Again no-one reported in MISPER and I don't know what further action DI Jackson initiated. All I do know is that I was told not to poke my nose in . . . ma'am.'

Flick sat and gazed at the telephone on her desk. Her first reaction was to go round to Tubby Jackson's house and ask him what the hell he was playing at.

The second was to wonder if this was what the Chief had been on about. Was one or both of these deaths important? Of course all death was important, but had these or at least one of them been so sensitive Tubby had reported direct to DCI Westcott who had told him to keep what he knew under his hat? That was a possibility of course but wouldn't explain why Tubby hadn't filled her in on a handover/takeover. Flick could think of no possible scenario where such information would not be passed on to her as senior officer taking over.

Should she go and ask the Chief? But what if this was Tubby being devious? Had he plotted the whole thing to drop Flick in the mire once he, Tubby, was well away? Well, if so, he wasn't going to get away with it.

'Get your coat,' she said to Booth. 'You're coming with me to see ex Detective Inspector Jackson. I need a witness and a strong arm of restraint.'

Dave Booth was alarmed. 'You don't think he'd try and hurt you do you, boss?'

'No. But I won't answer for what I might do to him.'

Wednesday

Unaware of the two new bodies his wife had on her patch, Andy sat at his desk hoping she could clear up the Fail to Stop murder quickly.

He was very fond of his mother-in-law, Amanda Faucherand, and more grateful to her than words could express for coming to their rescue when the twins arrived. After his accident she had even uprooted herself from her beloved London, leaving behind relatives and life-long friends to help the Fraser family settle in their new home. Amanda had been a true friend and support ever since the twins were born.

But when she had decided to return to her roots and set up home with her sister Andy'd welcomed the change. Until lately he hadn't realised how constricting the presence of a third adult in the house had been. Andy grinned remembering how, with Amanda back in London, he had "comforted" Flick yesterday evening once the twins were fast asleep. The cosy sitting room fire had not gone unappreciated, an indulgence normally unthinkable with Amanda in the house.

'He's home then, boss,' said Booth, noting Tubby Jackson's W reg Vauxhall in the drive of the semi-detached house.

'Good.' Flick was in no mood to put off the confrontation with her ex colleague. 'You just switch on

75

your memory and stay schtum.' The Yiddish slang from her old London patch still came easily to Flick's lips. Whatever passed between Jackson and herself she didn't want Dave Booth putting in his oar. This was her fight and one she was definitely going to win. No question. She stalked up the path, rang the doorbell and banged the ornate knocker for good measure.

She heard the bell sound somewhere in the house but no-one came to answer her summons. Flick's lips tightened. 'If Tubby Jackson wants to play silly buggers and try to ignore me, he's got another think coming,' she said to Booth. 'You go round the back and see if he's in the garden. I think you can get through that small gate beside the garage.' She banged the knocker and then put her finger on the bell-push, and kept it there. The noise went on and on. Surely no-one could bear that racket for long?

Booth reappeared beside her. 'No sign of him there, boss. In fact the place doesn't look lived in.'

'What do you mean?' Flick took her finger off the bell.

'Well, it's too tidy. Nothing on any of the kitchen surfaces. I peered through the other ground floor windows. There's nothing in the sitting room. No papers left lying around. No slippers by the hearth. His wife left him you know a while ago and I would never have taken him for a house-proud guy. Quite the opposite. I think he's a bit of a slob – at work anyway.'

Thinking of Jackson's desk, the state of which had always irritated her, and his sloppy table manners in the canteen, Flick had to agree. Although, she had always thought Jackson exaggerated those habits just to annoy her. She bit her lip and frowned. 'We'll just come back this evening, and again tomorrow and again and again until we get him. I'm not giving up,' she said.

As they turned to leave, an overweight woman laden down with shopping bags came puffing up the next-door driveway. 'No use you ringing there, dear,' she said. 'He's out.'

'Yes,' said Flick. 'Have you any idea when he'll be back, Mrs . .?'

The other woman hesitated.

A good neighbour wouldn't advertise when the house would be empty to just anyone, thought Flick. She pulled out her warrant card and identified herself.

The doubtful expression on the other's face disappeared to be replaced by a beaming smile. 'Cracken, Inspector, Mrs Violet Cracken. Been a neighbour of Mr and Mrs Jackson's for donkey's years. Sad the way their marriage ended, but there you are, I don't think he would have been an easy man to live with, and keeping odd hours and all, but you'd know about that yourself. Got family, have you?' Once Mrs Cracken's distrust was allayed, the flood of information and interrogation seemed endless. She never stopped for breath. Booth turned away to hide a smile. Flick waited for a gap into which she could put her questions.

'Do you know when Mr Jackson will be back?' said Flick. She was blowed if she was going to give him his rank.

'No idea. He didn't say. I was in the corner shop when he cancelled his papers. Said he didn't know for how long but he'd let them know when he got back.

Although he wasn't at home during the weekend. But just to fly off again the next night. Well, he might have said something. He knew we'd keep an eye on the house for him. And he just stuck a note in the milk bottle.' She saw Flick's raised eyebrows and hurried on. 'We share the same milkman, Jerry, that is, and he told me. Bit of a rum do, he thought, going off so sudden like that.'

Rum, probably not, thought Flick but very convenient to be out of town when he must have known Flick would come looking for answers. Once she had sorted out Mrs Cracken's various references, she smiled at her. 'Did you say Mr Jackson flew to his holiday destination? He obviously didn't take his car.'

'I don't know, dear, I mean, Inspector. I didn't see him go.'

'Thank you, madam, you've been most helpful.'

'Which is more than can be said for bloody Tubby Jackson,' she muttered as she and Booth got back into their car.

He waited, aware how Flick's anger was simmering still, just below the surface. It wasn't often she lost her cool, but boy, when she did it was best to keep his mouth shut and preferably remain invisible.

'I suppose now I shall have to go and see the Old Man,' Flick muttered. 'I can't go groping round in the dark and maybe there is a good reason Tubby didn't use you, Dave, or any other of the usual team.'

Booth heaved a quiet sigh of relief. The use of his Christian name alone signalled he had been forgiven.

'But that doesn't explain why the stupid plonker didn't do a proper handover/takeover,' went on Flick.

'I'll have to go and see the boss, but not before I've found out more about these other two. Let's hope Fred has been his usual efficient self and sent copies of his notes up to me.'

Later that afternoon, having been admitted by DCI Westcott's secretary, Flick had to wait while he finished a telephone call. She guessed, from the content, it was with his wife.

While she waited she thought over the conversation she'd just had with Marion Harvester. Marion was the media liaison officer and as such was always kept in the loop, ready to fend off the press or otherwise deal with news dissemination. If anyone knew about the three bodies, surely Marion would?

But Marion's answers to Flick's question were unhelpful. 'Yes, Flick, I saw it in the log. A Fail to Stop, a suicide and a beating. But nothing ever came of any of them for my attention. Tubby told me they were all out of towners, no MISPERS involved and nothing newsworthy. He managed to keep them under the radar, thank goodness.' she smiled. 'Makes my job easier.'

'But didn't you think it a bit odd there was no big investigation? After all, quiet little Ridminster doesn't often get three suspicious deaths in one week.'

'But they weren't really suspicious, were they? A drunken tramp staggers into the path of a passing car; a bloke betrayed by his girlfriend tops himself; and a Saturday night brawl ends in tragedy. Sad all of them, but nothing heavy.'

Flick couldn't believe her ears. 'Is that what DI Jackson said to you?'

'Yes. Why do you ask? Look, I'm sorry, but I must go. I've to be in Bristol in an hour and the traffic is murder. If you need me you know how to get hold of me.'

Flick didn't detain her. She knew Marion had a desk in Taunton where she spent a couple of days a week and the rest of her time she was here, there and everywhere doing what she did best, that was keeping the press and public off the backs of hard-working officers, or at HQ. But what would Marion have said, or done, if Flick had told her Lenny's death was murder?

'Sorry about that, Inspector. Now what can I do for you?' DCI Westcott's voice was cordial enough but his eyes flickered towards the clock on his wall. Flick had the distinct impression his thoughts were elsewhere.

'Nothing to report, I suppose?' he went on. 'No. You'd have come right up. So what is it?'

Flick had been trying to rehearse what she would say but without success. After the last bollocking Westcott had given her she couldn't just walk in and complain about Tubby's lack of investigation. She felt her way. 'Sir, is there anything DI Jackson has been reporting directly to you on? That is, something, not for general release to the rest of the squad?'

Westcott looked astounded, as though he thought she was mad. Then his words confirmed it. 'Don't be bloody silly, Inspector. You know better than to ask that. I thought you were ideally cut out for this job, but I'm beginning to wish DI Jackson was still with us.'

Flick opened her mouth to defend herself, ask what the boss meant and explain her problem with the bodies and no paperwork, but the telephone rang again.

Westcott raised his hand like a traffic cop to stop her speech and answered the phone. 'Yes. Yes. No. Go ahead. No, wait a moment.' He turned to Flick. 'That will be all, Inspector, and please keep your mind on the job.'

Flick found herself outside DCI Westcott's office more confused than when she had entered.

'I just don't understand what's going on, Andy,' she said later that night. 'If I didn't know better I'd say the Old Man has lost the plot. What am I going to do? The boss has lost his marbles, Tubby Jackson has done a runner, and I'm left with three unidentified bodies that no-one wants.'

Andy thought for a moment. 'Follow the trail,' he advised.

'But there isn't one,' cried Flick. 'Jackson has either taken or destroyed the files. The trail has gone cold. Who's going to remember or care what happened weeks ago?'

'Well, I image the people who own the house where the suicide took place will care, when they come home. You could start with them. No-one will have interviewed them as they were away. Perhaps they know the victim?'

Flick smiled. 'You're right, of course. There must be all the evidence the CSI team collected. I just have to find it. I wonder if Jackson conned the Detained Property Store to just hang on to it as something not over important, or somehow made it disappear? Surely even he wouldn't do that? I'll start from the beginning, as if it's just happened. After all that's what we did with Lenny and now we know that he was murdered and who he is.'

'Yes, and all you have to do is find his killer,' smiled Andy. 'I'm glad to have you back Inspector Fraser. For a moment there I thought I'd lost my wife and some imposter had taken her place. Not like you to get so down, pet.'

'I know. Sorry, love. But it's this Tubby and the Old Man business. He was so unfair, which I admit isn't like him, and he just didn't give me a chance to tell him I haven't a clue what he was on about the other day. Right, me lad. Bedtime. I want to be bright of eye and bushy of tail to start my *three* investigations tomorrow. The troops won't know what's hit them?' she laughed.

She got up and began to tidy the sitting room. 'And I suppose I'd better give Mum a ring tomorrow and see if she can come down. I've a feeling we're going to need her.'

Andy raised his eyes to Heaven. He'd surely been tempting fate when he counted his blessings this morning.

Thursday

The early bird catches the worm, thought Flick. Well she'd certainly done that but now she wasn't at all sure what to do with it. She looked without seeing at the three whiteboards she had had set up in the biggest briefing room. Each one was accompanied by its corkboard for pinning up photographs, newspaper cuttings or anything pertinent to the investigation.

But where would she pin up her latest find, if she could? Did it have anything to do with any of her bodies? Probably not, but it had been a bit of a shock to see Paddy Murphy here in Ridminster.

Last time they'd met was in the pub round the corner from her old nick, celebrating the successful end of a long investigation. Like her, Paddy had served with the Vice Squad. So what was he doing here? They'd met on the staircase so he could only have been coming from the top floor, which is no doubt why he had admitted having been in to see DCI Westcott. Played his cards very close to his chest Paddy did - always had. But when Flick had asked him what he was doing here, Paddy had looked surprised, almost as though she should have known. Now what was that all about? Flick frowned.

'Here you are, boss.' Dave Booth's voice interrupted Flick's ponderings 'What's going on here, then?'

'We're going to practice being jugglers,' she said and grinned at the puzzled frown that crossed Booth's pleasant young face. 'You've heard of keeping three balls in the air at once? Well substitute cases and you get the picture.'

'You mean . . .?'

'Yes. We're going back to square one and investigating all three deaths. They may not be suspicious, except for Lenny Strickland who we know was murdered. No-one accidentally accelerates towards someone standing in the middle of the road. But the other two were sudden and so deserve our best attention also.

'As far as I can make out nothing was even done to identify them. There may be grieving relatives to inform.'

'No MISPERs registered, boss.'

'Perhaps for once Tubby was speaking the truth when he said they were out-of-towners, whether he knew it or not. But even so we'll have to ID them. I want you and Derek Jarvis and Barry Spence on this. We'd better have Harry Whiteman too while we're about it.'

Booth grinned. DC Harry Whiteman was known for his encyclopaedic knowledge of every pub in the area. If answers could be found in the watering holes of Ridminster, Harry Whiteman was the one to send.

'Call in Barbara Hurle and Jane Best from Uniform too. They can cover the shops. Back here in twenty minutes,' said Flick, hoping the team she had chosen would be enough to get the investigation moving.

In her office she read through the copy reports Martin Barnes and Fred Updike had sent her. She shuffled photos on her desk then gathered everything up and walked across the corridor to the briefing room.

'Settle down, people,' she said. 'We have three investigations that I intend to run side by side. Although they are not connected, the ground work for each will start off pretty much the same. DS Booth will put up what we have on the boards as I speak.

'We start with Lenny Strickland deliberately rundown on the old Bristol road.' Flick went through all she and Booth had managed to find out about Lenny. 'So who were the two friends he was with at some time before he died? Will they know if he had any enemies or perhaps owed money to some "heavies"? We need to ask around the places Lenny frequented, the bookies, the pub, the roads he walked along to and from his work. I'll go back and ask Mrs Baker if she can give me a better description or if she had ever seen them before. DS Booth will go back to the bookies for any more information on Lenny including who he spent his time with. Someone must know who his friends were.

'Next we have the suicide. Not unusually he'd taken sleeping pills, washing them down with a bottle of whisky before the carbon monoxide fumes finished him off. When the householders return I shall interview them. Perhaps they will know who he is, although the postman who has been delivering their letters for the past two years didn't recognise him. He was pretty sure it wasn't one of the family. In the meantime I want his photo shown round.

'Same goes for the chap who was beaten up. Martin Barnes has cleaned him up pretty well but he's still not a pretty sight so be careful who you show the pics to. We don't want any old ladies fainting with shock.

'DS Perkins, I want you to go through the evidence bags, such as they are. We're looking for anything that can help us ID these men. Old bus tickets, cinema stubs, cigarette packets, you know the drill.'

Tom Perkins was the oldest person in the room. Figures were his passion. He was never happier than poring over ledgers and bank statements chasing phantom money someone had tried to conceal. But puzzles of any kind interested him and he was quite content to examine evidence so minutely not a single hair or out-of-place fibre would escape his gaze.

'Right you are, boss.' He nodded his agreement to Flick, delighted not to be pounding the beat on exhaustive and often fruitless enquiries. 'Can I bring them up here?'

'Yes,' said Flick. 'Let's have each bag on a table by the respective boards. Now,' she went on, 'the only times we can fix for any of them are when they were found and the pathologist's estimated time of death.'

Dave Booth began a time line for each victim with the meagre details. Apart from the time line, Lenny's name and approximate age and a brief description of the other two, the whiteboards looked very empty. On the corkboards were pinned the photographs Fred Updike had sent to Flick. Taken at the scenes of the crimes they recorded everything in minute detail.

'Right. Off you go and bring me back something we can work with. I'm going to try and clear my desk before we really get our teeth into this little lot,' she said.

Everyone did their best. But the people who knew or thought they might have seen Lenny couldn't remember him having any friends he drank with or knocked about with generally. And in spite of showing the photographs around and asking questions, no-one seemed to know who the other two victims were.

Stan Hatcher at the Global bookmakers was impatient with their renewed presence in his establishment and almost hostile at their continued interest in Lenny. Police attention was bad for business according to his way of thinking and the little runt was hardly worth all this fuss.

The landlord of the Crown and Sceptre was away at a Brewers' convention but his wife and the barman on duty couldn't help with identifying the photos they were shown.

Tom Perkins carefully examined every item of clothing on the tables in front of him. There was surprisingly little in the way of personal effects. One man had a few pounds in his pocket and the suicide had a crumpled piece of paper on which *I'm sorry* was scribbled in pencil. Tom spent quite a long time examining the lighter with the windshield. He hadn't seen one like that for years. It was almost with regret he returned it to its bag with rest of the suicide evidence on the table.

Flick had dealt with the usual run of the mill paperwork on her desk, answered several phone calls and was just about to call it a day when her phone rang again. It was Fred Updike.

'Flick? Can you spare a minute?'

'Now? I was just about to go home, at a reasonable hour for a change. Won't it wait until tomorrow?' She couldn't think of anything about Fred and Martin's "guests" that would warrant haste. They were going nowhere.

'If you wouldn't mind. There's something Martin and I think you should see.'

Thursday evening

Flick bit back a dismayed comment. 'Okay then, if you think it can't wait. Just give me a minute to ring home and I'll be right with you.' She ended the call, paused for a moment, then dialled home. She listened to the bell ringing at home and smiled. Which of the twins would win the race to answer the call?

'Hello,' panted the winner.

'Hello, Nat darling,' said Flick. 'Have you had a good day?'

'Brill,' enthused Natalie. 'Mum! NanaManda is coming back. Isn't that just fantastic? Get off, Ju!' she shouted, nearly deafening Flick.

'Yes, it's lovely. Does Jude want to talk to me? And please don't yell in my ear like that.'

'Sorry, Mum, but he's such a pest. He was trying to pull the phone away while I was speaking and that's rude, isn't it?'

'Yes. Tell him he'll have his turn in a minute. I may be late home so do your homework and help Dad with the dinner, but leave some for me. Okay? Now if there's nothing more you want to tell me pass the phone to Jude.'

'But, Mum, there's a new girl in our class. She's really brown, well black I suppose, and she says she comes from France. But black people don't live in France do they, Mum?'

'Don't be daft, pet. That's like saying black people don't live in England, isn't it? We'll talk about it at bedtime. Now put Jude on.'

After an interval when Flick could hear her children arguing Jude finally got possession of the phone.

'Hello, Mum.' Flick smiled. Her son was the less volatile of the twins, although he had his moments. She liked to watch "the wheels go round" as he worked out some new piece of information before committing himself to speech on the subject. 'I told Nat she was daft saying a thing like that,' the loving brother said. 'Francoise used to live in Marseilles but then her Dad was moved to Angers and now he works in Bristol. She's got a brother too and he'll be coming to our school but he's been ill so he won't start till next week. He's a year older than me but I think he'll be in our class because although Francoise says he's very clever it will be hard for him learning in English won't it Mum?'

Flick shook her head. Twins! You couldn't let one give out important news and stop the other from doing so. 'Yes, son. I expect it will, but like I said to Nat, we'll talk about this at bedtime. Now please ask Dad to save me some dinner. I'll be home as soon as I can. Bye, darling.'

She gave her desk a last tidy then made her way to the basement.

She found Martin Barnes with Fred Updike in Fred's office in the basement. Fred's big table had been cleared of its usual amount of material of all kinds and held only a selection of photographs spread out. Flick glanced down at them. They were all of bodies and body parts. Whenever she attended PM's she always felt a stir of pity when she saw the dead lying in the full glare of the harsh uncompromising overhead lamps. Their remorseless light uncovered every detail below. There is no hiding place in a morgue. The photographs revealed every detail

She cleared her throat and spoke up. 'So what have you two reprobates got that wouldn't wait till morning?'

Fred Updike turned without returning her smile. 'Possibly another murder for you, Flick. Although, as we know this chap was beaten so badly he couldn't survive, it is already a murder.'

Flick frowned. 'And this couldn't wait?'

'We thought you'd want to know what we found without delay,' offered Martin Barnes. 'The fact is after you told us you had identified a man who had been treated as a vagrant, I began to get an uneasy feeling about the other two who had been brought in just before Tubby Jackson departed. I asked Fred if he would come over and assist at a second autopsy.'

'And?' prompted Flick.

'There is something very peculiar about this death. At the time I was somewhat concerned at the lack of blood at the scene,' said Fred. 'Martin confirmed my belief that the body had been beaten up almost immediately after death.'

'What? I don't understand,' said Flick.

Martin pulled forward the photograph of a man probably in his late thirties or early forties. Even after he had been cleaned up for examination it was evident he had received a vicious beating. Traces of the make-up Martin had used to enable a reasonable photo to be taken for identification purposes remained on his face which was bruised to such an extent there was barely an inch of skin without some leathery-looking contusion. Blood had been washed from his hair which was long enough to reach his shoulders and which now lay spread out on the table below him

'It's not really the face that gives it away,' he said and pushed together photos of the torso. The familiar Y shape of the incisions pathology makes for examination were criss-crossed with the sutures used to close up the cavity caused. 'You see here and here,' Martin pointed, 'the ribs are cracked and broken enough to perforate the lungs. Both arms and legs have several fractures and the flesh is pierced where some kind of bludgeon has been used with force.'

Flick saw where the blows had landed, so many and so deep, she flinched at the thought of the malevolence needed to inflict such damage.

'With this kind of trauma there should have been pools of blood around the body.' Fred took up the tale. 'But there was very little and that mostly surface. On careful examination Martin found the place where this man had been stabbed.' He pointed out the picture where Flick could see the small slit between two of the lower ribs on the right hand side of the chest. It looked insignificant.

'How deep was the wound?' she said, 'and how could such a wound cause sudden death? It can't have reached his heart unless the blade was at least twelve inches long – not from that position, surely?'

'Ah.' Knowing she was really interested Fred had always taken the trouble to explain his findings in detail to Flick. Now he looked so pleased at her grasp of the present situation she feared he might almost pat her on the head for being such a good student. 'That is, of course, the anomaly. And that,' he went on, 'is where Martin and I became real detectives.'

Flick smiled. 'I always thought you were,' she said. 'You give me the answers the eye can't see.'

'Nice to be appreciated,' smirked Martin.

For a moment Flick wondered what a civvy would think if he were present. Except for the harrowing examination of dead and mutilated children or particular crimes, there was often a sense of levity in the mortuary. There was always respect for the dead but, like her own team, the pathologists couldn't possibly operate if they were always weighed down by the reality of man's inhumanity to man. A little light relief now and then made the job bearable.

'So what's the answer?' she went on.

'We don't know. But we did open him up to trace the route of the knife thrust and found something very strange. Normally the path of the wound is easy enough to follow. The blade pierces first the skin and then moves through the innards, causing damage to veins, arteries, and major organs on its way until the length of the blade is reached. It is at the point when the blade is withdrawn that most damage is done and exsanguination occurs. If the heart is still beating, blood under pressure will be lost from the wound.

'But this wound and the subsequent wounds when the body was battered hardly bled at all. Which suggests the heart stopped beating almost immediately.'

'So what on earth was the weapon like?' asked Flick. 'A sword? Or something like that?' She peered at the photo again. 'The slit is small so it would have been long and thin. A rapier?'

Martin shook his head. 'I've never seen anything like this before. The depth of the incision finished after piercing the subcutaneous layer, but the resultant damage was catastrophic.' He shook his head again in disbelief. 'It was almost as though something had smashed right through from the entrance wound right to the heart, pulverising everything in its path.'

'And causing instant death?'

'Certainly. The heart was destroyed. The cavity of the body was full of blood from the various arteries that had been ruptured but I would say from the second the knife - as we must continue to think of it - from the second it entered the body, the heart stopped and the victim was dead. Which is why there was no appreciable amount of blood coming from the later surface wounds and abrasions.'

'Well, you've certainly given me something to think about and you were right to call me today. I don't quite know how, but we must find out what weapon could inflict that kind of damage. But that's for another day, gentlemen. And I'll bid you good night. Unless you have any other horrid surprises up your sleeves?'

'Not really,' said Fred. 'The other chap was suicide fair enough. He had enough temazapam and alcohol in his system to knock out an elephant.'

Flick thought of the photos of the crime scenes she had been looking at earlier. Photos taken in the garage before the body was moved to the mortuary. 'Can you tell if he took the pills with the alcohol? How much of the whisky did he actually drink?'

'Whisky?' said Martin. 'Was it whisky? We can only say for sure that it was alcohol of some kind. Whatever it was he must have had at least half a bottle.'

For a moment she didn't answer while her memory ran through the photos again. Surely it had been a whisky bottle? And rather an expensive whisky at that. While she questioned her memory Fred spoke again.

'We may have some good news for you. We believe the van that ran Lenny down was a Volkswagen Transporter.'

That caught Flick's attention. 'Why? Why that particular van?'

'We looked at Lenny again also and in the strange way the body has of telling its secrets, the bruising on Lenny's torso has become more easily identifiable. A severe blow to the chest, especially over the right atrium and ventricle can cause sudden displacement of blood into the superior vena cava. Internal bleeding may occur for several hours after death. Where the tissue is shallow as in the chest the bone of the rib cage impedes the progress of the kinetic energy.'

Flick felt her eyes glaze over. Perhaps Fred noticed for he suddenly speeded up his delivery.

'Well, never mind all that. In short an intradermal bruise occurs in the layer of skin between the epidermis and subcutaneous tissue. This can hold a pattern of the object that has struck the victim. In Lenny's case his chest has taken on the pattern of a logo. Closer observation has convinced Martin and myself that it is the Volkswagen logo and according to the reference books we studied this particular logo appears on a Volkswagen Transporter van.'

'Someone said we were looking for a white van man,' said Flick. 'It looks as though they were right.'

'I hope all this is helpful to you,' said Martin.

'So do I,' said Flick. 'But at the moment, gentlemen, your answers have only raised more questions. I now have to find, from all the Volkswagen Transporter vans in the country, the one that ran down Lenny. I have a victim stabbed with an unknown weapon that no-one, despite your combined experience and expertise, can identify. And I have a suicide victim with an empty expensive whisky bottle at his feet. Thank you, gentlemen, for my triple headache. Good night.'

Thursday evening

DS Tom Perkins was fretting. Give him a puzzle and he would worry at it until he found the answer. But he had to have enough pieces and the trouble with this investigation was lack of pieces, or evidence.

Tom's wife was visiting her mother so that evening he made himself a meal in the immaculate kitchen of his home. He enjoyed the "woman's touch" as well as any man but in his wife's absence the house remained as pristine as when she was here to care for it. Neither of them could stand untidiness. In that as in so much else they were in complete agreement.

As he ate, sitting in solitary state at the dining room table, Tom reviewed in his mind the articles he had studied in the briefing room. He had perfect recall of every item.

Lenny's evidence bag had held so little. Apart from his clothes, torn and dirty from being dragged along the ground, and the pitiful contents of his pockets, there was nothing for Tom to get his teeth into. But the very absence of information suggested someone wanted Lenny to remain unidentified.

The suicide also wanted to remain anonymous. There was nothing personal on him. No letters; shopping lists; bus tickets or receipts. Just a packet with two cigarettes left in it and his lighter. Tom smiled. It had been a long time since he'd seen one like that. The only clue to the dead man's state of mind was the piece of paper with the two words *I'm sorry* scrawled on it. What had he been sorry for, or about? His clothes were nondescript items that could have been worn equally by university students, market traders, or in fact half the population of the British Isles. Worn trainers, jeans, T shirt and biker jacket. Also the ubiquitous baseball cap so beloved of a certain type of male. Tom associated them with souped-up cars and loud music. Underwear from Bhs which might point to him not being from Ridminster as there was no British Home Stores store in the town. Or it could simply mean a doting aunt had sent them for his birthday, or he had picked them up in a charity shop. Tom sighed. The only thing that might make people remember him had been the gold earring tucked into an envelope with the lighter. A lot of men did wear earrings these days, pop stars and football idols, but in Ridminster it might still cause remark. When the toxicology report came back they would see if he had taken any pills with the whisky from the bottle found in the car, but that was all it could reveal. That, and details of his last meal.

The final bag had belonged to the assault victim. The clothes were dirty and torn in places. Some bloodstains remained where the skin had broken. The shirt was a flannel check. There was a leather waistcoat and the boots were the type worn on building sites, with steel toe-caps. Had it been similar boots that had inflicted such damage on the body? The underwear and socks were from Messrs M&S. There were a few pounds in the pockets of the jeans, so it would seem robbery was not the reason for the attack. There was also a used tissue, or rather a piece of kitchen roll used as a handkerchief, and a rubber band.

Tom frowned. Now that was odd. Surely there must have been something else. To find *nothing* personal on a body was not only unusual, it was downright strange. Had the bloke been robbed, his attacker might, in haste, have just emptied every pocket of its contents hoping for something useful or valuable. But the idea this guy had been beaten up and then his attacker had removed everything but his money was ridiculous.

Tom cleared the table, washed up his dishes and put them away, then poured himself a glass of Theakston's Old Peculiar. He walked into the conservatory and gazed out into the beautiful garden. But Tom saw nothing of his wife's pride and joy. He was wrestling with an idea that wouldn't go away. Three bodies inside a week. Unusual for Ridminster. On the face of it three isolated incidents. One Fail to Stop, one suicide, and one extreme mugging.

But does a suicide bother to remove all identifying items from his person before doing the deed? There were two bodies killed by a third party, that was obvious. Both had been rendered anonymous. Why? And by whom? But so was the third. Was it possible the suicide had murdered the other two and then been overcome by remorse? Unlikely. It was all very well to read about beating someone to a pulp but much more difficult to do and be sure of death. And wouldn't the victim have defended himself? And why had the suicide then made sure he was anonymous? To spare family embarrassment or grief? Unusual behaviour in one who had screwed himself up to the point of death or who had arrived at the conclusion life had nothing left for him. If he had not committed suicide, had his death in fact been murder disguised? And if all three had been murdered, why?

And by whom? There seemed to be no connection between them. If only Tom had more pieces of the puzzle. But he would certainly voice this theory to DI Fraser in the morning.

Satisfied he could do no more that evening, Tom switched on the television to watch and criticise 5 USA's CSI programme.

Dave Booth sat in his Volvo in the station car park. It wasn't a new car but if cars matched their owners his was a perfect fit - big, sturdy and reliable.

He contemplated his options. He'd left the boss at her desk with a mound of paperwork in front of her. The more he saw of that part of police work the less he liked the idea of taking his exams for promotion - although the extra money would be useful. DI Fraser had assured him there was nothing more he could do for her that night. So what was it to be? There was no rugger practice, no current girlfriend and nothing on at the local cinema he fancied watching. He could phone a mate to come out for a beer and maybe a curry afterwards but somehow he couldn't be bothered.

Booth frowned. He should do something with this free time because it looked as if it was going to be in short supply for the foreseeable future. DI Fraser was determined to clear up these three cases that Tubby Jackson had slipped under the radar. And that was a rum do and all. What had the man been thinking of? In all the years Dave had worked with Tubby he'd known he was an idle sod who would try and shift as much of the daily grind as possible onto someone else, but to hide cases? It didn't add up.

And not only was DI Fraser going to clear up Tubby's old cases, she seemed on a mission to shake up the whole department. Perhaps that would be a good thing. Tubby's rule had been slapdash, sometimes allowing juniors to get away with late arrivals, early leaving, sloppy records and other poor policing, but at other times he would snarl and bully. Woe betide who got on the wrong side of him then.

At the back of Dave's mind something nagged. What had the DI said down in the morgue? A white van man. Well if there were any "sus" white vans in this area Dave knew who would have the answers. James Pillings had his ear to the ground on every aspect of his own business. Dave put his car in gear and drove off.

'I told you guys already, it's nothing to do with me. I checked the chassis number. That one's never come through my workshop, and I'm the only business in Ridminster that deals with vans ,' said James Pillings.

'Hang on a minute,' said Dave. 'What are you talking about? I only asked if you knew of any vans stolen in the last few weeks.'

'And I told you like I told the uniformed copper it was never in my shop.'

'What wasn't? What copper?'

Pillings sighed. 'Don't you lot ever talk to each other? Your uniformed guy gave me the chassis number of the burned out van they found on the old factory site. You know - that derelict area between the railway lines and the back of the High Street.'

'And when was this?'

Pillings thought for a moment. 'It was a Saturday morning when he came in. That must have been two weeks ago. It'll be exactly a fortnight this coming Saturday. Someone reported the burning van late Friday night. The Fire Brigade were called out but that was a formality. Nothing left – as usual. Kids probably. You see them driving round the streets these days. They can hardly see over the steering wheel. Most of them look through it. Joyriding they call it. I'd give them joy.'

'Was that all the description he gave you, just the chassis number?'

'No. He knew it was a Volkswagen but he hadn't got the plates, at least I don't think he had. He came to me because he knew I'm the only one around who deals with vans. And even if someone was "moonlighting" I'd know about it,' he grinned. 'Not much in the motor trade gets past me.'

'Glad to hear it,' said Dave. 'Always good to know where the expert is. I think I might be seeing you again fairly soon.'

Deeply satisfied, he got back into the Volvo. At Briefing tomorrow morning he'd have something to offer the boss. Something they could get their teeth into. If only he could tie the van to Lenny's murder he would score big brownie points with the DI and hopefully scrub out her poor opinion of him. Suddenly it mattered very much that she should think well of DS Booth.

On the way home he got himself a fish supper and planned how he would make his report to DI Fraser in the morning. She would be really impressed at being presented with a possible murder vehicle for Lenny, complete with make.

Friday

How the hell did she do that? Dave was pissed off at being robbed of his moment of glory. The first thing the DI had done that morning when everyone had settled down was write up on Lenny's whiteboard *Volkswagen Transporter*. Then she had announced this was the type of van that had run Lenny over. And that scuppered Dave's big announcement. But hang on, next she said it was a priority to find that van. Dave put up his hand.

'Yes, DS Booth? Have you got something?'

'I hope so, boss.' Dave went on to explain his visit to Pillings and the resultant information. 'I haven't had time to go into Traffic this morning, but if it is our van we should be able to trace it through the DVLA.'

'Absolutely. Well done, Dave.' Flick surveyed the room. 'This is the kind of initiative I like to see from my team. Don't be afraid of following up ideas, or bringing theories to me. I will always listen and where credit is due, it will be given.'

After Tubby's reign where any personal action had been taken as an affront; fresh ideas had been jeered at, and individual initiative had been positively discouraged as "arse-licking to them upstairs", this kind of encouragement was both novel and exciting.

'It may be that Traffic - I suppose I should call them the Road Policing Unit these days, but what a mouthful – they may have been too backed up to prioritise this

104

matter,' Flick went on. 'Get the chassis number from them, Dave, and if they haven't done a trace through the Cardiff licensing office, take it down to Andy. He's on duty this morning. Ask him if he can do a quick call to the DVLA and find our van. I feel it's too much of a coincidence that Lenny is run down by a Volkswagen Transporter and a Volkswagen van is burnt out in the same twenty four hours.'

'Right, boss, will do,' said Dave.

'Just to help things along I want you, Jarvis, and you, Spencer, to go over that waste ground with eagle's eyes. Start at the seat of the fire and work outwards,' said Flick.

The two constables exchanged nods. It could be a boring and painstaking job but it got them out of the office.

On a sudden thought Flick asked, 'Does anyone know if the van is still there? Or has it been towed in for examination?'

No-one knew. 'Tom, go with Dave to Traffic and find out everything that has or has not been done with that van. If it is still out there I want you to go and give it the once over in your usual immaculate fashion.' Flick smiled. DS Tom Perkins's enthusiasm for minutiae was well known.

'Right you are, boss,' said Tom, 'but first can I run something past you?'

'Go ahead,' said Flick. 'This is just the kind of start to a day that I enjoy. Everyone on the ball and full of ideas.'

'I feel it's just possible all three deaths were murder by the same person or persons,' said Tom.

All round the room people sat up straighter as they took in what he had just said. Puzzled glances were exchanged; some shook their heads. Had Tom flipped, or what?

Flick's eyes narrowed. 'Go on, Tom. I'm sure you have a good reason for this idea.'

Tom explained his thoughts of the previous evening and finished by counting off on his fingers. 'Three violent deaths within a week – very unusual for Ridminster. No, absolutely no, personal items on any of the bodies – strange coincidence and, again, very unusual.'

'You're certainly right about one thing, Tom. There were at least two murders,' said Flick and told of the unidentified weapon that had killed the victim found behind the nightclub. 'No way was that a fight or mugging that got out of hand. It just shouts deliberation. I agree there are similarities that look very suspicious but we need something much more solid to go on before we can think of them as connected. However we'll keep it in mind.

'Now, let's look at the photos from the suicide.' She spread them out on the table. 'If you want to think of this as a possible murder, how was it done? There's the whisky bottle on the floor of the car just below the victim's left hand. He's in the driver's seat so it appears he drove the car into the garage. But we know appearances are deceptive. Did he drink the whisky? We can't tell from the stomach contents. All alcohol presents the same way in the corpse. Was it his usual habit to drink whisky? Was the bottle there from a previous occasion? Or has someone made a mistake?

We must find this chap's identity. Then I want to know if he is left or right-handed and if he ever drank whisky.

'Next the actual scene. What happens in a suicide by car fumes?'

Encouraged by Flick's earlier speech, Barry Spencer spoke up. 'He'd run the car into the garage, close the garage doors and maybe put something round them or at least at the bottom to keep the fumes in. Then he'd put the hosepipe from the exhaust to the window next to his seat, close the door and switch on the engine.'

'Good so far,' said Flick. 'Anyone see a problem with that?'

Derek Jarvis pointed to one photo. 'He's stuffed something round the hose where it's keeping the window from shutting tight,' he said.

Flick nodded. 'Yes. Anything else?'

'Hang on,' said Dave. 'If he stuffed that material in the crack from inside, shouldn't there be more on the inside than the outside? It's a big piece of cloth. What is it? A curtain? Was it in the garage or did he have it in the car? They usually come in pairs. Where's the other one?'

'All good questions and all needing answers,' said Flick. 'I think you're right, Dave. I'll need to go and talk to the CSI to make absolutely sure this is how the material was. It is possible that when the victim was found, someone tried to clear away anything that would stop fresh air getting to him. We just don't know enough yet. That will be my job for this morning. Dave and Tom you have the car. Jarvis and Spencer forget the waste ground. There will have been too much coming and going to leave any useful traces and there must be so much rubbish lying about there who could possibly say what might or might not be relevant. Instead I want you to take the photos and go round the town. I know uniform have already done a sweep without any luck, but someone must know who these guys are. They didn't just come here to die.'

After a quick visit to her office Flick made her way once again down to the basement.

'You just can't keep away, can you?' came Fred's cheery voice as Flick put her head round the door of his office. 'Shall we run away together?'

Flick smiled. 'Don't let my Andy hear you,' she said. 'Were you on the suicide shout?'

'I was, and a rum do that one. No-one local seemed to know the chap. No-one had seen him in the area before and the house owners are away on holiday. They're due back on Monday so maybe they'll be able to give us an ID.'

'If they are away, how was the body discovered?'

Fred looked at Flick and frowned. 'Come on, young Flick, what's going on? This is the second case where you've come to ask elementary questions that have all been covered in the initial report. Why don't you just look in the file?'

Flick hesitated. She had tried to keep what Tubby had done under wraps. But why? He certainly wouldn't have done the same for her. But then she would never have destroyed files in the first place. It would make life easier to come clean and it surely couldn't do Tubby any harm now he was retired.

'The truth of the matter is there is no file, Fred. Not for this case nor for the hit and run, and not for the body behind the nightclub either.'

'What? What do you mean, no file? I sent them up to Tubby myself. I even hand-delivered one as I was on my way upstairs.'

'That may be the case but the last time they were seen was on Tubby's desk on the morning he left. DS Booth saw three of them lying there. By the time I came in later that day for a handover/takeover there was no sign of them and Tubby Jackson assured me there was nothing outstanding at all.'

For a moment Fred said nothing. Then slowly he shook his head. 'What a bloody idiot,' he said. 'Trying to play the big man to the last. Nothing could be left undone on Tubby's watch. Wanted to impress you did he?'

'You must be joking. He couldn't stand the sight of me. He's resented me being here from day one and made my life hell one way and another. I did think, when I realised what he'd done, that he was trying to drop me in it, but why, when he wouldn't be here to see me get it in the neck? It didn't make sense. So please humour me, Fred, and tell me everything you can about the scene in the garage.'

'The postman heard the car engine. He knew the family were away for another week because he'd been warned to push the mail right through until it fell onto the mat. He went up to try the garage door and smelled the fumes so he dialled 999. We arrived the same time as the Fire Brigade. When they got the door open and I'd been issued with a gas mask it was obvious to me there was no chance of reviving him.'

'Hang on a minute. So far that's just what Booth said, but can you go back to where you entered the garage? What did you see?'

'The car was nose in to the back wall. A hose ran from the exhaust to the driver's window. A piece of material was stuffed into the crack left between the top of the window and the door-frame.'

'Right. Now please think hard. Did anyone move that material for any reason?'

'No. Why should they? The hose was disconnected from the exhaust, then we just opened the door – it wasn't locked – and switched off the engine. Once the door was open I could get access to the body. But it was too late. There was no need to move any material. There was very little inside the car anyway. Most of it hung down the outside of the door.'

'Fred, I could kiss you,' beamed Flick.

'What have I said?'

'Imagine you are going to commit suicide in a car. You've got a piece of material to stuff in the crack of the window. How would you go about it?'

Fred closed his eyes. Flick watched his hands as he went through the motions.

'I'd bung up the outer door first. But in this case he didn't. Then I'd get in the car with the hose coming through my window. I'd push the cloth into the crack all along and round the hosepipe so hard until I couldn't get any more in. Then I'd turn on the engine.' Fred opened his eyes. 'Or in his case I'd take my pills and wash them down with booze. Then, when I felt them working, I'd switch on the engine. We should test the whisky bottle for prints to match the victim, or not.'

'And if they don't or there are none?'

'It rather looks as though you have another murder on your hands. The material *outside* the car is a definite factor.'

'So we now have three murders,' said Flick. 'If this is murder, not suicide it's no wonder there was nothing blocking air round the garage door. The killer would have to leave that way.' She saw Fred nod in agreement. 'Tom Perkins thinks they may be linked,' she went on. Fred's eyebrows rose in surprise. 'Even committed by the same person. What do you think?'

'If that is true he must be strong, to overpower the bloke behind the nightclub, and to position the suicide body behind the wheel - not an easy task. He has a knowledge of anatomy, knows just how to position that knife or whatever the weapon was to destroy the heart. He's vicious. I have rarely seen a more savage battering than that inflicted on the nightclub body, and he is also cool headed. He either orchestrated or took advantage of a disturbance in front of the nightclub to cover his activities there, and if the postman hadn't delivered to the house, the body of the car victim would not have been discovered until Monday. That gives him nearly a fortnight to cover his tracks, establish an alibi after the event – people are very susceptible to suggestion you know. And the lapse of time makes things fuzzy in people's memories. Yes, our killer is resourceful and well-prepared. But why he should want to kill these particular three men is up to you to find out, my dear.'

'Thanks. But you say "he" all the time. You don't believe it could have been a woman?'

Fred shook his head. 'I know this is an age of equal opportunity, Flick but I just don't believe it, no matter how strong she may be. I just can't see a woman doing this.'

Saturday morning

'I'm in the chair,' said Major Carver, 'what'll it be?'

The bar of the Ridminster Golf and Country Club was crowded. A pleasant hum of conversation created a friendly atmosphere in the large room.

'No, no,' said DCI Westcott. 'After the way I played this morning I should be in the chair for the next month as penance.'

Because both of their usual partners were away on holiday Carver and Westcott had found themselves as partners in the usual Saturday morning fourball. In time-honoured fashion the losers bought the first round.

'Could happen to anyone,' said Carver. 'I can think of several occasions when I've been right off my game. Golf is played in the head as much as with the body. When my mind can't focus because I'm stressed over something, it always shows up in my score.' He smiled. 'Now, what's it to be? Peter and Harry aren't coming in, so it's just the two of us.' He laughed, 'I think they're a bit under the thumb if you know what I mean. Are you on the wagon because of driving or can I get you a decent drink?'

'I'll have a pint, thanks. My wife dropped me off this morning and I'll get a taxi back. She's off for the day, shopping with our eldest girl.'

'Very nice, too . . . but no need to get a taxi. Clive Manners, my man, will be coming to collect me when

I'm ready and we'll take you home. It's not far out of our way. Two pints of Theakston's, please, Helen,' he called to the pretty barmaid. 'And a couple of whisky chasers. We'll take Glenmorangie. No, no, old chap,' he said as Westcott demurred. 'You don't need to worry about driving.'

Westcott smiled. 'You're very fortunate to have a chauffeur always to hand.'

'Yes. I don't know what I'd do without Manners.'

'Do you ever drive yourself?'

'Rarely, but on occasion, yes, it has been known,' said Carver. 'And now with your good lady out for the day I assume you're in no hurry. Which is very fortuitous,' he went on, 'as I'd like a quiet word in your ear.'

When their drinks were ready they picked up their glasses and moved away from the bar to make room for other groups continually entering as the morning rounds finished. They managed to find seats at a small table in the far corner of the room and raised their glasses in salute before taking that first long satisfying swallow of the cool beer.

'Ah, that's better,' said Edward Carver,' with a smile. 'Nothing quite like it after fresh air and exercise.'

Westcott agreed, then, 'You wanted a word?' he said. 'Nothing wrong I hope?'

'No, yes, at least nothing personal. But as a member of the *Police meet the Public* committee I do hear things others might not. Just lately very disturbing whispers about drugs have been reaching me. Now, of course, I know you can't discuss any police business . . . that is actual business. I wouldn't ask or expect you to. But as a concerned, a very concerned, member of the public I would like some kind of reassurance something is being done. Of the two young people taken to hospital the other day I gather, although one has escaped harm, the other has not been so lucky. There will be lasting damage of some kind. How badly are these 'F's entrenched in our community?'

Westcott's lips tightened. 'I envy you your contacts,' he said.

Carver shrugged. 'Well, a man in my position hears things, and not being official helps, of course. But I am sure my informants know I will pass anything I am told straight to you.'

'Which is appreciated. Obviously you know there is something new on the patch, but I can assure you we are dealing with it. Apart from one other unfortunate child, or I should say, young person, who had to receive treatment there hasn't been any sign of a flood on the market.'

'It could be I suppose that the dealers have learned not to prepare it in such a strength as to draw attention. If it's that new they may still be in a learning curve in gauging what is safe and what is not?' suggested Carver.

'I sincerely hope you're wrong.' Westcott shuddered at the possibility. 'The Drug Squad found nothing at the hospital to suggest there was more of the stuff around. And the two dealers identified by description have not been seen again in the area. I hope the kids' bad reactions have warned them off our patch at least. Although I would prefer to apprehend them here, the next best thing is to know they've moved on.'

'Quite so.'

'I can assure you and your committee that we have pulled out all the stops on this and the feed-back I am getting is that things have quietened down again. I am of the opinion that an outsider tried his hand, tried to muscle in on our ground and was warned off. Not by us, unfortunately,' he smiled briefly, 'I wish it was. No, I think it was our regular dealers, whom we can't pin down, although we have them under constant observation, who will have got rid of the opposition.'

'I'm sure you're right. I do think the danger is passed. Our young people will have to get their fun another way. That does relieve my mind.'

'I'm in the chair I think,' said Westcott and stood up to go and order another round of drinks.

'And so our good Chief Inspector believes the drug invasion threat has gone,' said Carver to his driver. They had dropped Westcott off and were on their way back to Marylands.

Manners smiled. 'I'm so glad you were able to reassure him,' he said. 'So unsettling to have nasty business like that on our doorstep, so to speak. We like Ridminster to be a quiet, uneventful place, don't we, sir?'

'Indeed we do, Manners, indeed we do.'

It was only when DCI Westcott was settling down to sleep that night he realised he had no idea how Carver had found out what new drugs were on the patch. Neither the Drug Squad nor his own people involved in that business had said anything to the hospital staff. When the youngsters had recovered enough to identify their purchases as 'F's they were still an unknown quantity. Until the forensics had been done and analysis made of the stomach contents, no-one knew what they were. Had Carver's words been innocent or did his reference to *fun* actually mean Fantasy Fun? Just how much did the man know and from where was he getting his information?

Saturday

On Saturday morning after Andy had left to run Jude to football practice, Natalie wanted to watch an Open University programme on Art. Flick settled her in front of the television and went through into the kitchen. Much to the twins' delight Amanda had come to the rescue once again, arriving on Thursday evening. Effortlessly she had slipped into her old role.

'Mum, I'm just going to nip next door to see Elaine. I would have had a word yesterday evening but she was out.'

Amanda looked up from her task of wiping down the units. 'Secrets? Or can anyone join in?' she smiled.

'No secrets. I just want to ask her if she remembers anything more about seeing Lenny that Thursday you two were in town.'

'Well, I'll come with you. Two heads are better than one, they say. Nat will be glued to the "box" for a good half hour and Andy will be home soon. He wasn't going to wait for Jude. He said Peter – whoever he is – had offered to drop Jude off in passing. I trust he doesn't mean literally.' She pulled off her rubber gloves, fluffed up her short hairstyle and joined Flick at the kitchen door. 'Come on then, let's sleuth.'

With a helpless shake of the head Flick followed her out.

Settled in Elaine's sitting room with coffee in dainty china cups and tiny biscuits arranged on a plate in front of her, Flick looked around. The room was as softly feminine as its owner. Knicknacks abounded together with crocheted doilies and crystal vases full of flowers. Flick appreciated the fact Elaine never put away her treasures when she was watching the twins. She trusted them to treat her possessions with care and respect. So far there had been no mishaps. Which in itself was a miracle Flick prayed would continue. With two twelve year olds given free rein, and twins at that who couldn't seem to let an hour go by without arguing, accidents were always just an instant away.

'Now then, Felicity, dear,' said Elaine. 'What was it you wanted to ask me?'

It was no good. DI Fraser didn't exist here. Between her mother and Elaine, the pair of them could make Flick feel about six years old. She took her notebook out of her bag and found the page she wanted. 'You said you and Mum saw Lenny Strickland on Thursday afternoon.'

'That's right, dear. On the old factory road it was, wasn't it, Amanda?'

Flick's mother nodded. 'Yes, you mean that little chap with the other two?'

'Yes, I remember thinking how good it was to see him with friends his own age.'

'Not friends, Elaine, surely?'

'What? Why not? I remember they were laughing.'

'One of them was laughing,' corrected Amanda. 'The one with that silly baseball cap. And the other one just looked bad-tempered. But Lenny, the little one in the middle, he wasn't laughing at all. In fact I think he was frightened.'

'Surely not, dear. What makes you think that?'

With the bit between their teeth Flick was sure the two older women had forgotten her existence. But as their conversation was producing the information she wanted she was quite happy for them to continue.

'Well you might link arms with friends while you walk along but you don't clasp their arms tightly do you? They each had a good grip of him and seemed to be marching him along whether he would or not.'

Elaine frowned, looking back to the scene at the time. 'Perhaps you're right, dear,' she said. 'I didn't really take that much notice.'

'I am right. Maybe I wouldn't have looked so closely if it hadn't been for that silly earring the laughing one was wearing. And then when I looked back I saw them practically shove little Lenny into that van of theirs.'

Enough was enough. Time for Flick to take charge. 'Hold on a minute. Can you describe the two men with Lenny?'

'Well they were both taller than him,' said Elaine.

'Yes, and the other laughing one had a gold earring in his ear, a baseball cap and a leather jacket,' said Amanda. 'I didn't really notice the other one so much except he looked fed up.'

'He had a pony tail,' said Elaine.

'Did he? I didn't notice. But the van they all got into was one of those white vans that always go too fast and think they own the whole road,' finished Amanda indignantly.

Flick finished taking notes and chewed the end of her pen. Another white van? Or perhaps the same one? What would that mean? Lenny and the other two, not friends, drove off in a white van on Thursday afternoon before tea. Two of them went willingly. But Lenny is dead by Friday morning and the van burnt out on Friday night. Was it the van that killed Lenny? And had one of the others been driving? Had they both been there, in it together? But, if they killed Lenny, why? Surely they couldn't be that upset about losing betting money? There must be something else and they must be identified. The ponytail and earring would be a help. At that thought she remembered the fan of hair below the head of the stabbing victim. And hadn't there been talk of an earring in one of the evidence bags? Were the two bodies in the morgue Lenny's so-called friends? She got to her feet. 'Well thank you both very much. That has been helpful. I must go and make a few phone calls. No don't bother, Mum, you stay. I heard the car, so Andy's home and I won't be all day. Just want to verify a few things. Bye, now Elaine, and thanks again.'

'Not at all, dear. Anytime you think I might be able to help. Bye bye.'

Flick could hear Andy and Nat in the kitchen so she slipped into what they called "the den" which was really a study she shared with Andy and where the children were allowed to do homework that called for peace and quiet. She opened her mobile and dialled hoping it would be answered, even on a Saturday morning.

'Tom? Flick. Sorry to bother you on your off duty. Just a couple of quick questions. When you were going through the evidence bags did you see a gold earring? You did? Great. And what was the owner wearing?'

As Tom Perkins listed the biker's jacket, baseball cap and the rest, Flick nodded. So the laughing guy was the

121

suicide who they believed had also been murdered. She shook her head. This was bizarre. 'What about the other one?'

'Workman's boots,' said Tom. 'You know the steel-toecap kind. Check shirt and leather waistcoat.' He went on to list the clothes right down to the boxers.

'Anything to distinguish him?'

'No. No watch, jewellery, or headgear. Just a rubber band and a few pounds in his pocket, so robbery not a motive.'

A rubber band to hold his ponytail, thought Flick, taken off by the pathologist to examine the back of the head and meticulously included with the other items in the evidence bag. 'Has that burned out van been left on the waste ground?' she queried.

'Yes. No idea it was a crime scene and nothing to connect it to any that had been committed. I suppose it will be down to the council to move it if they can't collar an owner.'

'But you did go and have a look, didn't you?'

'Yes, boss, for all the good it did. Whoever torched it made a good job of it. They'd removed the plates but either didn't know or didn't care about the VIN plate.'

That gave Flick pause for thought. The arsonist had carefully taken off and away the number plates, the easiest way to identify a vehicle, but had left the Vehicle Identification Number plate intact, riveted to the engine. Why? Too difficult to remove? Too little time to do so? Or didn't they realise what and where it was? Now she knew who her other corpses were the task remained to identify them. If these murders had been just committed she would have called in the whole team even though it was the weekend, but the trail was already very cold. Letting her guys have their weekend break should keep them sharp for Monday. Then she would expect results.

Natalie's voice from the kitchen penetrated her thoughts. Flick smiled. She would have what she was giving to everyone else – a pleasant work-free weekend.

'Hi folks,' she greeted father and daughter busy at the kitchen table. 'What on earth's going on?' Thin card lay everywhere in different shapes. Paper; two bottles of glue; drawing pins and paperclips were strewn across the surface. Nat's paintbox lay open.

Natalie turned a glowing face to her mother. 'We're making a pyramid, Mum,' she explained. 'Dad's helping me.'

'So I see,' smiled Flick wiping a smudge of brown paint from Andy's cheek. 'But why?'

'Nat's class is studying the Ancient Egyptians in History, and for homework she has to bring in something relevant to the period,' said Andy. 'We did think of making a scarab beetle out of mud and baking it in the oven but thought it would make a mess.'

'Let me be thankful for small mercies,' said Flick, opening her hands to encompass the table and its contents. But she was delighted to see Andy being creative again. Before the accident he had enjoyed DIY and making things for and with his children. Afterwards he had felt useless until by perseverance he had taught himself to use his left hand as well as he had formerly used his right. Then when the wonders of modern science provided him with his new prosthetic arm and hand he gradually became more and more adept in its use. Now he would even attempt the fiddly business of glueing cardboard shapes together. She frowned down at the mess. 'What's it supposed to be? I know you said a pyramid but I don't understand why you need all those little bits.'

'It's a cross-section,' said Natalie importantly. 'So we can see the inside and how it was all done. We have to have the passages leading to the tombs. That's the King's chamber, right in the middle,' she pointed to a pencil sketch of their project. 'We're nearly ready to glue all the bits together to make it fit. Dad's the . . . what did you say it was, Daddy?'

'I'm the architect,' said Andy. Natalie started to giggle. 'What's so funny, young lady? I'll have you know I think I've done a very passable job.'

'Yes, you have, Daddy. I think it's super but when it's finished I'll have to kill you,' she continued with a beaming smile.

Flick felt her mouth drop open. 'What did you say?'

The giggle came again. 'I'll have to kill Daddy when he's finished my pyramid. Although he should really only die after me.'

Flick shook her head. 'We don't joke about killing people in this house, Natalie.'

As her mother usually called her Nat and when she was cross with her used her full name, Nat's face fell. 'I wasn't joking, Mummy,' she said. 'That's what they did. The pharaohs. It took years to build pyramids and they had hundreds of slaves. When it was finished some of them who'd worked on the secret bits were killed. They were ex . . .ex . . .'

'Expendable?' offered Andy.

'Yes. What Dad said because they could always get more slaves. Then when the pharaoh died his servants carried lots of gold and jewels and furniture and food and even boats into the pyramid. And they had to stay there and sometimes they were given poison to drink. When everything was inside, the architect,' she said the name with care, 'he went in too and pulled a lever. The King's tomb was sealed up and all sorts of traps opened and filled the pyramid passages with sand so no-one could get out. They all died so no-one would know the secret of how to get to the treasure.'

Flick smiled. 'I see. You've certainly been paying attention to your lesson. Well done. But I think you should spare Daddy. You might need him another time. Now I must get us some lunch while you finish your masterpiece.'

As she boiled pasta and made a spicy sauce Flick's mind went back to her problem. What was the connection between Lenny and the other two? Why had they killed him, if indeed they had been driving the van that hit him? Who had killed them and why?

With a wooden spoon in one hand and the salt pot in the other Flick turned and looked back towards her daughter. Slaves, servants, and the architect, all dead to preserve the secret. Was that the answer? Out of the mouths . . .? But what was the secret and who was the architect?

Monday

Andy was on duty on Sunday. So Flick was thankful Amanda had come back to help out. True to her silent promise Flick left her team in peace for the rest of the weekend but her own family found her distracted. All the puzzle pieces in her head went round and round, but she was convinced there were too few of them. Finally Amanda took the twins out to the park and left Flick to her problems. On Sunday evening she drew up her battle plan.

Bright and early on Monday morning she had already entered on the white boards and time lines all the new information gathered before the weekend. As people straggled into the Briefing Room bearing take-away breakfasts and cardboard coffee cups balanced on their notebooks the atmosphere in the room changed as they saw the results of Flick's labours.

'Good morning everyone,' she greeted them, only when the last arrival was seated. 'Let's get down to it. I want some answers.'

She took the cases one by one, going over what they already knew of the victims and the crimes. Some of what they heard was new to most of the room. The object of this briefing was to bring everyone up to speed on progress.

'So we have three victims all within a short period of time. We can connect Lenny with the other two by sightings but we still don't know their names or how they fit in with him.

'We want to find the connection between the three of them and one or more other people who would benefit from their deaths.'

She told them of Natalie and her pyramid. She smiled. 'It's surprising what you can learn from kids, isn't it? But it makes sense to me. The only questions are, what is the secret, and who is behind it all?

'I want renewed house to house round the bookies and down Hyacinth Terrace. Show the photos everywhere. Someone must know these two. They might not be locals but they have enough familiarity with the area to know Lenny and his route home.

'I shall go to interview the householders where our suicide was found. Before anyone gets smart, I know he wasn't a suicide but until I have a name that's who he is. The . . .' she consulted her notes, 'Pargiters, the family who own the house there, are due back from holiday today. Let's hope they can help us.' A uniformed officer stuck his head round the door. 'Yes, what is it?'

'Message for you ma'am,' he walked across to where Flick stood with her back to the boards and handed her a piece of paper.

'Thanks,' she said, read the message and shook her head. 'It doesn't get any easier, does it, folks.' She looked round the room. 'Apparently our burned out van belongs in Swindon. So what was it doing here? How and when did it arrive and who was driving? Just a few more questions for us to answer. You could look into that, Dave. Okay, off you go and remember all the info we want. Keep your eyes and ears open because in

127

answering or not answering one question, people can sometimes shed light on another.'

Back in her office Flick looked in the mirror she kept hanging behind the door. She looked her usual neat and tidy self but she smoothed her hair again and adjusted the collar of her shirt with fingers that weren't quite steady. She had requested an interview with DCI Westcott and this time she was determined to have her say.

'Take a seat, Inspector. I hope you've brought me news, but if so you should have made it a priority.' DCI Westcott's face was solemn. 'You understand the seriousness of this business. Your part may be small but it is vital. Now what's happened?'

Flick gazed at him, thrown completely off her stride by his words.

'Come on, Inspector. Don't waste my time. What action did you take and why wasn't I informed immediately?'

Flick took a deep breath. 'Sir, I have no idea what you're talking about. I have come to give you an update on the three murder cases we are at present handling.'

'You what?' DCI Westcott almost rose from his chair with the force of his exclamation. 'Murders, what murders? I am talking about Operation Country Ride.'

'What?' It was Flick's turn. 'What Operation? Like I said at the beginning, I have no idea what you are talking about, sir.'

He seemed to swell before her eyes until he filled the room. The sensation was nerve-wracking but Flick curled her toes in her shoes and stayed silent. She saw the effort with which he controlled himself and swallowed. She had never seen the Chief lose his temper. As far as she knew, no-one had, but he had just come perilously close to it.

'What have you done with the mobile phone Inspector Jackson gave you?' was his next question.

Flick shook her head. 'I have had no mobile phone from Inspector Jackson, sir.'

William Westcott sat back in his chair and closed his eyes. He took three deep breaths then looked at Flick.

'When DI George Jackson did a handover/takeover with you on his retirement, he gave you a mobile phone with certain instructions on its use. It was to be carried on your person at all times.' He spoke quite quietly but distinctly as though Flick were a small child or half-witted.

Bloody Tubby again. She felt her temper rise and pushed the emotion down. 'No, sir.'

'What do you mean, no sir?'

'I mean Inspector Jackson did not give me a mobile phone or instructions. In fact we didn't have a handover/takeover.'

This time she really thought he would explode, he gave her such an incredulous look. She couldn't blame him. When one officer was handing over charge of a case or position to another there was always a handover/takeover to exchange the necessary information for the incoming officer to do his job. She hurried on.

'I wasn't due back from leave until the Monday morning, but I came in on Friday afternoon to do the takeover. I thought it would save DI Jackson coming back in on Monday.' She hesitated. She was about to drop a fellow officer into mire so deep he would never recover. Not that he was still on the force, but it still went against all her instincts.

'Go on.'

Flick swallowed. Her throat was dry. What wouldn't she give for a glass of cool water. 'DI Jackson was surprised and not particularly pleased to see me,' she went on. 'He informed me there was no need for a handover/takeover as he had tidied everything up and there was nothing left for me to do. Before I could remonstrate with him he pushed past me out of the office holding a cardboard box I assumed contained his personal possessions. Unfortunately I now have reason to believe it also contained the files relating to three open cases. The ones he concealed from me.'

'Be careful, Inspector. That is a very serious allegation to make. I know DI Jackson is retired but I warn you to be careful what you say.'

Suddenly Flick felt ice-cold. She was in the right and could prove it. If DCI Westcott wanted her resignation after this he could have it. She was fed up with him belittling her and believing her capable of such stupidity and downright spite.

'Those are facts, sir. The files were seen on his desk before I arrived back that day. He did not pass them to me. Of course these cases eventually came to light, as they would have to. In following them up I have come to the conclusion they are most probably related.'

'Three murders you say?'

'Yes, sir.' Flick went on to outline her actions; her findings, and her reasoning for linking the three deaths. She gave credit to her team and to Fred Updike and

Martin Barnes for their findings of the so far unknown weapon.

'And why are you only now coming to tell me of this?' demanded Westcott.

'Twice I have come to your office to tell you about it, sir, and twice you have stopped me. The first time you stopped me before I was able to explain, because you thought I was trying to traduce DI Jackson, and the second time we were obviously talking at cross purposes. You dismissed me when you answered your telephone.'

She watched DCI Westcott's eyes narrow as he thought back over the past few days. She had always thought him firm but fair and she was not disappointed.

'It would seem I owe you an apology, Inspector.'

'Accepted, sir,' said Flick. She couldn't do anything else.

Westcott nodded, 'Thank you.' He paused. Flick could almost see the wheels going round as he decided what to do next. 'I'll start from the beginning,' he went on. 'Operation Country Ride is an undercover operation that has come onto our patch. It had its origins in London and from there I believe the centre moved to Swindon and now we have them here. The Vice Squad are trying to net the whole operation so haven't shut off anybody along the way, just noted and watched. When it does come to fruition this op will have an incalculable effect on the whole of the South of England. Obviously they have set up a safe house away from the station but DI Patrick Murphy is our liaison on this.'

'Yes, sir,' put in Flick. 'I saw him on the stairs the other day. No wonder he gave me a funny look when I asked him what he was doing here. He would have thought I knew.'

'Precisely. I gather you know him from your days with the Met?'

'Yes, sir. We worked on one or two things together. He's a good officer.'

'It's fortunate you know him. Have your people got enough to do at the moment?'

'Yes, sir. There are several things we need info on. We don't yet know the ID of the other two vics, nor how they fit in with Lenny – apart from possibly having killed him. But on that point, sir, there is now another possible connection between my murders and your op.'

'Go on.'

'The van we believe ran Lenny down was burned on the waste ground that was the old factory site. By the VIN plate we traced it to a garage in Swindon. I know it's a slim thread, sir, but I don't like coincidences and why would a Swindon van be burnt out on our patch?'

'As you say, it is slim but we will keep it in mind. I want you close by me on this op now, Flick. It is vital we support them in every possible way. Which brings us to ex-Detective Inspector Jackson and the mobile phone.'

The tone of Westcott's voice gave Flick an involuntary shiver. She had no love for Jackson, but she felt almost sorry for the guy when the Chief eventually caught up with him.

'I want you with me when I interview him,' went on Westcott. 'We need that phone.'

Flick was puzzled. 'Why is it so important, sir?' she queried. 'Can't we just get another one?'

'This phone connects us to a very brave undercover officer known to us simply as Mike. We hope and believe, he has penetrated the inner workings of the drug-trafficking network. Although he would report to his safe house on a reasonably regular basis, this phone is what you might call his panic button. The one he carries and ours are modified to only work with each other. If he presses any key on his phone it will ring on ours and alert us to his position by way of an inbuilt tracking device. If anyone else should use the telephone you, or supposedly DI Jackson, would identify himself simply as Uncle John for him. I suppose you'd better be Aunty Johanna.' Westcott allowed the ghost of a smile to soften his severe expression. 'But first we need it in your possession. Come along, Inspector. I want a word with DI Jackson.'

'But he's away, sir. At least he was when I went to confront him about the missing files. His neighbour, the milkman and the paper shop, all told me they didn't know when he would return.'

Westcott bit back an expletive, then his eyes gleamed. 'I wonder,' he said. 'I wonder. Stand by, young Flick. I'm going back to my youth.'

Flick kept her face expressionless. What was the guv. up to? She would go along with anything that helped their cause and now he was once again addressing her by her Christian name, as he used to do informally in the past, she could relax and concentrate all her energies on solving the puzzles Tubby Jackson had left them.

They went down the stairs to the lower floor. 'Wait here,' ordered Westcott and disappeared into one of the open-plan offices. He was back in a moment looking very satisfied with himself. Flick kept her mouth shut.

'I'll sign out a pool car and you can drive,' said the Chief. 'Let's see if Tubby is home yet.'

Flick couldn't make him out. She'd told him about Tubby being away indefinitely. Why did the boss think he might be back and why did he seem to be inwardly amused? Hers not to reason why, and certainly not to question anything the Chief Inspector wanted.

When they arrived at Tubby's house, Flick saw at a glance he hadn't been home. In spite of his instructions, a piece of mail stuck out of the letterbox. When she looked through the ground floor windows the house had that air of abandonment Dave Booth had noticed; too tidy and a light film of dust showed on the polished surfaces in the late Spring sunshine. Perhaps that was the norm in Tubby's house but she didn't remember it from her last visit. She shook her head. 'It's no use, sir. He hasn't come back.'

'Well, I think we'll just have to have a little look round on our own then, won't we?

Flick was shocked. Her eyes opened wide. 'We're not going to break in, sir . . . are we?'

'Not at all, Inspector.' Westcott was grinning. 'Without a warrant that would be illegal. But I don't have time or patience for a warrant. We don't need to break in. We have a key.' He held up a shiny key, then slid it into the front door lock.

Monday

Flick followed the Chief Inspector into the house

'Don't look so worried,' said Westcott. 'These days there are very few people left around here who remember that Tubby Jackson and I joined the Force around the same time. After a while it became clear that Jackson liked the booze a little too much. Not enough to lose him his job, but enough to affect his promotion. Hence I am a Chief Inspector and he retired as Inspector even though he cleaned up his act. Once upon a time we shared an office and I remember Tubby locking himself out of his house. His wife, Marge, was away and he'd taken advantage of the fact to go on a bit of a spree. After that he taped a spare door key to the bottom of a desk drawer. The gods are smiling on me today because, when I looked, it was still there.'

'You remembered which desk it was?' said Flick.

Westcott smiled. 'After the hours I spent looking across the room at it?' he said. 'Yes, indeed. Good solid wood in those days and unlikely to be replaced for cosmetic reasons.' His expression became serious once more. 'Perhaps our entry is not quite kosher,' he said, 'but I want to keep this as quiet as possible. We can't explain what we are looking for and it's a case of least said, soonest mended. Now glove up and we'll start at the top and work our way down. Bedroom first, I think.'

'What exactly are we looking for?' said Flick.

'Initially, the mobile. I just hope to God he hasn't taken it with him, or worse still, thrown it away. Surely even with whatever game he's playing he wouldn't do that. He must know he would be putting a fellow office in jeopardy. But while we're looking keep your eyes open and be aware of anything that might give us a clue why he is behaving like this.'

Flick said nothing about Tubby's loathing of her and his past attempts to put her in the wrong at every turn.

They went up the stairs of the eerily quiet house. There was no sound, even from the street outside. Flick felt uncomfortable to be delving into Tubby's private life, but she had no option.

One bedroom was obviously a spare that yielded nothing beyond drawers containing remnants of female occupation. When she left Mrs Jackson had abandoned some of her clothes and personal possessions. Had Tubby kept them there in the forlorn hope she might return? It painted him in a pathetic light, an object of compassion. Or had he been too idle to clear them away and just moved himself into the other bedroom? Much more likely, thought Flick.

The other bedroom had been occupied by a man. There were signs of a hasty departure; one sock kicked half under the bed, an old sweater stuffed into the wastebasket and a solitary tie draped over the back of an upright chair.

'Sir?' said Flick, when she opened the wardrobe.

'What is it, Inspector?' Westcott was bending over the bedside table sorting through a jumble of letters, receipts, and two paperbacks he had found in the drawer.

'Sir, I don't think Inspector Jackson is planning on coming back.'

Westcott straightened up sharply. 'What do you mean?'

Flick indicated the open wardrobe. Apart from a very heavy winter coat, and a pair of boots on the floor, it was empty. 'You don't take all your clothes when you go on holiday, sir, surely?' She crossed to the chest of drawers and found them empty also. A dressing gown hung on the back of the door, possibly overlooked, but they were the only items of Tubby's clothing left upstairs in the house.

The bathroom yielded a shrivelled bar of soap and a half-used can of deodorant. In the cabinet there was aspirin, paracetemol, Vaseline and hair gel, a few Kirby grips and a bottle of dried-up nail polish. Possible indication of his intention not to return but offering nothing towards his state of mind.

The third bedroom, or rather the boxroom for it was so small, held a large assortment of odds and ends, no doubt shoved in to be dealt with later or forgotten about.

Westcott sighed. 'I hope to hell we don't have to go through that lot,' he said.

Flick smiled. 'You should put DS Perkins on it, sir. That's just the kind of muddle he would enjoy straightening out. He'd have it sorted in no time.'

'Let's hope it won't come to that. I want to keep this whole business as low profile as possible.'

Downstairs was tidier. Dining room, sitting room and hall yielded nothing of interest. There was a desk against the sitting room wall that was stuffed full of papers and old photographs but a cursory examination proved them to be dating from the time of Jackson's marriage, the letters addressed mainly to Mrs Jackson and of no interest to the present searchers.

That left the kitchen. By this time DCI Westcott's face had taken on a stormy look. Flick kept her mouth shut and concentrated on the matter in hand. Westcott began opening the cupboards methodically and examining the contents.

Flick looked into the oven and then the empty fridge. 'The power is switched off, sir,' she said. She tried the taps over the sink. 'And the water. So he evidently meant to be gone some time.'

Westcott grunted in acknowledgement.

Flick looked about and eventually found what she wanted. A rubbish bin stood at the side of the unit nearest the back door. She lifted the lid and wrinkled her nose as the smell of rotten food rose up. It would seem Tubby had emptied his fridge into the bin and then forgotten to transfer the contents into the dustbin outside for collection. Why? She held her breath and rooted through the debris inside. The heel of a loaf; a butter wrapper with about 150 gms left on it, two eggs, one miraculously intact; the usual bits of vegetables and half a pizza. Flick moved them to one side and found the edge of an envelope. Carefully she lifted it out, picking off whatever was stuck to it rather than brushing it off and destroying any evidence on the paper. She turned it over. 'Sir? This probably arrived on the day Jackson left. It's first class post, dated the day before. No return address or indication of the sender but the lab might be able to find something. It's a funny thing to put in this bin with the food.'

'Why do you say that?'

'Last time we came I looked in his outside bin. There were old newspapers there and also envelopes, circulars and other junk mail. This was stuffed at the bottom of the refuse bin under the contents of the refrigerator and smacks to me of fear or haste.'

'Right, bag it and we'll take it along. I'll continue with the cupboards. You start on the drawers.'

Just as he spoke a telephone rang. Flick and Westcott looked at each other. Like a double act they each checked their mobiles. Flick took a step towards the telephone in the hall, but it was definitely a mobile ringtone.

They looked around. Nothing in sight. Flick opened the unit drawer nearest to her. Westcott started from the other end. As Flick opened the next drawer the sound was louder. Frantically she scrabbled through the assorted utensils; string; old birthday cake candles and recipe cards, desperate to answer the call before the ringing stopped. At last she found the phone and flipped it open. She took it to her ear and held her breath.

'Hello.'

Flick frowned, then answered. 'Hello?'

'What's your name?'

No doubt about it. It was a child's voice. Had the undercover agent entrusted the phone to this child in a last desperate effort to summon help?

'My name's Felicity,' she said. 'What's yours?' She shook her head at Westcott who was beckoning imperiously to take the phone from her. She held up her hand to stop him, palm out like a traffic cop.

'My name's Timmy,' said the child. 'I can talk to you.'

'Yes, of course you can,' said Flick. Perhaps Timmy had a message to pass on?

'This is my phone now. Our Kennef said it didn't work so that's why he give it me. He couldn't talk to his mates. Said it was a useless bit of junk. But I got it to work, didn't I? I'm talkin' to you.'

'Yes, Timmy,' said Flick and tried to silently mouth a description of her caller to Westcott whose face wore a thunderous expression. 'You're a very clever boy. But you know your Kenneth is right. That telephone won't work properly because it's special. It belongs to a friend of mine. Do you know where Kenneth got it?'

'He found it when he was out on his bike. He stopped for a pee and there it was on the grass,' the child giggled. 'Good job he didn't wee on it wasn't it?'

'Yes. Now Timmy I am very glad you have got my friend's mobile. I know it's yours now but he would really like to have it back. If I gave you five whole pounds would you sell it to me?'

For a moment there was silence. Dear god, thought Flick I hope he hasn't dropped it or wandered off. 'Timmy? Are you still there?'

'Make it a tenner and you've got a deal,' quoted the child.

'Done. My goodness you drive a hard bargain.'

'So does my brother, at least that's what our Mam says.'

'Timmy if I'm going to give you ten pounds you'll have to tell me where you live.'

'Oh no, you don't,' said the street-smart child. 'Our Mam said you don't give where you live to no-body you don't know.'

'Mum is quite right,' said Flick, now painfully aware of Westcott's growing impatience. 'So shall we meet somewhere there are lots of people? Do you know where the park is?'

'Course I do. I'm there now, in't I?'

'Good,' said Flick. 'You wait by the swings and we'll come and meet you.'

'Who's we? You said *you* wanted my mobile.'

'My friend is with me and we'll see you in fifteen minutes. Is that alright?'

'Okay.' And the phone went dead.

Timmy and Kenneth

It was an uncomfortable ride to the park.

'I'm sorry, sir,' Flick had explained, 'once I knew it was a child I daren't hand over the phone. He was obviously quite young and they get bored or distracted so easily. I had to keep him talking until we could get a contact organised.'

'Very well, Inspector. I'll let it go this time, but if you ever give me a *stop the traffic* hand again there will be consequences.'

Flick was concentrating on her driving and didn't see the glint of amusement in William Westcott's eyes. At that moment the mobile rang again.

Flick smiled. 'That will be Timmy checking up to see if I was telling the truth,' she said. 'Can you hold it up to my ear, sir? We don't want him doubting us, do we?'

Westcott slid open the mobile and held it up for Flick.

'Hello, Timmy,' she said.

'How'd you know it was me?'

'I told you it's a special phone and only rings to me and my friend.'

'Okay. Just checking,' said Timmy and the phone went dead.

Flick laughed. 'That's one bright kid,' she said. 'Would you like to check the phone, sir, and see if his brother tried it? Timmy said it didn't work, but it did work for us. I wonder how long it's lain in that drawer?' she mused. 'It must be at least since Tubby went away.'

Westcott was fiddling with the mobile from Tubby's house. 'I've found the call history,' he said.

'But there shouldn't be one, should there? If it could only work for Mike calling Tubby?'

'Right. There are several missed calls lately but I suppose that's Timmy's brother. But much earlier on there's voice mail. It's scratchy and faint. Sounds like "lined the throne",' said Westcott.

'Lined the throne? What on earth does that mean? Do you think it was Mike?'

'I don't know who else it could be. But what does it mean? Had he found some plot against the Queen?'

'Or is "throne" a slang word for something else, sir, like Cockney rhyming slang,' offered Flick.

'I don't know. We'll hand it over to the lab boys and see if they can come up with anything. Now we just have to get the other half of the comms setup.'

Flick parked the car outside the grand main entrance to the park, where the scrolled and gilded gates were kept permanently locked. They made their way on foot through the pedestrian side gate and went towards the swings in the play area near the northern end. She rooted in her bag to find her purse.

'Er, got a tenner on you, boss?' she said. A stain of embarrassment flushed her cheeks.

This time Westcott really did smile. He pulled out his wallet and handed over a note. 'You'd have been in a bit of a fix if I hadn't, wouldn't you, Inspector?'

Flick's grin was saucy. 'I'd have thought of something. But thanks, anyway. Look. That must be Timmy.'

A small boy with crumpled jeans riding low on his skinny hips, and a brightly coloured Tee shirt showing under his anorak was leaning against one of the metal swing supports. He was passing a mobile from one hand to the other. He straightened up as they got nearer.

Westcott hung back a little to let Flick do the talking. A woman's touch had worked so far.

Flick bent down to bring herself on eye level with the child. 'Hello, Timmy. Thank you for waiting for us. I see you've got the phone.'

'Told you I had didn' I? You got my tenner?'

'I have indeed.' Flick showed Timmy the note in her hand. 'Do you think your brother – Kenneth - isn't it, would remember exactly where he found the phone?'

Timmy grinned. 'Where he had his wee?'

Flick smiled. 'Yes, there.'

Timmy shrugged. 'I dunno. Maybe.'

'Could we come home with you and see your Mum and ask Kenneth if he can remember? Will you show us where you live?'

'I spose, but where's my tenner?'

'Here you are. Fair swap. One mobile for one tenner.' Flick held the note out to Timmy who reached for it but they were interrupted.

'Ere, you! What d'you think you're doing with that kid? You clear orf out of it before I call the police. I know your sort.' The speaker was a large middle-aged woman who had been sitting on one of the benches round the swing area. Several shopping bags were on the seat beside her and she held a voluminous handbag on her knees. With somewhat of a struggle she stood up. 'I can see you. I know what you're up to. Now clear orf.'

Flick had to bite back a snort of laughter at the look on DCI Westcott's face. The mortification of being accused of child molesting and the sheer astonishment of being the object of such an accusation held him speechless. To make sure the child didn't run off, Flick took Timmy's hand. This made matters worse.

'Take your hand off that boy. You let him go. Don't think I'm helpless,' cried the woman, ''cos I'm not.' She raised her voice to a shout 'Help! Help!'

At last Westcott took action. Not before time, thought Flick. He took out his ID and held it in front of the shouting woman.

'Madam,' he called. 'Madam. We *are* the police.'

But it wasn't until the woman had to stop to get her breath she heard his words. In that time two or three mothers had drawn nearer, grasping their children's hands tightly, but ready to come to the rescue. Already one had a mobile out, no doubt prepared to dial 999.

Timmy squirmed round to look up at Flick. 'You're not a copper are you?'

She smiled at him. 'Yes, Timmy, I am. And so is my friend. He's a very important copper indeed. He's my boss. Let's go and join him and explain to that lady why I was giving you ten pounds.'

But by the time they had reached the others, Westcott had already explained why they were with Timmy and the reason for money changing hands. Flick managed to slip the mobile into her pocket. Not much chance of spoiling any trace evidence when they had no idea how long it had been lost or who had handled it since. The vigilant woman wanted to see Flick's Warrant Card, examined it closely and, when they left the park with Timmy, she followed behind them until they were safely at his home. Only once they were inside his house did Flick feel free of those suspicious eyes.

'I suppose I should feel grateful there are such people around keeping a lookout for children who are not with their parents,' she murmured, 'but I could have done without the public attention.'

Westcott snorted. 'How do you think *I* feel?'

'Mum,' called Timmy as soon as they were inside the house. 'I've got two coppers and they want to see Kennef.'

'Oh, Lord,' said Flick. 'How to make friends and influence people. The poor woman will think we've come to arrest him or something.'

'Timmy, what have you done now?' A harassed woman emerged from the back of the narrow hall. She wiped her hands on the skirt of her apron as she approached.

'S'not me, Mum. It's our Kennef.'

'Mrs? I'm sorry, Timmy didn't tell us his surname?' said Westcott, moving forward with hand outstretched.

'It's Watts, Irene Watts,' said Timmy's mother. She shook the proffered hand and calmed visibly under the beam of DCI Westcott's smile. He could really be quite charming when he wanted to, thought Flick.

'Mrs Watts, there's nothing to be alarmed about. Quite the reverse. Timmy has been very helpful to us today and we would be grateful if your other son, Kenneth, could help us too?'

Mrs Watts frowned. 'Timmy, helping you?' she said doubtfully. Which made Flick wonder if young Timmy was more usually on the receiving end of a warning rather than thanks.

'Yes, indeed,' said Westcott and explained what had happened.

'That dratted phone,' said Mrs Watts. 'I told him to take it to the Police Station. But he said it was broken so there was no point. And now you say it works. Well, let him just wait till I get my hands on the little liar. I'll give him broken mobiles.'

'Please don't chastise your son, Mrs Watts. To him it would appear broken but to us it is valuable. A test piece, you understand.'

'Er, yes, of course.'

Flick hid a grin. That's right, boss, blind her with science.

'It would be very helpful if Kenneth could show us exactly where he found this mobile.'

'It was where he had his pee, Mum,' put in Timmy with a delighted grin.

Perhaps big brother would be in hot water for that too? wondered Flick.

'He's out the back,' said Mrs Watts. 'I'll give him a shout.' She hurried down the hall, presumably to the kitchen region and could be heard calling for Kenneth.

By the time he appeared with her it was evident he had received the rough edge of her tongue, whether for the mobile or the pee her visitors could only guess. Kenneth looked mutinous. Some years older than

Timmy, he was at that awkward age for boys when their arms and legs have sprouted length and the rest of their bodies don't seem to have caught up. He scowled at Westcott.

'I didn' do nothing wrong. I never nicked it. It were there . . . on the ground . . . and no-one about who might have dropped it.'

'That's alright, Kenneth,' said Westcott. 'We just wondered . . .'

'I got a tenner for it. They give me a tenner,' put in Timmy, before Westcott could finish.

The look of wrath on Kenneth's face was all his younger brother could have wished for but his glee was short-lived.

'You just give that back this minute,' cried Mrs Watts. 'That's stealing that is. We have no thieves in this family. Come on now, hand it over.'

Timmy's pleas were in vain and even Westcott assuring Mrs Watts it was worth that to recover the mobile wouldn't budge her. Timmy had to hand over the note.

'You go with the officers now,' said Mrs Watts, 'and find that place. Then you come straight home. I haven't finished with you yet, my lad.'

'We'll take you in our car,' said Westcott. 'I'll wait with you while Inspector Fraser fetches it.'

'Can I come too,' pleaded Timmy. 'I'd like to ride in a police car.'

Flick left Westcott explaining to a disillusioned Timmy why his car didn't have "blues and twos". She smiled as she hurried back through the park. Jude would have felt just the same. Come to that so would Natalie.

Because the Watts lived in a terraced road parallel to the park, and only two streets deep from the road surrounding it, Flick easily retraced her steps to the park gates.

By the time she arrived back at their house, Timmy had got over his disappointment and Mrs Watts, no doubt happy to have a period of peace without the boys and knowing they were safe, had agreed he should accompany his big brother on the outing.

'Now then, Kenneth,' said Westcott when the boys were strapped into the back seat of the Mondeo. 'You tell us the way.'

'We were just messing about on our bikes,' said Kenneth. 'We went along beside the park and then we played that game, you know, where you take the first turning on the left and then the right and see where you get to.'

Flick grinned. She remembered teaching that one to the twins. 'Alright,' she said 'here goes. As you were on your bikes I suppose it's not far away is it? I won't go too fast in case we miss the spot.'

'Where Kennef had his pee,' put in the irrepressible Timmy.

'You shut up, or else,' threatened his loving brother.

'Just pay attention to where we're going, Kenneth,' said Westcott as Flick turned the car into a road that led them away from the town, heading into the country and becoming more of a lane as they progressed.

'There,' said Kenneth. 'There. Over by that tree. That's the place.'

'Are you sure?' queried the Chief.

'Yeah,' said Kenneth, 'that's it alright 'cos I leaned me bike against it.'

Flick pulled the car over and parked. They all got out and approached the tree in question. It was a beautiful oak, looking incongruous all alone beside the road. In fact it must have been there far longer than the lane, thought Flick judging by the height of it. When she looked back she could see that in fact the lane had diverted around it. Behind the tree ran a high wall. It too had diverted from the straight on the other side, forming in effect an island of grass around the mighty old oak. Flick held an eager Timmy back while Kenneth moved slowly forward his eyes on the ground.

'I stopped and put me bike here.' He gestured to the trunk of the tree, 'and then I moved a bit away and faced the wall.' He took a few steps. 'And there it was, lying in the grass, just about there.' He pointed to a spot. 'I didn't pee on it,' he reassured Westcott. 'Just near it.'

'Thank you for that, anyway,' said the DCI. 'Just wait with Inspector Fraser a moment will you?' He leaned closer to the grass and slowly moved around, his eyes focused for the slightest hint of anything out of place.

Flick waited with the boys, then saw her boss straighten up and shake his head. 'It's no use,' he said coming towards her. 'Dear knows how long it was there or what might have been dumped or blown onto that spot since, but we'll get someone discreet out to have a look anyway.'

'Fred Updike's your man for this, sir. Close as the grave,' she added, 'and he does know Tubby's gone AWOL.'

'Who's Tubby?' said Timmy. 'There's a boy at Kennef's school called Tubby because he's a greedy pig. Is your Tubby a greedy pig?'

'Will you shut up,' moaned Kenneth. 'You wait till I tell Mum what you said.'

'That's enough boys,' said Westcott. 'As you have both been so helpful I think you deserve an official police reward.'

Two pairs of eyes fixed on him with eager attention.

'Can I have my tenner back?' said Timmy.

'No. Your mother made that clear.'

Timmy drooped.

'But in recognition of your services to the police you shall each receive five pounds.' This restored the good humour all round even though the official wording might have gone over the boys' heads. 'Now we must get you home,' ordered Westcott having handed over a note each to the two thrilled lads.

But the loss of Timmy's tenner still wrankled. 'What if Mum makes us give it back?' he said.

'We won't tell her?' offered Kenneth.

'I shall tell her,' said Westcott, 'and explain. Now home please, Inspector.'

Later that night Flick regaled Andy and Amanda with the story. 'You should have seen Westcott's face when Kenneth assured him he hadn't pee'd on the mobile,' she laughed. 'Just for that I'd have given him a fiver myself.'

Monday, Tuesday, Wednesday, Thursday

Back at the police station Flick explained to Fred Updike exactly where the DCI wanted him to search and gave him the mobile to pass to the lab, then she made her way upstairs. As she went through the main office DS Booth called over to her.

'Hey, boss, we've got the other two.'

Flick crossed the room to Booth's desk. 'What other two? Please don't tell me you have more bodies?'

He grinned. 'No, but I can tell you who the ones we've got are. Ponytail is called Jake Brand and the one with the earring is Lawrence Hardy. They are, or we think they are, delivery drivers.'

'What took you so long?'

'It was the landlord of the Crown and Sceptre who clocked them.'

'But I thought all that area was canvassed first time around. Uniform took the pics into every address.'

'Yes, they did, boss, and no-one recognised them but then PC Hurle thought maybe there were different employees on different shifts so she went back.'

'Smart thinking. And so someone knew them?'

'Not just someone, boss, but the landlord himself. He'd been away at some conference or other the first time the pics were shown. He says he doesn't believe they are local but come here regularly. I suppose that would fit in with a regular delivery run.'

'But delivering what, and from where?' wondered Flick.

'He didn't know, boss, but said he'd seen the van down the side of the bookies. Maybe they were delivering there?' said Booth

'What kind of delivery would a bookie need on a regular basis?'

'Betting slips?' offered a voice from the back of the room. There was a quiet ripple of laughter.

'How regular is regular?' said Flick. 'You could get a million betting slips in one of those white vans. You wouldn't need a regular delivery.'

'Well, I don't know what else they use,' said Booth. 'And of course they probably have other drops to make each time to different addresses. It wouldn't only be here in Ridminster, if they come from Swindon. If it is the same van then the garage manager said he had reported it stolen, so it may not be the same one, or have the usual driver or drivers. But there's lots of places they could service between Swindon and here.'

'Yes, thank you DS Booth. I am aware, and chasing them all down can be a headache for you perhaps. I don't think we can do much more today but I want to know everything there is to know about those two. I'm getting good accurate photofit pictures printed in the local paper. Less likely to give people nightmares than the photos,' she explained. 'Hopefully someone will recognise them and come forward. In the meantime, keep digging. Goodnight.'

Because first the children and then Amanda were constantly around Flick couldn't say anything to Andy until they were in bed. Briefly she filled him in on the day's events.

'I thought it wasn't like the Old Man to jump down your throat like that,' he said in satisfaction at a problem solved. 'No wonder he thought you were being dim when you were at such cross-purposes. But what the hell can Tubby Jackson have been playing at?'

'I have no idea, and you should have seen the Old Man when he realised what had been going on. I never wanted to get on the wrong side of him before in a general kind of way, but after today I reckon I'd do practically anything to keep him sweet.'

'Not anything?' grinned Andy.

'Don't be daft,' she laughed. 'But seriously, And, I'm getting a very bad feeling about this whole business. And the silly part of it is I keep thinking they're related.'

'Who?'

'Not who, but what. My three murders; Tubby doing a bunk; and the undercover drug thing.'

'Surely not? Tubby and your murders, yes, because he tried to cover them up, but only for his own vanity, I guess. Then when the silly plonker realised just what he'd done he got the hell out of it for a long holiday as fast as he could.'

'I suppose you're right, but it still feels wrong to me somehow.'

'Well, shut up about it now and come here,' said Andy, pulling her into his arms where he very satisfactorily took her mind off her problems.

Tuesday and Wednesday passed with no new developments. Routine took over. Paperwork was slightly reduced. Two consecutive very amateur burglaries were swiftly and successfully cleared up when the police sniffer dog traced the criminals by their scent, comprising a strong amount of stale alcohol, back to their own homes where the four sat still consuming their ill-gotten gains. There were three calls for "domestics". One was resolved before the police car arrived to find the two combatants weeping in each other's arms. The other two needed separation and mediation to sort out their problems. In other words it was a typical two days. Flick felt restive. And the frown deepened on DCI Westcott's forehead.

On Thursday morning Flick called Dave Booth into her office.

'I'm giving you this task because you know Tubby Jackson has gone away,' she said. 'But I don't want it talked about in the squad room. Do the work and keep shtum. OK?'

'Yes, boss.'

'No exceptions. None. Understood?'

'Right. As the grave,' he said. 'What do I have to do?'

'Find out where he went and how he got there. He didn't take his own car so you could start with the taxi firms. Then find out which Travel Agent sold him his tickets. Even if he did the first part by train and bought his ticket at the station he must surely have booked a seat either on a plane, a cross-Channel ferry, or the Eurostar. And hopefully that will give us a destination and maybe a hotel or resort to follow up with. Okay. Go.'

'Will do and report directly to you?'

'Yes. Don't worry. If we get anything useful I will tell the DCI your part in it.' Flick grinned.

Dave nodded and opened the door. He turned before he went out. 'Good luck for tomorrow,' he said.

Flick frowned. Tomorrow? Tomorrow was Friday. What was so special about Friday?

'Hey,' she called as the door was closing. 'What's so special about tomorrow?'

'Your school visit,' said Booth.

'What school visit? This is the first I've heard of it. Are they coming here and if so how many?'

Booth came back into Flick's office. 'No,' he said. 'It's the day of your visit to the Priors Parveneau school to give the usual "we are your friendly Police Force and this is what we do for you" speech.' he said.

'Back up,' ordered Flick. 'I have never heard about this. I certainly didn't arrange it.'

'Ooops!' said Booth. 'No, ma'am. I believe it was DI Jackson who took the call and arranged the details'

'Well I'll hand that on,' said Flick.

'They'll be terribly disappointed. Apparently the Head Teacher was over the moon when she heard you would be there in person.'

'Pull the other one,' said Flick.

'No truly. She said, and I quote "how lovely that someone so important would take the time to come to a little school like ours" end of quote.'

Flicks eyes narrowed. 'So if you can quote the conversation, you were there?'

Booth was trying hard not to laugh. 'Actually, Tubby, that is DI Jackson repeated her words, mimicked her as it happens and that was the first time I saw him smile while you were away.'

'Go on,' said Flick. Her voice was ominous.

'He said . . .

'and you quote.'

'Yes. He said, "let's see how Mrs High and Mighty Metropolitan Officer Fraser likes that little duty", ma'am.'

'Well I shall,' said Flick. 'I'll take Andy in full rig and we'll give those kids the works. What time tomorrow?'

'I think Tubby arranged it for eleven. The teacher said it would nicely fill the time before lunch. DI Jackson said he would put it in your diary.'

Flick turned over the page of her desk diary. 'Guess what?'

'I'm sorry, boss. I should have thought to mention it earlier.'

'No sweat. I just wonder what other little surprises DI Jackson has secreted to delight me with.'

Friday

'Okay, let her rip,' grinned Flick on Friday morning.

'Anything you say, ma'am,' said Andy. His eyes crinkled with amusement as he switched on "the blues and twos". So with lights flashing and the siren wailing he steered the marked police car through the gates of Priors Parveneau school and brought it to a halt in the playground.

The sight of eager little faces pressed to the windows gave Flick great satisfaction. It quite outweighed the irritation she had felt at being landed with this chore in the middle of a murder investigation. Her team all knew what they had to do in her absence and she would give the kids her best shot.

Andy killed the engine and the siren. As they climbed out of the car Flick looked with pride at her husband. He made an impressive sight in full sergeant's uniform, ready for patrol. His hot pursuit days had given her a few bad times culminating in his accident, but now he was safely behind a desk she could enjoy the memories of his past bravery with a quiet mind.

A slim young woman with shoulder length rich brown hair came across the playground with hand outstretched. 'Hello, I'm Kate Roberts, the Headmistress. Thank you so much. You have made this day for the children. They have promised to sit quietly and listen to what you say and I hope they will, but your arrival has practically sent them into orbit.'

Flick grinned as she shook hands and introduced herself and Andy. 'I hoped you wouldn't mind, Miss Roberts.'

'Kate, please.'

'Kate,' said Flick, 'but having kids ourselves, we couldn't disappoint them.'

Kate Roberts nodded as she led the way into the school. 'I thought you must have a real understanding of children. That just confirms it. How many and how old?'

Flick explained her family as they walked along a corridor towards the sound of excited children corralled in one place.

'Twins. How lovely,' said Kate. 'Go for one and get one free,' she laughed. 'Very modern.'

It said a great deal about the type of teacher Kate Roberts was when the hubbub died down as soon as she opened the door of the large classroom and entered with Flick and Andy. The children were obedient to her instruction to sit down but not in the least in awe of their Head. They quickly settled, sitting cross-legged on the floor and looked up at the visitors with big smiles and wide eyes, waiting to be entertained.

Small chairs and tables had been pushed to the back of the room which, Flick guessed, was used for various activities and not just for academic lessons. Large windows let in the daylight that showed up the bright colours of the furniture and the cupboards round the walls. The children's drawings and writing were displayed on corkboards and on tables that ran under the windows. One was a Nature table complete with a jam jar full of wild flowers and an abandoned bird's nest. Another held cut-outs of a Saxon settlement and a third was devoted to the Romans. But it was the sight of a sand tray holding a cardboard pyramid surrounded by tiny palm trees that made Flick really smile. That was something to tell Natalie.

It had taken only a moment to take in details of the whole room while Kate Roberts was telling the children who Flick and Andy were and reminding them that policemen and women were their friends and there to protect them.

'Good morning, children,' said Flick and went on to give her usual talk, starting with the role of the police in general and then getting the children involved in answering her questions as to their viewpoint of the police. That was the part she had found often gave her food for thought and sometimes in the past a sense of despair. But here in the heart of the countryside the results were all good.

She moved from her questions to questions from the children and stored up one gem to relate to Amanda. A wide-eyed little girl in the front row was so sympathetic that Flick couldn't wear a "pretty uniform" like the policeman, with "all the fun things" on it.

Next it was Andy's turn to show and explain just what the fun things were, how they worked and why he had them with him. He called them out in fours to hold most things, from his extending baton to his handcuffs. When he had laughingly refused to manacle two bright sparks together Flick took over again. She explained that although the police were friends of the people, their servants in fact, the job they did was very serious and no-one should ever want to feel handcuffs on their wrists. Having got the children into a sober frame of mind and sure she had got her message across, she then offered the opportunity to sit in the police car and have the "blues and twos" going.

Kate and her assistant teachers organised the children into orderly lines and the treat went off without a hitch five children at a time. Then it was all over, for the kids and for Flick and Andy. A small boy swelling with importance stood up and gave a vote of thanks he had no doubt been practising for days. He got through it very well and in turn Flick thanked the children for their patient attention and reminded them they could always ask a policeman or woman for help. Then the children marched off to the dining hall and Kate walked with Flick and Andy to the door.

'That was brilliant,' she said. 'The kids will never forget it. Thank you so much for coming and giving them so much of your time. Mind you,' she added with a smile, 'you didn't tell them how long it might take for the police to take any action.'

Flick frowned. 'What do you mean?' she said.

'I reported that incident weeks ago,' said Kate 'and I haven't heard a dicky bird.'

'What incident?'

'That guy I saw in the woods. But perhaps you haven't been told about it? I reported it over the phone. Would it be to someone at the front desk? Anyway when

I phoned back he said it had been passed on to CID. That's you isn't it?' she asked Flick.

Flick's heart sank. Not another Tubby Jackson cock-up?

'Yes, it is me, and no, I haven't heard anything about it. Would you mind going over it again?' Even if it was a load of nonsense, she couldn't risk it being another of Tubby's ways of putting her in a bad light. And Kate Roberts didn't strike Flick as the kind of person who would waste police time. But a man in the woods? A pervert?

'Sure. Come into my office and have a seat. It won't take long.'

Once they were all seated Kate began. 'It must be about five or six weeks ago now. I was jogging along the back road to Ridminster quite early. If it's fine I like to go for a run before I have to stay indoors when the sun is shining.' She smiled. 'The children aren't the only ones who look longingly out of the window.'

'What day was this?' asked Flick

Kate looked at a calendar on the wall beside her desk. 'It must have been a Thursday, because I rang as soon as I got back, and then I waited a whole week, and rang again on the following Friday. And that takes us to exactly a month ago.'

'Right,' said Flick and made a note in her book. 'So what actually happened?'

'Like I said, I was running along the road past the woods on one side and the hedge bordering the Hall lands on the other. The fields there rise steeply from the road but the hedge is quite high, so that stretch is not overlooked. By the trees there is a sort of passing place.

The locals use it to park their cars when they go walking in the woods. It's a pretty wood and a favourite place for families'

'And dog walkers?'

'Not so much. It is just that bit farther out of the village. Not enough to warrant getting the car out for a dog, but maybe a bit far to walk there and back.'

'I've got the picture,' said Flick. 'Go on.'

'I noticed this white van parked by the road and didn't think much of it. But later when I turned to run back I saw a man come out of the woods carrying a spade. He threw it into the van and then got in and drove off, nearly knocking me over in the process.'

'Do you mean he tried to run you down?'

Kate hesitated. 'Probably not. It was more like he resented me being there and gave me a scare to make a point.'

'So what happened next?'

'I couldn't think what he would be doing in the woods at that time in the morning with a spade. It just seemed fishy so I walked down the little path leading into the woods from the point he had been parked and then I saw it.'

'Saw what?'

'He'd marked the spot with a piece of that tape you see on building sites or round holes in the road where men are working. Red and white stripes. There it was tied to a tree.'

Flick frowned. 'What exactly was he marking?'

'A big bank of bluebells. I don't know if my appearance changed his mind. He might have seen me pass the first time and decided to leave it till later. Or he may have been marking them for someone else to come. But I could see where he had started to try lifting the whole bank of them.' Kate's eyes shone with indignation.

Andy looked at Flick. 'Bluebells?' he said.

'They are a protected wildflower,' went on Kate. 'And now we have the menace of these Spanish ones mixing with ours. Soon our native bluebells will disappear altogether. I have no idea how much he could sell them for or if he wanted them himself but I stopped his little red wagon,' Kate said with satisfaction.

Flick controlled the involuntary twitch of her lips and daren't look at Andy. 'What did you do?'

'I untied his wretched tape, rolled it up and brought it back here,' said Kate. 'And here it is. I kept it to show whoever came to investigate. But no-one turned up,' she finished with a frown. 'I could have kicked myself later because I didn't take the number of the van.'

'Yes. That is a pity,' agreed Flick. She thought for a moment. Why would anyone mark a bank of bluebells? Surely there would be more than one in a wood? And the white van? How did that fit in? Was it *her* white van or another one altogether?

'Don't worry,' she heard Andy say, 'that's just what she looks like when the wheels are going round.'

'So you are taking me seriously?' asked Kate.

Flick smiled. 'Oh, yes, indeed. Tell me, could you show me the exact spot you took the tape from?'

Kate nodded. 'Of course. I know the woods well.' She glanced at the clock on the wall. 'If we go right now I can be back in time for playground duty after lunch. In a small school like ours it's a question of all hands to the pump,' she smiled. 'No standing on rank as you would say.'

'Stop just there,' Kate indicated. 'In that small layby. That's where the van was parked. I'm afraid it's a bit muddy after the rain we've had.'

'Not to worry,' said Flick and she and Andy followed the teacher along a track so narrow it had probably been made initially by rabbits.

After a couple of hundred yards when they were just out of immediate sight of the road, Kate took an even less distinct track on her left and walked with confidence to a thorn tree. 'Here we are. The tape was tied just here.' She showed them a branch just above shoulder height.

'High enough it would be unlikely a child would take it,' mused Flick. 'The tape itself is official enough it would be unlikely an adult would remove it, believing it served a purpose of some kind.'

'And so it did,' averred Kate. 'That rotter or a mate of his meant to come back and take our lovely flowers. Look. You can still see where he started to dig because there are dead plants along the length of the bank.'

It was true there was a distinct line of wilted vegetation at the base of a large clump of bluebells that were now past their prime.

Flick crouched down and felt with one finger along half of the length of that line. She had a telltale tickle between her shoulder blades. She didn't know why, couldn't even begin to credit these bluebells with any importance, but she had once ignored that particular tickle to her cost. She straightened up, took out her

165

mobile and dialled the station number. While she waited to be put through to the Dog Section she turned to Andy.

'Will you take Kate back to school? I'll wait here. You can pick me up afterwards.'

Kate raised her eyebrows. 'Dogs?' she queried. Then she laughed. 'Don't worry I won't embarrass you by asking questions you can't answer, but please let me know what happens. After all, it was my initial report.'

'I will,' said Flick, 'Goodbye and thank you.' She turned her attention to her phone.

While she waited for Andy to come back and a member of the Dog Section to arrive Flick just hoped she wasn't making a fool of herself. If the man with the spade had really been stealing bluebells why hadn't he taken them with him? It may be illegal but surely not so heinous a crime he would be frightened off by a passing jogger? A lone young female at that?

Flick was just beginning to feel she had made a right idiot of herself when a thought struck home. She fished out her mobile and phoned the school.

'Sorry to bother you again, Kate, but how close were you to the man you saw. Could you describe him?'

At Kate's answer Flick gave a sigh of relief. 'A ponytail, you say, like an ageing rock star? Right. Thank you, Kate. Thank you very much; and keep all this to yourself just now would you please?'

So this white van man and Lenny's white van man would seem to be one and the same. What could a killer be doing in Priors Parveneau woods so early in the morning? Flick remembered the disturbed earth. Not

166

another body surely? Perhaps she had asked for the
wrong kind of sniffer dog?

Three quarters of an hour later she had her answer. But
once again the answer simply threw up more questions.

Handler Kevin and his spaniel dog, Rags, had arrived
sooner than Flick could have hoped. Once in the wood
Rags started pulling at his lead even before they had
reached the turnoff to the second smaller path. Flick
stood back and let Rags lead Kevin straight to the bank of
bluebells. She had warned Kevin to bring a spade. When
he inserted the blade into the line of decaying weeds and
lifted it gently, Rags nearly turned himself inside out
with excitement. His stumpy tail wagged so hard it was
just a blur. His whole body quivered. Kevin patted and
praised him, then gave him a doggy treat to eat.

'Definitely drugs,' said Kevin. 'What kind I don't
know. Rags has been trained to find two or three different
ones. But let's see what's underneath here?' He bade
Rags "Sit" and then handed the leash to Flick. 'Hang on
to him, ma'am. I don't want to jab the spade in too hard
in case I burst a package. That is if there is anything here
at all. It may be all the boy is getting is residual scent.'

But as he gently eased up the clods of bulb-bearing
earth it could be seen a package lay under the soil.

'Hold it up a minute, can you?' said Flick. 'I don't
want to kill any more wild flowers and I think I can reach
the package. Here, Andy, can you hang on to Rags?'
She passed the leash to Andy and pulled a pair of her
nitrile gloves out of her pocket. Once she was gloved she
knelt down and reached into the hole Kevin had created.
Soil went up the sleeves of her coat making her wrinkle

her nose, but she ignored it otherwise and persevered. She got a purchase on the edge of the packet with her fingertips. 'Can you push the spade farther in alongside my hands?' she asked the handler, 'and raise it just a fraction more?'

She felt the cold blade of the spade slide along her right hand, shuffled forward on her knees and reached farther into the hole. 'Got it,' she panted and scooted back on her heels, the precious package in her hands. It was about the size of an A4 padded envelope that had a line of staples running along each end for extra security. At the back of Flick's mind something niggled. What was there about this envelope that bothered her, apart from its place of concealment and the almost certain fact it held some kind of drug? And what connected Lenny and the ponytail man with his white van and drugs? Was it too far-fetched to think that they might both - or rather all three, for there was also Gold Earring to remember - be connected to Operation Country Ride? One thing was sure, the sooner she could inform DCI Westcott of this latest piece of the puzzle, the better. She turned to Handler Kevin. 'I know you don't sound off about your finds outside the nick,' she said, 'but for reasons I can't explain at the moment I don't want you reporting this find to anyone, inside or outside the station. Okay? '

He frowned. 'What do I put in my log, and what do I tell the Sergeant?'

'Tell the Sergeant it's a "need to know" and in your log you can put a reference to DCI Westcott. Alright?' She softened the order with a smile. 'When I can, I'll tell you all about it. Promise.'

'Ma'am,' he grinned and went off down the track with Rags.

I just hope the day will come when I can explain, thought Flick. But it won't be until we've got a hell of a lot of answers.

Friday

DCI Westcott listened intently to Flick's account of her visit to Priors Parveneau school and the results. He gloved up and then examined the package but agreed with Flick it should go to Forensics intact.

'I'll have a word. See if they can give it top priority. It's just possible they could lift prints from the outside but I think it would be a miracle if they found anything useable considering the circumstances. The paper is quite tough but the damp has already started to soften it.'

'It has been there a whole month, sir. It would be surprising if there was no damage. I can't think it was meant to remain this long or they would have made sure it was water-proof.'

'Agreed. And we have the Head Teacher's quick action to thank for this little windfall?'

'Kate Roberts, yes sir, that and her passion to preserve the wildflowers of England.' Flick smiled, then sobered. 'Do you think this links our three bodies with Operation Country Ride, sir?'

'If they're not linked it's a hell of a coincidence we find our white van driver involved in drugs apart from the ongoing investigation. And I don't believe in coincidence to that extent.'

'And didn't you say that F's seem to have disappeared off Ridminster streets for the last week or so?'

'Yes. There's been nothing reported for over a week,' said Westcott.'

'And just ten days ago Jake Brand, that's the one with the pony tail, and his mate with the earring, Laurence Hardy, were found dead. Normally that would smack to me of a local interest clearing out a pair of strangers trying to muscle in,' said Flick.

'Agreed. But not in this case you think?'

Flick frowned. 'It just doesn't feel right. There are too many loose ends. Where does Swindon come into it? The op moved here from London via Swindon you said. Brand and Laurence don't seem to have set up any kind of base that we know about. We do know they bumped off Lenny, but why? As far as we are aware he never had any drug connection with the locals and he belongs to Ridminster so would be more likely to be involved here rather than with incomers.'

She and DCI Westcott sat either side of his desk both wracking their brains to find some kind of thread to follow; some kind of connection that would lead them further along with the investigation.

A tap at the door came as a welcome diversion. When it opened DI Paddy Murphy looked in. 'Could I have a word, sir?' he began, then noticed Flick sitting by the desk. 'Sorry, sir. I didn't realise you were engaged. I can come back.'

'No, Inspector. Come in. I'm glad you're here. I would have sent for you otherwise,' said William Westcott.

Murphy walked into the office and closed the door behind him. He nodded to Flick, 'Afternoon Inspector Fraser,' he smiled.

'Hello, Paddy,' she said. 'Your timing is spot on.'

DCI Westcott outlined everything that had happened from the time Flick discovered there were three murders on her patch. What he left out was any reference to Tubby Jackson.

The Old Man is keeping our dirty linen under wraps as long as possible, thought Flick.

'So Forensics has got the mobile?' queried Paddy.

'Yes, and will have this package asap,' confirmed Westcott, 'but where does that get us?'

'We obviously have to look at the Swindon angle, but really have very little to go on,' said the undercover liaison. 'Mike, our man, was convinced of the trail but had very little hard evidence. The only people he could point out were, in our opinion, small fry we've let run on but with covert surveillance. So far they've given us nothing apart from some disputes among themselves.'

Flick sat up straighter. 'What kind of disputes?'

'Difficult to say exactly but something seems to have gone wrong. There are angry and worried faces around Swindon. A hiccough in the smooth running of the business, at a guess.'

Flick's eyes shone. 'I think you're right. And the reason could be right in front of us. How many of these F's would you say would fit into an envelope of this size?'

Murphy shrugged. 'Difficult to say. We've never actually intercepted a shipment, but if they're treated like

172

other so-called recreational drugs they could be fixed on a sheet of some kind of light medium. Depending on their size you could get a few hundred on a sheet that size,' he said nodding to the package on the desk. 'Judging by the thickness of the envelope it could hold as many as 50 sheets or more. Say 500 individual F's per sheet and 50 sheets there, that would be a total of 250,000 doses.'

Westcott whistled and Flick's mouth dropped open. She nodded. 'Yes. So you see the loss of that package would mean a big disruption in the supply line.'

Murphy shook his head. 'I can't buy this "stuff it under a bush and I'll collect it later" form of delivery. It's far too amateurish for the people we're after. The boss in particular, the brains behind the whole thing is just too methodical and careful to go down that route.'

'But it wasn't him, was it?' said Flick. 'It was someone much farther down the food chain. And the one we know about has turned up dead. So do we think he was dealing a bit on the side, double-crossing his master, perhaps?'

'Some "bit on the side",' put in Westcott. 'It smacks more to me of one of the drivers having a personal crisis and missing a pick-up. Then he calls his opposite number and asks for a favour to cover up his mistake. All would have been well had it not been for the teacher. The goods would have been picked up and maybe the boss would never know?'

'That's a distinct possibility I suppose,' said Paddy Murphy. 'Certainly retribution would be swift and final if or when his boss found out. The man is ruthless. If these are connected they wouldn't be the first who have paid the price of disobedience. And that's what sticks in my gullet. The man rules by fear and as far as we can tell he's canny enough to remain anonymous to those who work for him. I know Mike tried to get his identity from various sources but no-one knows him. He's just "The Man". I don't suppose you've heard from Mike?' he queried.

Flick and Westcott looked at each other. Flick held her tongue. It wasn't her place to pass on information when she had her boss with her. It was his call.

'That's the other reason I wanted to see you.' Westcott smoothed into the story of the found mobile. Flick could only admire the way he managed to leave Tubby completely out of the story.

Murphy frowned. 'This is bad news,' he said. 'That leaves Mike really hanging in the wind if things go pear-shaped. Of course it was only a last resort kind of thing, but I'll tell you in confidence we are getting worried. Mike has never been out of touch for so long before. He was quite excited last time he managed a brief word. Said he hoped to get a line on the power behind the throne. So somewhere there is a front for what is going on. Perhaps a perfectly legitimate business? They might not even know they are being used. I tell you this guy is one of the cleverest and most devious we've come across.'

'But you'll get him in the end?' said Flick.

Murphy's smile was grim. 'Yes, in the end we will. But at what cost?'

That evening when the kids were in bed and Amanda was visiting with Elaine, Flick filled Andy in on what had happened after they had got back to the station from the Priors Parveneau woods.

'It's such a mess, And,' she said. 'Nothing seems to lead anywhere.'

'But it's not the first time you've felt like that is it?' said Andy as he refilled her glass of wine. 'Remember at the Met you used to say you'd got so much information and nothing fitted together? It was usually just before you found the one bit of the puzzle that connected the other pieces.'

Flick grinned at him and raised her glass in salute. 'You do know how to say the right things, don't you, mate?' she said. 'Like Paddy Murphy said, we will get there in the end.

'But the big worry is where Tubby Jackson fits into all this. The Old Man very carefully made no mention of him when Paddy was in the office. I think our revered boss is hoping to deal with Tubby very, very quietly.' She gazed into the cheerful flames of the sitting room fire, then went on 'It all depends on just what Tubby has been up to. What has he done? Or not done? Well, let's forget Tubby and the nick for the rest of the weekend. Paddy is chasing up the garage in Swindon where the van came from and Forensics have got the package and the phone. Dear knows how long it will take them to get a result. They said they're snowed under and short-staffed.' She pulled a long face. 'So what's new?'

Saturday

'That's more like it, old boy,' smiled Edward Carver as he and William Westcott took seats at a spare table in the large lounge bar of Ridminster Golf Club. 'Not a thrashing, but we did beat them and that's what counts. You were certainly on better form than last week'

Westcott nodded with a wry smile. 'Couldn't have been much worse, could I?' He would dearly have loved to give his Saturday morning golf game a miss today. He had so much on his mind. But he was firmly of the opinion showing his face here and in other areas of Ridminster life reassured the public their police force was part of the whole fabric of the town. It was another reason he backed every initiative that integrated the force with civilians. Such as Flick Fraser's visit to Priors Parveneau yesterday and just look what that had yielded.

'Hello. Earth to Westcott,' chanted Carver beside him.

Westcott blinked and smiled. 'Sorry, miles away. Just trying to remember what it was my wife asked me to pick up on the way home,' he lied smoothly.

'Ah, the ladies,' said Carver. 'What would we do without them?'

But he does, doesn't he? thought Westcott and realised he knew very little about his companion. 'Have you ever been married?' he asked.

Carver shook his head. 'I could say no woman in her right mind would have me,' he joked, 'but truth is I've never met any one particular member of the fair sex I felt inclined to share the rest of my life with. The other bar is of course it's not an easy life for a woman. Left alone for long periods of time, with worry her only companion.'

'I suppose it takes a certain strength of character to be able to do that,' agreed Westcott. 'Seen much active service have you?'

Carver hesitated, then smiled. 'Need to know old boy,' he said and tapped the side of his nose, 'but I've done my fair share. Here come the drinks,' he finished as their two opponents in the game just finished advanced from the bar carrying glasses.

As soon as the drinks were finished the losers left, but Carver insisted on buying the second round. 'Bird can't fly on one wing,' he said and carried his and Westcott's empty glasses to the bar.

When he had returned with his lager and whisky chaser and another half pint of orange and lemonade for Westcott he pushed himself more comfortably into his chair, looked around to see if they could be overheard and quizzed Westcott. 'Glad the others left,' he said. 'Couldn't talk with them here, but wanted the opportunity to ask you how it's going.'

Westcott raised his eyebrows, 'Going?' he said.

'The matter we spoke about last week. Lord it seems so much longer ago. I keep my ear to the ground and I gather there have been no more cases of drug overdose? Very happy to learn that, as you can imagine. My committee was getting twitchy about the police capability. It doesn't take much you know.'

Westcott hid his irritation and growing dislike of the man beside him. 'My people have got things in hand,' he said.

'Of course, of course. And when are we going to meet your new Inspector? A very attractive young lady by all accounts. Will she be joining us at our "meet the people" meeting? Or are you going to take over that role personally?'

Westcott frowned. 'New Inspector?' he queried, although pretty certain he knew who Carver meant.

Carver mused for a moment. 'Let me see what was the name? Frances? No, of course, Fraser. Is she Scotch? Pretty little thing so I hear.'

'I think you'll find Scotch is the drink,' Westcott forced a smile. 'Inspector Fraser is married to a Scottish man but she is by no means new to us. She has been a valued member of my force for six years now.'

Carver grinned and winked at Westcott. 'Very p c old chap,' he said. 'But now Inspector Jackson has retired she'll have to do some more grown-up police work no doubt.'

Westcott changed the subject and until they had finished their drinks the discussion centred on golfing matters. They parted in the car park with mutual congratulations on their morning's win and Carver got into the classic Jaguar that waited for him. Westcott admired the sleek, graceful lines of the powerful machine. Sun shone on its immaculate bright red paintwork. This car made a statement. Here I am. Look at me. Aren't I beautiful?

178

No anonymous black modern car for Edward Carver. The silent grey-suited driver seemed out of place in such a machine. What a contrast. As it drove out of the Club car park Westcott climbed into his Volvo and sat, thinking.

What was there about this morning's conversations with Carver that had left this sense of unease? His antenna was twitching. The man was obviously an out of date, patronising idiot. Not a misogynist. He claimed to enjoy the company of women. But certainly he didn't respect their mental abilities. Where did that come from? And who had described Flick Fraser to him as an empty-headed, young and incapable officer given promotion to keep the numbers right in this "politically correct" regime? Only one person sprang to mind. Tubby Jackson. He had been the police rep with the "meet the people" team. Westcott had seen him in conversation on several occasions with Carver and never thought anything of it. That was part of Tubby's remit in that role. But hadn't Carver stayed behind after the lunch on Tubby's last appearance? One of the other officers present had mentioned to Westcott, in passing, that Tubby had thoroughly enjoyed the drinks Carver had treated him to – for his retirement.

Westcott started up the Volvo and drove home but his wife found him distracted over lunch and in the afternoon he booted up his home computer and started making a few searches.

Major Carver was in an expansive mood. 'What's for lunch, Manners?' he said.

Manners glanced into his rear view mirror and saw the smile on the Major's face. 'Lamb cutlets, sir?' he offered.

'Very nice too.'

Carver proceeded to relate his conversation with DCI Westcott, then chuckled. 'You would think he would be missing Inspector Jackson. But I think he has another agenda for the delectable Inspector Fraser.'

'Sir?' Manners was at his most wooden.

'You should have heard him fire up in her defence when I suggested she wasn't perhaps up to her new role as Inspector Jackson's successor.' Carver grinned. 'I wonder if our dear Chief Inspector is playing away from home? I haven't heard any whispers but then there are so many cliques in Ridminster I can't keep up with them all and they'd be very discreet, very discreet indeed,' he chuckled again. 'I don't suppose you . . .?'

'No, nothing, sir. Do you really think so?'

Carver shrugged. 'I don't know but it's not beyond the realms of possibility. He wouldn't be the first and no doubt won't be the last to make a false move over a pretty face and compliant body.'

'I understood the lady to be married, sir?'

'Yes, to a deadbeat, passed over Sergeant, according to Inspector Jackson. If she's ambitious, what better way to secure her rise than to bed the boss? A step forward older than Adam, or rather Eve.'

'Sir?'

'Didn't she seduce the snake?'

Manners allowed his lips to twitch in what passed with him for a smile.

As Carver pushed away his cheese plate and placed his linen napkin on the table he heaved a satisfied sigh.

'You are a prince among servants, my dear Manners. And now I think you should share your talents with others.'

'Sir?'

'We are going to give a party.'

'A party? Yes, sir. An intimate dinner perhaps? There is a way of doing fallow buck, still in season, that melts in the mouth. And perhaps red mullet or sea bream before?'

'No. That won't do. Not nearly enough scope to give themselves away. We'll have a cocktail party and invite Westcott and Inspector Fraser, with their partners of course.' Carver rubbed his hands together as his idea took wing. 'And the sooner, the better. We'll make up the numbers with the Captain of the Golf Club and his lady, and the Mayor and Mayoress. Even if the young inspector feels intimidated, all to the good. She'll be looking to her boss and boyfriend for support. We want enough people to feel like a crowd. Let the booze flow and keep our eyes open. They'll give themselves away. People in their situation always do. They think they're so clever, but it only needs a look, a touch, the shape of a body movement and to a trained eye it's like a bugle call. We'll include Councillor and Mrs Raybourne. She'll eat us out of house and home but he's been useful to me. And Darling, from the Bank, with his wife. How would that do?'

'A very good selection, sir. But with six couples and yourself that would make thirteen.'

'Superstitious, Manners?   Not to worry about that. You'll be there so that will make everything alright.'
    'Indeed, sir.'

Sunday

On Sunday morning Andy woke with the Black Dog on his back.

Flick took one look at his pale face and dull eyes and her heart sank. No, please, no. Dear Andy. It's not fair. He's suffered so much, fought so hard. Why? And why now? It must be nearly eighteen months since the last one. He was fine yesterday. We had a lovely time with the kids in the park and then ice creams and Mum made drop scones for tea with her own raspberry jam and double cream from Mr Tesco. I shouldn't have let Jude eat so much cream. He was nearly sick with laughing when we played Jenga before bedtime. So not the kids, and surely not Mum? They are so fond of each other and he really appreciates her coming down to help out. So what? Was it something I said, or did, or didn't do?

But she knew it was no good guessing. After one of his bouts of deep despair Andy had told her.

'It's not anything anyone says or does as far as I can make out. I don't brood. It doesn't build up from any word or action. I don't get any warning. One day I can be as happy as Larry and the next, there it is. I'm sorry pet. I know it's rotten for you. It's pretty rotten for me too.' He'd managed a small smile. 'But I have at least agreed to take some anti-depressants when it happens. I know I resisted for ages and I'm still not sure they do any good but we do know the attacks, moods, call it what you like are getting farther and farther apart and less severe, so I'll try anything.'

These episodes had begun when Andy lost his arm. Immediately after he'd been told his arm had been amputated, he had seemed so upbeat. He'd talked of coping in new ways; of rebuilding his life. But as the truth really came home he had wished himself dead. He had even ranted at Flick she would be better off without a useless cripple to look after. Those had been hellish times and ones she wouldn't by choice revisit, even in memory. But Andy had pulled himself out of it and been so brave through many weeks and months of pain and physiotherapy. They had really thought they were through the worst. He had a new arm and was learning to be as dextrous with his left hand as he had been with his right. Eventually he was back working for the police, not in the job he loved but in the same ambience. Even behind a desk he was among people who thought like he did, understood the job and solidly backed each other. All seemed fine and then one day, out of the blue came the Black Dog. They'd given the state he was in this name to have something to fight against. Name something and it is far less frightening. The unknown is always the most terrifying enemy.

Flick left Andy in bed and organised her family for the day.

'I've got a heap of paper work to do so Nana is going to take you two on the train to Bristol and the Zoo. A double treat.' To children more used to travelling by car, the train was indeed a thrill. Amanda had made the offer when Flick told her of Andy's condition.

'Perhaps a little peace and quiet might help? Elaine from next door said she'd like to come along too. She does enjoy the twins.'

'Thanks, Mum. I don't know if it will make him better but he won't have the added strain of trying to appear normal for the kids.'

Once she had seen off the Zoo party, Flick made a warm drink for Andy and took him his anti-depressant pills. She knew they contained a mild sedative and hoped he would go back to sleep and work through whatever was happening in his mind. He swallowed them meekly and turned on his side under the duvet. But she knew his eyes stayed open, gazing unseeing at the wall beside their bed. She drew the curtains, left the bedroom door slightly open, then went downstairs.

Soon she was immersed in her notes on the two cases now almost certainly joined. Using a technique she had found successful before she wrote the known facts on different cards and laid them out on the dining room table. For the next hour she grouped them this way and that, placed them together than changed the order, made time lines involving different people. And still she could make no sense of it.

Finally she pushed the heap of cards together and opened a new page in the large pad at her side. What she knew hadn't helped so perhaps she would come at it from a different angle.

She had just compiled a list of questions she needed answered when Andy walked in.

'Hello, love. Feeling any better?' she asked.

'I don't know why you put up with me,' he said.

'Perhaps because I love you?'

'I can't think why? I'm so useless.'

This was Andy's normal feeling when he was hit by his Dog. Flick knew she couldn't talk reason to him because he was unable to accept the truth of her love and need for him in every way, as lover, husband, father to their children and best friend. Heaven knew she had tried in the past. His brain seemed just incapable of seeing beyond a huge heavy cloud of deep despair, not centred on any one thing but just there.

'Just take my word for it,' she said.

Andy's dull eyes scanned the table. 'You working?'

'Yes, just sorting out a few questions that need answers. I'm going to make a sandwich for lunch. Do you want to help me?'

He shook his head and wandered out of the room. She followed him and watched as he sat in a chair in the study, gazing out into the garden. She wondered what demons he was wrestling with as she went into the kitchen.

By the time Amanda and the children got home Andy was back in bed with a sleeping pill Flick hoped would keep him under until the morning. She listened to the twins' excited account of their "brill" day. The Zoo had been fabulous and they'd even visited the centre of Bristol, seen some of the old buildings there, and window-shopped, spending small fortunes on the way.

'But Nat's daft,' said Jude.

'Daft yourself,' retorted his loving sister.

'What brought that on?' demanded Flick.

'It was the display in the window of the furniture shop,' explained Amanda. 'There was an antique and particularly beautiful chair.'

'It was a throne,' said Natalie.

'Stupid. It wasn't,' said Jude. 'Elaine told you.'

'She said the king sat in it,' said Natalie.

'Yes, but not just the king. And only when he was eating.'

'What are they on about?' demanded Flick of her mother.

Amanda smiled. 'It was a carver. You know, darling, the chair with arms that sits at the head of the table and sometimes at the other end as well. The chairs at the sides of the table have no arms. It took Nat's fancy for a throne and I must say it was a beautiful chair, quite worthy of the title. But Elaine did explain it was called a carver because the head of the household, who sat there, would usually carve the roast or bird for the whole company.'

'I see,' said Flick. I just can't seem to get away from carvers or Carvers, she thought.

'Well I'm going to have one and it will be my throne,' said Natalie. 'So there.'

When peace and order had been restored, Flick took two Paracetemol to counter her own nagging tension headache. Please God Andy would be better by the morning.

Better, he was but not his usual bright self.

'Sorry, pet,' he said as soon as he woke. 'What a day it was yesterday, but I am better this morning.'

187

'Fit for work?'

'Yes and I'm not on till later. I'll be fine.'

Flick cuddled into his arms and they lay peacefully until the alarm went off.

She kissed his cheek as she uncurled herself from the comfort of his body. 'Stay there until we've gone, then it will be easier for you,' she said.

Amanda was already in the kitchen sorting out the twins' breakfast when Flick went down. Beyond raising enquiring eyebrows in Flick's direction Amanda said nothing.

'Right, you monsters,' said Flick, giving each a kiss on the top of their heads in passing, even Jude, although he tried to duck out of the way. 'Dad's on "lates" so keep the noise down and let him have a bit of a lie in.'

She looked out of the window where April showers looked more like winter storms. 'If you're ready in time, I'll run you to school in the car. Is there anything you need from the shops, Mum? It looks like this is set in for the day and I could pop to the supermarket at lunchtime. No sense in you getting wet.'

'I don't think so, love. But if there is, Elaine said she was going into town this morning. I might go with her.'

'Okay, but if you think of anything, just give me a ring.'

It was a relief to walk into the station and resume her role of Inspector. Flick tried to put all thoughts of Andy and his misery out of her mind. She was reasonably successful as she paid a visit to the top floor

'I've heard from Inspector Murphy that the garage in Swindon was visited. The van was stolen from their forecourt but didn't belong to them. It was, as we expected a delivery van from a firm called . . .' Westcott consulted a note on his desk, "Speedy Drive". According to the manager of the garage they do small deliveries all over the South of England.'

'What's the name of the garage, sir?'

Again Westcott looked at his notes. 'Raymond Hill Motors of Swindon. And I've heard back from Forensics about the mobile. Not much we can use. Many overlaid prints, one adult, probably Mike, Murphy's man, and at least two smaller. That will be young Master Timmy and his brother. The lab managed to get part of a message, presumably from Mike, but very crackly. A whisper but garbled. As far as the boys in the lab can make out it said "lined the drone".

'Drone? As in bees?' said Flick. 'A sting of some kind? Why lined? Drugs,' she went on, musing all possibilities that came to mind. 'Lines of coke, perhaps?'

Westcott shook his head. 'I have no idea. With only this fragment it's impossible to tell what he was trying to say. But, according to Inspector Murphy, as Mike used his "panic button" phone it must have been important.

'The envelope from Tubby's bin again gave no useful prints but when they opened up the staples they found the corner of a fifty pound note.' Westcott's face was like granite. 'It had most of a serial number on it so could possibly be traced.'

Flick didn't speak or move. What on earth was Tubby up to? Messing her about was one thing and very irritating. But getting brown envelopes of money through the post opened up a totally different can of worms. Brown envelopes, stapled each end. Surely not? Could it be a real coincidence? She swallowed on a throat suddenly gone dry and hoped Westcott would make the connection himself. Surely he had seen both envelopes?

But he was giving her that piercing look few had ever resisted. 'What is it, Inspector?' he said. 'You have something on your mind?'

Flick swallowed again. 'Envelopes, sir.'

'Yes. What about them?'

Here goes, thought Flick. Am I about to be bawled out again for traducing a fellow officer? 'Two brown envelopes, similar type and both closed with a line of staples at each end. One turned up in T . . .ex Inspector Jackson's waste bin and the other we found on Friday in Priors Parveneau woods. Sir.'

There was silence in the office. From deep in the building Flick heard someone call out, a door slammed, another call, possibly answering the first, a telephone rang, muffled by distance. She waited. Finally DCI Westcott heaved a sigh.

'We must find Tubby Jackson,' he said.

'I've got Sergeant Booth doing a check of Travel Agents and Booking Offices.'

Westcott nodded. 'Let me know if he finds anything. Dismissed, Inspector.'

Downstairs Flick called a briefing meeting.

'You were all here on Thursday so know what we have so far. It's what we haven't got I want to concentrate on now. There was a note on my desk this morning. In answer to the photofit picture in the paper we have two calls from the public. One lady says she is or rather was landlady to both men. PC Hurle I want you and PC Best to go and interview her. Get everything you can, including any gossip she may come up with. You never know when a kernel of truth might pop out.'

The two young female constables smiled and nodded.

'DC Whiteman, the other caller was an irate motorist, swearing those two maniacs, and I believe that is a quotation, were driving a white van that nearly ran him off the road. Again as much info as possible. Too much to hope for he got the number of the van but you never know. Date, time and place is what we need. Tracing their movements must be a priority. We want to know where they went, who they spoke to, when and why.'

'Right, boss,' said Harry Whiteman.

'Tom, I want you to concentrate on a garage in Swindon called Raymond Hill Motors and a delivery company called Speedy Drive, also I believe in Swindon. I want everything; financial status; Boards of Directors or owners or both. Full background check on those individuals as well.'

'Are we looking for anything in particular?' said DS Tom Perkins.

'I don't know, Tom. But I think there's something there.'

'Got a hunch, boss?' called a voice from the back of the room.

'Yes,' said Flick. 'I can feel it in my water,' she quoted to general amusement. 'Right, folks off you go. You all have something to keep you out of mischief. Booth, my office.'

Once Dave Booth had closed the door of her office, Flick filled him in with Friday's events.

'Drugs?' he said. 'That figures I suppose, but why didn't you tell the others?'

'We're not sure if this find puts our other investigations into something much bigger that's going on at the moment. It's on a "need to know" until further notice, so everything you find comes through me and otherwise keep stumm.' Flick considered for a minute. 'There's something else you can keep under your hat. The envelope we found on Friday and the one recovered from Tubby Jackson's wastebin are identical.' She watched the wheels go round as Booth thought through the implications. 'Have you found anything out about his travel arrangements?'

'Not so far. Needles and haystacks spring to mind. You should have put Tom Perkins onto it.'

'No way. The fewer involved the better. More so now when dear knows what shit could hit the fan. Okay, keep at it. The DCI knows you're looking into it. You could do yourself a bit of good there, Dave.'

Booth grinned. 'I'd better get back to it then, boss.'

For the rest of the day Flick dealt with routine paperwork but Andy's unhappy face came between her and what she was reading. There was no phone call from Amanda so Flick got a sandwich brought in from the High Street by Derek Jarvis who happened to be on the lunchtime run that day. Later she found an excuse to go by Andy's desk and give him a brief word and smile. He was still pale but his eyes were brighter. Flick noticed a packet of Paracetmol half hidden by a stack of papers.

This time they'd got off fairly lightly and he was obviously keeping his headache under control. She counted back on her fingers. Yes, it was certainly over a year since his last attack. That was an improvement. But how much longer would they have the spectre of his Black Dog at the back of their minds? And all because of some bloody so-called joy-rider.

Monday

A phone call established the Pargiters had returned from their holiday and were only too anxious Flick should visit them and explain the state of their garage. She phoned home to talk to the twins and tell Amanda she would be late.

'I shouldn't be too long so try and save me some dinner from the ravening hordes, Mum,' she laughed. 'See you later. Bye.'

On the way through the squad room she gathered up Dave Booth.

'You wouldn't have been doing anything exciting on a Monday evening would you, Sergeant?' she asked straightfaced. 'You can drive. It's Waterloo Road, number fifteen or Shangri La, whichever you prefer.'

'Up the posh end,' said Booth, and swung the Vauxhall out of the station yard. 'Do you think they've got any connection with the case, boss?'

Flick shrugged. 'Which one? Or all? Or none? Time will tell, but it seems very odd if someone commits suicide in your garage, without breaking in and you knew nothing at all about it or the victim. I am very interested in interviewing Mr and Mrs Pargiter.'

Shangri La was a large detached house in its own grounds. The garage was built on to it at one end. Normally Flick would have visited the scene before the body was removed. It bugged her she only had photos to give her a picture of how it had looked. But from them she knew there was an inner door leading from the garage into the house. Because of Tubby's idleness she felt at a disadvantage, and could only trust the CSI team had missed nothing of importance. Once they had finished, the garage had been made secure again and there had been no valid reason Flick could make for breaking in a second time.

A woman answered Flick's ring on the doorbell. Her deep tan was mostly covered up by an elegant pair of slacks and a roll-neck tunic Flick judged was made of cashmere. She fiddled with a rope of pearls at her throat and light sparked off diamond studs in her ears. They matched the large solitaire diamond worn with a wide gold wedding band on her left hand. Her appearance fitted in with Booth's comment that Waterloo Road was the posh end of Ridminster.

'Mrs Pargiter?' said Flick. She and Dave showed their Warrant Cards. 'I am Detective Inspector Fraser. I spoke to you on the telephone. And this is Detective Sergeant Booth. May we come in?'

Mrs Pargiter swallowed visibly and hesitated. She seemed nervous. Guilty conscience, wondered Flick? Then Mrs Pargiter stood back, and opened the door wide.

'Yes, of course, come in please.' She closed the door behind them and led the way across a wide hall and through another door into a large lounge where French windows opened onto a well-manicured garden. 'Please sit down. I'll just call my husband.' She went back into the hall. Her footsteps sounded on the polished parquet, retreating into the distance.

Flick looked around the beautifully furnished room and wondered if it was the Pargiter's taste or the product of a professional designer? Everything matched or blended. There were two large flower arrangements and various ornaments on the gleaming wood surfaces. Several pictures hung on the walls and two rugs gave splashes of colour against the neutral wall to wall carpet. Money seemed to be plentiful but, lovely as it was, the room lacked soul - a stage set without players. Unlike Flick's very lived-in home. She glanced at her watch. Mrs Pargiter had been gone five minutes. How long did it take to call a man who had known in advance when the visitors would arrive? Were they getting their stories straight?

However when Mr Pargiter strode into the room, Flick revised her ideas. It would be far more likely Mrs Pargiter had been trying to calm her husband down, but without a great deal of success. The man's jaw was clenched and the flare of his nostrils spoke of temper barely under control.

Without so much as a greeting he burst into speech. 'About time too. It's taken you long enough to come and apologise, Inspector,' he said to Dave Booth.

'Frank.' Mrs Pargiter put her hand on his arm.

He shook it off. 'Be quiet, Celia. Now then, Inspector. What do you have to say for yourself? I go away for a well-earned holiday and come back to find the police have broken into my property, no doubt stamping their size sixteens all over my home and poking into what doesn't concern them.' He stopped to draw breath.

Flick stepped in front of him, into his "space" Natalie would have said, thought Flick. Just what she intended. This bully was not going to take over the interview. She held her Warrant Card about a foot from his face. 'Inspector Fraser, Mr Pargiter. Shall we sit down? I have a few questions to ask you.'

His eyes popped open wide as he looked from her Warrant Card to where Dave Booth still sat on the settee. There was no apology forthcoming. With a surly 'Hrrmph, get on with it then.' He moved over to a deeply carved "partners" desk and leaned his backside on it.

Flick took her time replacing her Warrant Card, made sure Dave had discreetly palmed his notebook and spoke to Mr Pargiter in a calm voice. 'Now then, sir. Can you tell me if you recognise this man?' She held out a photo of Lawrence Hardy.

Pargiter barely glanced at it. 'No.'

'You're sure, sir? Please take a good look.'

'I said no, dammit.'

'Mrs Pargiter?' Flick held the photo out to the woman, who did look at it with care and a sick fascination.

'Was this the man? The one who was in our garage?'

'Yes, madam. Do you know him?'

Celia Pargiter shook her head. 'No. I've never see him before. But how did he get into our garage?'

'That is what we'd like to find out. Who else besides yourselves has keys to this house?'

Pargiter spoke before his wife could answer. 'No-one. I'm not fool enough to give the keys of my property to anyone else.'

197

'No relative perhaps, or friend, who would come in to water your plants while you were away?'

'No.'

I'd be surprised if he had any friend close enough to offer, thought Flick. 'You don't have staff who would get the house ready for your return?'

'No. How many more times do I have to tell you before you can understand? No-one had access to my house in my absence. No-one. That's why I spend a fortune on intruder alarms.'

'That gives us rather a puzzle then, sir. Because some-one entered your house without doing any damage and without triggering that expensive alarm system. Now it is possible an experienced intruder could pick a lock, but how did they get past your precautions? I suppose you did set the alarm before you left, sir?' Flick's expression was bland. She kept her face straight even when she feared Frank Pargiter might burst a blood vessel in his rage. Obviously no-one ever questioned his actions in the normal course of events.

'Of course I bloody set the alarm, woman. What do you think I am, stupid?' he yelled.

'Frank,' said Mrs Pargiter.

'Shut up, Celia.' He rounded on her, his eyes narrowed. 'Don't tell me you've been daft enough to give a key to one of your feather-brained friends?'

She looked shocked. 'Of course not.'

'I should think not indeed, when I expressly forbade it. But you can't trust women,' he muttered almost to himself.

Flick asked again. 'Can you think of anyone who might know the code for your alarm? Mrs Pargiter?'

Celia Pargiter shook her head. 'I'm not really sure of it myself,' she confessed.

'Mr Pargiter?'

His nostrils flared again in irritation. Flick felt for two pins he'd smack her face for impudence. 'Mr Pargiter?' she repeated.

He spoke deliberately as to a child or someone slow of understanding. 'Inspector, I do not give my keys to anyone. I do not go around telling people security codes to my home, my bank accounts, my safe or even my dog kennel – if I had one. I should have thought it obvious my house was secure. That is until your PC Plods broke into my garage. And who is going to pay for the repairs might I ask?'

Flick ignored the sarcasm and replied to him with a question of her own. 'How then was it possible for someone to open your front door, shut off the alarm, enter your garage, open the garage door, murder a second party and leave the premises again after resetting your alarm, Mr Pargiter? Because if you set the alarm before leaving, that is what happened.'

Celia Pargiter's eyes grew huge in a white face. She clutched the pearls at her throat and seemed to lose her fear of her husband. 'You idiot, Frank. That's your fault, you and your stupid friends at the Club. Next we'll be murdered in our beds'.

'Be quiet, Celia. You don't know what you're talking about.'

Flick looked from one to the other. 'If you would care to explain?'

'My wife's talking rubbish. How do we know the intruder didn't break into the garage? We only have your word for it. All *we* know is it was unsecured when we got home, except for being nailed up from the inside and very inconvenient it was too.' He paused, frowned, then continued. 'Yes, indeed. How did you manage that, Inspector?'

'When our officers and the Fire Brigade responded to a 999 call from a member of the public, an engine was running inside the garage of a house that should have been empty. Exhaust fumes were seeping out of the join where the door met its jamb. In these cases either service would effect an entry. When the alarm continued to sound we contacted your Security Company who shut it off at distance, without revealing your code. When we had finished, they reversed the process. But that still doesn't answer my question. How did someone effect entry in the first place?'

'That's your problem. You're the detective. Find out. I've had enough of this harassment and shall be writing to your superior. My wife will show you out.' Frank Pargiter stomped out of the room before Flick could say any more.

'I'm sorry, Inspector,' began Celia Pargiter. 'My husband was very upset to find there had been a break-in. We have a lot of expensive items in the house.'

Flick couldn't believe her ears. 'We are not talking about a burglary here, Mrs Pargiter. A man died.'

Celia Pargiter bit her lip. 'Yes, I know and it's very sad, but we didn't know him and why would he choose to commit suicide in our garage while we were on holiday? It just doesn't make sense.'

'He didn't commit suicide. He was murdered. And I think your house was chosen for the site of the murder just because it was empty and therefore the body might not be found for some days. From the murderer's point of view it was unfortunate there was enough petrol in the tank to keep the engine running until the postman arrived the following morning. Now, Mrs Pargiter, tell me who knew of your plans. Who knew when you were going to be away?'

She frowned. 'Well, no-one really. That is, my tennis four knew, because they had to find someone else for our regular game. And then I suppose the milkman knew and the postman. Just the usual people you tell, Inspector. And, of course, Frank's four at the Golf Club.'

'Would that be the club to which you were referring earlier?'

Celia Pargiter, chewed her bottom lip. 'Yes,' she admitted finally, then seemed to make up her mind. 'It was so stupid. I'd gone to pick Frank up and he wasn't ready. They had another round of drinks. I had an orange juice,' she assured Flick.

In the background Dave Booth scribbled in his notebook.

'When was this, Mrs Pargiter?'

'About a fortnight before we went away. They were talking about security and remembering codes and like an idiot Frank told them.'

Flick frowned. 'Your husband told them the code to your alarm system?'

'No, of course not. But he told them his way of working it out. He said you take a four letter word you won't forget, change it to numbers, and then you put it in backwards.' She beamed. 'Isn't that clever?' Then her face fell. 'But just before we left, Major Carver said he bet he knew what word Frank would use. Frank said he couldn't possibly know and then Major Carver said "golf" and I'm sure Frank's face gave it away, although he swore the major was wrong.'

'So you are saying Major Carver knew your code at home was,' Flick paused as she worked it out, but Dave was ahead of her.

'7,15,12,6, entered backwards, boss,' he said.

'Celia Pargiter looked terrified. 'Oh, hush,' she said. Her eyes were on the door through which her husband had disappeared.

'I thought you didn't know the code?' said Flick.

'Of course, I know it. How do you think I get in and out when Frank locks up after him? But he prefers to think I don't know. He likes me to be dependent on him.' She shrugged. 'Men!'

'Was anyone else in earshot when . . . Major Carver, did you say?' Celia Pargiter nodded. 'When Major Carver guessed the code?'

'No, the others had gone. There was only him and Frank and me. But he wasn't whispering, so someone else must have heard him, mustn't they? I mean, the Major. He'd hardly be a burglar would he?'

'So our Major Carver wouldn't be a burglar?' said Flick as they drove away from Shangri La.

'Hardly, boss,' said Booth. 'Pillar of the community, the Major. Sits on all sorts of committees, even with DCI Westcott. You're not thinking of him for the murder, are you?'

Flick shrugged. 'It seems he had the code so he must be on the list of suspects.'

'Or whoever he passed it on to?' said Booth.

Monday

The man looked up at the night sky. He enjoyed the dark. It was his natural habitat, seeing yet unseen.

All was well. Traitors had been punished, loose ends tied up.

On Wednesday it would be a month since settlement day. Pity about that. The buzz of the game had been enjoyable while it lasted. He'd been a worthy opponent. Quite like old times.

Pity too about Brand. He'd been a useful tool for a long time. One of the amazingly few who knew the man's identity or rather the one he used to use. But he should have known better than to step out of line. The others were just collateral damage; of no importance.

A gust of wind made him shiver as the cold penetrated his light-weight jacket. He could stand the cold if it was necessary but not by choice.

Give him central heating and streetlights any day. Who'd be a farmer?

He went to bed and slept the dreamless sleep of one with a quiet mind.

Tuesday

At Tuesday morning's Briefing Flick was greeted by a different atmosphere. She could almost taste the interest in the room. Everyone sat up straight: no lounging over coffee mugs or doodling on notepads. Eyes were bright and expressions keen. What had brought this on?

'Good morning everyone,' she greeted the room in general. 'I hope you have something decent to report. I know this case, or cases, whatever, have been frustrating, but only by keeping on chipping away can we progress. Let's start with the ladies first. PC Hurle, PC Best, what have you got for me?'

Barbara Hurle replied with a huge smile. 'The photos in the paper brought us Mrs Scales, ma'am. She was landlady to both Hardy and Brand. They'd been boarders with her for about two years. We didn't find anything of interest in their rooms. They certainly weren't expecting to leave in a hurry but there wasn't much personal stuff lying around.' Suddenly the young PC stopped and bit her lip. 'It was alright to go in, wasn't it, ma'am? It wasn't a crime scene.'

'Yes, that was alright, Barbara. Go on.'

'Mrs Scales said they never did bring much but kept the rooms on even when they were away. Their reason was they didn't like sleeping in strange beds, so they could get used to hers. She wasn't going to argue as the money was paid up front. "Money for old rope", was how she described it, ma'am.'

Barbara Hurle grinned. 'She was a bit stiff at first, suspicious like, but she got very chatty over a cup of tea. Said they came and went at odd hours and usually arrived with no warning. It was after the tea she let us see the rooms. We just had a quick look round, ma'am and explained to her she must keep them locked until someone from the nick had been and given them a thorough search. But we did get from her all the dates they were staying in Ridminster.

'Talk about chalk and cheese, ma'am. Even on first glance you could see the difference. Hardy's room looked like every mother's nightmare, even with so few personal possessions around. While Brand's was the opposite: so tidy and clean you'd have thought it wasn't occupied at all. Mrs Scales used to be in the Women's Royal Army Corps. I reckon she would have made Sergeant, ma'am. Had firm rules for her boarders she said but never any trouble from those two. Kept themselves to themselves they did and she said she'd seen barrack rooms less spruce than Brand's bedroom. But that was about it, ma'am. We know where they stayed and when and for how long but not much else. I don't know if it really helps?'

'Everything helps to fill in the big picture, Barbara. Well done. You too, Jane,' Flick nodded at PC Best. 'I'm sure you put in your three penn'orth.'

Best grinned. 'Yes, ma'am. Thank you, ma'am.'

'Next?' said Flick. She looked round the room. She caught DS Perkins eye. 'Tom? Have you got anything for me?'

'I've been looking into the garage in Swindon.'

Flick raised her eyebrows. 'And?'

Tom was not to be hurried. 'It didn't smell right,' he said.

There was a ripple of laughter round the room. Tom and his "feelings"; his notions of what smelt right and what didn't were well known. They had produced some surprising results in the past.

'Enlighten me,' said Flick.

'The manager or owner, I don't think it was established which he claimed to be,' began Tom Perkins, 'told Dave he had reported the white van stolen. That was on the day after Lenny the Hare, died. But he also said the van wasn't really used by his garage although it was registered in Swansea to Raymond Hill Motors. Under some kind of gentleman's agreement it was parked on his forecourt but used by a company called Speedy Drive.'

'We know about them,' said Flick. 'Haven't we established that's the company Hardy and Brand worked for?'

'Perhaps, but after a bit of digging I found that Speedy Drive and Raymond Hill Motors are both subsidiary companies of an outfit called Traktion Express.'

Flick frowned. 'So there's a definite link between the two? Do we know who owns Traktion Express?'

Tom Perkins shook his head. 'Not yet, boss. There seems to be a paper trail that pops in and out of various companies and I hope won't go overseas eventually. But I can tell you that Speedy Drive is registered at Companies House as non-trading.'

Flick frowned again. 'So how does a non-trading company have at least one delivery van and two drivers making regular runs?'

'Exactly. But there have been no trading company Returns filed under that name for the past nine years since it was bought by Traktion.'

Dave Booth waved his hand in the air to get Flick's attention. 'Boss. Why would the garage owner report the van stolen? Even if it was no longer on his forecourt one morning, surely he would assume it had been taken by one of the Speedy Drive drivers?'

'Good point, Dave. I think we might have to have a little chat with this gentleman. What's his name?'

'Kaplan, Sam Kaplan, boss,' said Tom.

'And are we convinced it is the same white van that ran down Lenny; was seen in Priors Parveneau woods; was – reputedly - stolen from Swindon; and was burnt out here?'

'I think so, boss,' said Dave Booth. 'The link is Hardy and Brand. They were seen putting Lenny into the van before he died; the school teacher identified the driver as having a ponytail which matches our description of Jake Brand; and the VIN number gives us the connection to Swindon where Kaplan confirmed Speedy Drive kept their van.'

Barbara Hurle put up her hand. 'Please ma'am. They told Mrs Scales they worked for Speedy Drive. She was pleased they were good lads in steady work in spite of ponytails and earrings.'

Flick smiled. 'Thank you, Barbara. That seems to tie in nicely. Any other offerings? No? Well keep up the good work. Tom, you concentrate on the companies.

Harry, I want you to liaise with CSI at the boarding house, and Barbara and Jane you have the happy task of getting all the paperwork up to date.' She got a meaning look from Dave Booth. 'DS Booth, my office.'

There were one or two glances across at Booth wondering if he was either on the carpet or assigned special duties but everyone had their own jobs to be getting on with and soon the room was empty.

Dave Booth followed Flick into her office and closed the door.

'I've been burning the midnight oil, boss,' he began.

'Why?'

'I didn't feel happy doing searches for Tubby Jackson in the office with folks around looking over my shoulder.'

'Good man. Any luck?'

"Yes. I traced the taxi driver who took him to the station the evening he left for his holiday. Tubby was in a hurry to catch a train that would get him into London in time to get to Heathrow for a flight to Amsterdam.'

'Amsterdam?'

'Yes. The driver said he seemed nervous, or worried. Kept looking out of the back window of the cab. And then Tubby said something about a jumping off place, but the cabbie couldn't remember or didn't hear exactly what it was. He seemed to think the DI was talking to himself.

'I've got in touch with Customs and Excise at Heathrow. They're probably the best people who can check to see if Tubby really did take a flight that night. I'm waiting for them to come back to me. There are two regular flights of an evening. One leaves at seven but might be too early for us. The other leaves at eight arriving local time at ten past ten. It would give him time to book into an hotel and have a meal before bed.'

'Good work. I'll see the DCI knows what you've done.'

'But Amsterdam's a big place, boss.'

Flick smiled. 'I know Sergeant, but we have our methods.' She tapped the side of her nose, unconsciously mimicking Major Carver. 'We have our methods.'

For the rest of the day Flick was busy clearing her In-tray and keeping up with her average normal work load. Just before four o'clock Dave Booth put his head round her door.

'We're on, boss. Tubby Jackson definitely arrived in Amsterdam on that evening. But that's all we know.'

'Thanks, Dave. At least I'll have that to tell the Old Man when I go up.'

'Good work, Inspector,' said DCI Westcott.

'Sergeant Booth stuck to it, sir, very discreetly in his own time.'

'Good man. But where do we go from here?'

'I'd like to get in touch with a contact I made when I was with the Met. Always useful to keep in touch. He's a jolly good officer and thankfully speaks perfect English as my Dutch isn't worth talking about.

'Brigadier Rudi van der Velde is stationed in Amsterdam. I could ask him to make discreet enquiries. If he gets curious I could always say Tub . . er . ex Inspector Jackson . . .'

'Oh for goodness sake, Flick, call the man Tubby. It's quicker and it seems he might not even deserve his old rank.' Westcott's voice was bitter. 'Do whatever you have to do to get your contact helping us. I trust you completely in this matter – as in all things,' he added.

Heavens, is that an apology for bawling me out when I hadn't a clue what he was on about wondered Flick.

'I hope you've got some good news for me,' went on Westcott.

'We certainly have some more information, sir.' Flick went on to report what Tom Perkins had found out. 'It seems more and more likely, sir, that what we have in Ridminster and Operation Country Ride are closely connected. Drugs and the two dead men, three counting Lenny being the links.'

'We knew that yesterday.'

'Yes, sir. But DS Perkins has uncovered closer provable links.'

'Who owns Traktion Express?'

'That we don't know as yet. DS Perkins is still digging. He feels someone has been very careful to hide exactly who the main players are. It's not uncommon apparently, for tax avoidance and general privacy. Some celebrities might not want the public to know just where their money comes from, especially if it could be controversial and they are figureheads for one campaign or another.'

'Right, let him keep on at it. Is that it then?'

'No, sir. Our photos in the newspaper produced the landlady of both Hardy and Brand.'

Flick repeated Hurle and Best's report in detail including the landlady's comment on the state of Brand's room.

'And that reminds me, sir. Mr Pargiter told a friend at the Golf Club how he worked out a code for his security alarm. Then the friend guessed what it would be. I wonder who he told?'

'Perhaps it might be worth asking him. Who was it?'

'Major Carver, sir. You know. The one who sits on the "police meets the people" committee with you. Shall I go and see him then, sir?'

Wescott frowned, pursed his lips and gazed at Flick until she started searching her conscience. Yet he didn't seem to see her.

Finally he muttered, 'Army; deliveries; code. No, Inspector, don't go and see the Major just yet. He is something of an enigma and if he is tied up in any way with this matter, I don't want him spooked.'

Flick gaped. 'The Major, sir?'

'He was very keen to pick my brains on Saturday morning,' went on Westcott. 'But when I asked him about his Army career he intimated he had been on such covert work he couldn't reveal what unit he was with. However a little searching on the internet and contact with an old friend from the Ministry of Defence gave me the information he had served with the RASC.

'Now although the Royal Army Service Corps is no doubt a very worth body of men, their main job is to provide everything logistically the Army needs to operate. Not, I would have thought, a state secret if you had served with them?'

'No, sir.'

'And if indeed his membership was a cover for more secret work then why didn't he say he belonged to the Corps?'

'I've no idea. But why is that important?'

'It may not be. But consider, Flick, in providing everything to the fighting men, millions of pounds worth of goods pass through the Corps each year, probably hundreds of millions.' Westcott smiled. 'My old Dad used to call them "the jam stealers". Very unfair I have no doubt, but unhappily there have been bad apples in the barrel in the past. Especially at the end of the Second World War when a starving Europe would give anything for such foodstuffs as tinned meat and coffee for example.

'You could get a Meissen figure worth hundreds of pounds now for a two ounce tin of powdered coffee. Of course it was strictly against the rules for the occupying forces to swap even their personal rations, stuff they could buy at the Naafi shop. The penalties were pretty severe.

'But there was always someone prepared to break the rules for enough profit and when they were caught it was the glasshouse for them, and then a dishonourable discharge.'

Flick smiled. She knew "the glasshouse" meant the Army prison. 'I expect your father had lots of yarns to tell you, sir?'

Westcott nodded. 'Yes. He had me late in life and always made time to spend with his only child. I miss him. I'd like to pick his brains on this one.'

'Do you really think the Major might be mixed up in this? He doesn't seem the type. No. That's a stupid thing to say, but why would he endanger his cosy life here where he is well-respected and a figure in the community?'

'He probably wouldn't, or didn't mean to. Didn't we think the Priors Parvenau drop was an unofficial one, an underling covering up a mistake? And didn't Murphy say our man was ruthless, getting rid of those who disobeyed? Say the two who died had by their actions brought attention too near to Major Carver, here in Ridminster. Would their punishment be death? Cutting off the lead to him and warning any others to be more careful in future? It's a hypothesis. But that's all it can be until we get more information. Let your people go on digging, Flick. We are getting there. Keep up the good work.'

Wednesday

Wednesday started off with an invitation to Detective Inspector and Mr Fraser to take cocktails at the home of Major Carver on Saturday 9th May at 6.30 pm. The invitation was a hand-written note apologising for short notice but explaining it was just a little informal get-together.

Flick frowned. She'd left home before the post was delivered and found the invitation with her mail at the nick. Did this mean Carver didn't know where she lived? Or was it to make the invitation more official? And what a cheek not to give Andy his rank. If it had been Mr and Mrs, or even Mrs and Mr, that would be fine but to call her a DI and leave Andy as a civilian, well that just wasn't on. Of course they wouldn't go   There was an e:mail address for replies, but it could wait until she had spoken to Amsterdam. She pushed the note into the In-tray with other matters to be dealt with and picked up her Address Book and the telephone.

Brigadier van der Velde was not at his desk but a message would be delivered and he would contact her as soon as possible.

Flick tried to concentrate on her pile of work but Carver's invitation kept grabbing her attention. Why on earth would he invite her and Andy to a cocktail party of all things? She had never met the Major and cocktail parties were not a part of the Frasers' social round. What did one wear? Not that it mattered because she wasn't going. She pulled the next file from the heap and read the first page.

It could have been Greek. Nothing was going into her brain this morning. Why had Carver invited her and Andy? And just after the DCI had put Carver on the "persons of interest" list.

When the phone rang she welcomed the interruption to her chaotic thoughts.

'Is that the beautiful Felicity?' said the pleasantly accented voice of Rick van der Velde.

Flick laughed. 'And is that the handsome Brigadier Rick van der Velde?' she countered.

'My dear Felicity, what a pleasure it is to hear from you. I hope it is because you are coming to visit us here in Amsterdam, preferably without your charming husband Andy.'

'Behave yourself, Rick. If I didn't know that you are a very happily married man with a beautiful young wife and a devoted father to your three sons I might think you are trying to flirt with me.'

'But of course I am, my dear. It is only from the safety of a happy and settled marriage that any man should flirt. But I have the sad feeling it is not my company you seek. How can I be of assistance?'

'I'm not sure you can. How good are you at finding needles in haystacks?'

'What is this talk of the countryside and needles?'

Flick chuckled. 'Sorry, Rick. Your English is so good I forget you might not know all our idioms. I need your help to find one man in the whole of Amsterdam.'

'Ah! Now I understand the reference. What a task you have given me. What do we know of this character?'

'He arrived in Amsterdam on the BA flight at twenty-two hundred hours, and ten minutes, on the evening of Monday 14th April, and that's all we know I'm afraid.'

'You have a description?'

'Yes. I can give you that. And his name is Jackson, George Jackson.' Flick gave Rick a detailed description of Tubby down to the bald spot on the top of his head and his bitten fingernails - a fairly recent habit attributed to his trying to give up smoking. 'So I'll leave it with you my friend. Give my regards to Anneka. We must try and meet up again sometime. Perhaps Andy and I will bring the twins over for a long weekend, or half-term?'

'As always you know my dear Felicity, you will be very welcome. Say Hi to Andy for me. I'll see what I can do about your missing person. Our hotels are legally obliged to make a note of every foreign visitor, but it may take some time.'

'Of course. I understand and am very grateful for anything you can do. Goodbye, Rick.'

'*Tot ziens*, Felicity.'

Flick had a smile on her face for the rest of the morning. It was always good to chat with Rick. He had managed to push thoughts of Carver's invitation out of her mind. At lunchtime she popped downstairs to tell Andy about her call and the half-promise to take the twins over to Amsterdam.

217

'Good idea,' he said. 'I'd like to see old Rick again. I remember that bottle of fire-water he brought over when he came.'

Flick laughed. 'You got your own back with that bottle of poteen we brought back from Ireland.'

They were both smiling at the happy memory of Rick's last visit to England when a uniformed officer stuck his head round the door. 'Phone call for you, Inspector.'

'Take a number please. I'll call them back after lunch.'

'It's from Amsterdam.'

'Your boyfriend wants another chat,' teased Andy.

'Heavens, that was a quick reply,' said Flick. 'I'll take it up in my office, Constable. Just give me a couple of minutes to get up the stairs. Bye, Andy, love. See you later.'

She hurried out of the room and was quite breathless when she got to her desk. Had Rick worked miracles?

'Hello! Rick, is that you? Have you got a result? My goodness that was quick,' she laughed.

'Hello, Felicity. In a way I hope I haven't succeeded in my quest.'

'What do you mean?'

'This man you are seeking. Is he a criminal?'

Flick hesitated. What should she tell him about Tubby? 'No, Rick, not at all. In fact he's an ex-colleague we wanted to consult about an ongoing matter and he hasn't left his holiday address. Not that he needs to now of course, since he's retired.' That should cover her interest in finding Tubby.

'That makes what I have to say worse, then.'

'What do you mean?'

'I hadn't even got around to making enquiries at any hotels when I was telling a comrade what I was about to do. When he heard the date your friend arrived in Amsterdam he remembered we have an unidentified victim from that time.'

'Victim?'

'Yes. This unfortunate man would appear to have been mugged and robbed, with such viciousness that he died. But the case is not as straightforward as it would appear.'

'What do you mean?' Flick repeated.

'Although he was left badly beaten and with no money or Passport, which would indicate an everyday street theft, when our pathologist examined the body he found something he had never seen before.'

'And is this man experienced?'

'Very. Beneath the dirt of the street and some blood, but not as much as one would have expected, he found a stab wound.'

Flick felt the hairs on the back of her neck stand up. Where had she heard these words before?

'Go on,' she whispered.

'On opening the chest cavity our pathologist found a scene of such trauma he couldn't believe his eyes. Nor could he explain what had caused it or how it had come about. He still doesn't know. Are you there, Felicity?'

Flick swallowed on a suddenly dry throat. What did this mean? 'Yes. I'm here, Rick and this man might possibly be the one we are looking for, but how do you know all this detail?'

'Our pathologist is in the basement of this building. I went and spoke to him as soon as my colleague told me of the victim. What happens now?'

'I must speak to my boss and then I'll come back to you. Thanks again, Rick. I appreciate your help and so will he.'

When she had ended the call, Flick sat back in her chair and gazed unseeing at the window. What did this mean? Rick had described almost word for word the same type of injury Martin Barnes had told her he had found on Jake Brand's body after he had been beaten up behind the Phoenix nightclub. Surely this couldn't be a coincidence? Two experienced pathologists in two different countries and both finding something they had never seen before? But if not coincidence, that would mean the same killer operating in both countries. Flick frowned. The only common denominator here was Tubby in both countries. Tubby who had written off Jake Brand's murder as an argument gone too far between a load of yobs. He'd also written off two other murders and now he was a victim himself. How did this all hang together? Had the murderer accompanied Tubby to Amsterdam and then killed him? Was he still there, or at least out of England?

She repeated the question to DCI Westcott half an hour later.

'That's what we need to find out,' he said. 'I think we need to send someone over to Amsterdam to identify the body and bring it back if it turns out to be Inspector Jackson.'

'Do you want me to go, sir?'

'I'd rather have you here. You say your contact speaks excellent English so we can send Sergeant Booth. He's known Jackson far longer than you and with the help of your friend can do all that's necessary. He also knows the ongoing situation with Jackson. Did you tell anyone in Amsterdam of our identical victim?'

'No, sir.'

'Good. Then hopefully it will be a matter of simple identification and then they'll release the body to Sergeant Booth. Warn him not to mention the unusual stab wound to anyone in Holland, or even at home here.'

'Why is that, sir?'

'If the Dutch authorities knew of our similar wound they may well feel this death is more than a straightforward mugging. If they opened a case file on Inspector Jackson we should be obliged to reveal our interest and our own findings. They may want to hang onto his body feeling - rightly so - that it was pertinent to the Dutch investigation.

'It may be that our drug problem will turn out to have a link to Amsterdam, but that's not for us to worry about, at least not yet. We'll pass what has happened on to DI Murphy and leave it to him and the Drug Squad to follow up or not. Interpol might be called in. But I have a feeling this is more a domestic operation. It seems to be run by one man, the Mr Big, or The Man as he has been referred to since no-one knows his name. You're frowning, Inspector. What is it? '

'These three murders Inspector Jackson covered up, because that's what it seems now. We've found they're all linked, and also linked to drugs, and now to Jackson.

Does that mean he was in on the drugs thing, whatever it is?'

DCI Westcott sighed. 'I am very much afraid it does. How deeply he was involved we may never know and he may have been foolish rather than wicked, but I don't like the way things are shaping up. No, I don't like the look of it at all.'

'You've known him for years, sir, haven't you? I assume he hasn't always been crooked. How does it happen? Could we have spotted anything earlier?'

'Good question, but I don't know the answer.' Westcott gazed at the far wall for a moment, then looked at Flick. 'We started out together, as I told you before. Tubby felt he was destined for great things but didn't seem to realise he had to put in the graft to get there. From odd things he said it appeared whatever he had aimed for or wanted in the past had just fallen into his lap. Whether jobs - he had three before he joined the force, each one better paid than the last - or girls who thought he was the bee's knees. And he was a good-looking lad, no doubt about it.'

Flick tried to imagine surly, overweight, Tubby with his nicotine-stained fingers and untidy dress as the kind of Romeo girls would swoon over, but her imagination failed her.

'As time went on and he didn't get the jobs or promotion he felt he deserved, Tubby's attitude changed. Unfortunately, it didn't encourage him to make more effort but he laid the blame on others for his misfortune, especially me. Apparently I had queered his pitch, as he put it, for my own ends. Of course when I got promotion it was inevitable we drifted apart. We rarely spoke

222

unless it was for work or,' Westcott's expression spoke volumes, 'or it suited Tubby's purpose to remind someone, usually of lesser rank, that he and the DCI, were old muckers.'

'But that wouldn't make him crooked, would it?'

'Not in itself. But bitterness can corrode. He lost what enthusiasm for the job he had had, became lazy and slipshod, piled whatever work he could onto others. It was chance that brought us back together in the same nick at this time. When I eventually found out how he was behaving I would like to have got rid of him but it was difficult to prove he was negligent to the extent he jeopardised any investigation.'

'Until now,' put in Flick.

'Yes, but now he's gone. As to his involvement in this affair I believe he was cleverly and gradually drawn in. Judicious flattery would work well on him, to get his cooperation in little things at first, gradually building up until, even if he realised he was breaking the law, he would be in too deep to do much about it without setting himself up for dismissal or even jail. The more I think of how chummy he became with Major Carver, the more I believe that chap is in this up to his neck.'

'That reminds me, sir,' said Flick. 'The oddest thing happened this morning. I got an invitation, for both Andy and me to go and have cocktails with him, Major Carver, that is. Have you ever heard anything like it?'

For the first time that day William Westcott smiled. 'As it happens, yes, I have. I received an invitation also this morning.'

'But I shan't go,' said Flick.

'Yes, you will,' said Westcott, 'as shall I and my wife.'

'But I don't know the guy,' Flick protested.

'That doesn't matter. A cocktail party is a good way to meet new people. The so called "movers and shakers" of this world often use it to that end for business purposes. Now why do you think Carver has invited not only me, who he knows – we even play golf together on occasion – but also you, Inspector Fraser.'

Flick looked horrified. 'You don't think he's looking for a replacement for Tubby do you, sir? But I'd never . . . how could anyone believe . . . ?'

'He may be looking for a replacement. But if not I think he just wants to size you up, see that you're not going to cause him any grief.'

'How do you mean?'

'From something he said at the Golf Club last time I spoke to him, he has got the impression you are rather a silly young thing, sidelined to the country because you couldn't hack it at the Met.' He watched Flick's indignant face with amusement. 'And, my dear Inspector, I think we'll let him go on believing in this delusion.'

'But, sir . . . .I mean . . . I don't really know what I do mean. What do you want me to do?'

'Ever done any AmDram, Flick? I think you should be perhaps a little overawed by your invitation to his wonderful house. You'd simply love to see over it. My wife could be useful there. It would be less obvious if you both expressed an interest. I'll brief her. And you'd better tell Andy why his sensible wife is behaving like a fluffy-headed nincompoop. Then keep a smile on your face and your wits about you. Without realising it, Major Carver may have done us a big favour. There's no way we could apply for a search warrant for his house. We haven't really got anything on him except suspicion. But as invited guests we may be able to pick up something useful. I'm almost looking forward to a week on Saturday. '

Before the party

When Flick told Andy about the fluffy-headed nincompoop, he laughed. 'The DCI hasn't seen you sometimes at home. It shouldn't be too hard to convince Major Carver.'

'That's enough out of you,' said Flick with a finger wagged under his nose. 'Any more cheek like that my boy and I'll put you on starvation rations. And I don't mean food,' she added.

Andy raised both hands in surrender. 'I give in. I give in. You know I didn't mean it. But what an extraordinary evening it's going to be. What's my role? Country bumpkin? Or just village idiot?'

'I think eyes and ears well alert should cover it. Wasn't there something I heard about a celebrity living at Marylands once? I think we should do a bit of homework on the house. The DCI has done the job on Carver. A less than glorious Army career apparently even though he tries to give the opposite impression. We mustn't let on we know the truth. Drink in any tall stories he tells you about his exploits, Andy, and if

Margaret Westcott and I disappear to view the house, all the better for you to pick up something useful.'

'Well, we've got over a week to dig farther into Carver's past and get "genned up" on the house. I'll ask around at the darts match in the pub tonight. It's not as though our presence at this cocktail party must be kept secret. There'll be others there who know who we are, so it would be only natural for us to be curious about the place.'

'Marylands?' queried Thomas Stebbins, the oldest member of the darts team at Andy's local pub. 'Going there, are you? Well I heard this new bloke puts himself about a bit. Fingers in a lot of pies. Not like the other lot.'

'What other lot?' said Andy.

'Them what built the place,' said Thomas. 'Great long-haired bunch they were. And dear knows what goings on. Carloads of folks down from London. Musicians they called themselves, but not chamber music.' Thomas laughed. 'A pop star that's what my daughter called him. Pop star. Must have had plenty of money anyway.'

'Ah,' said Andy. 'Now I get the name. Marylands - Gracelands. Thought he was a second Elvis did he? But who was Mary?'

'His Mum, seems like. Fifteen year ago it were. My brother worked on the building. Couldn't make out what it were at first. Great deep foundations. He thought it might be a swimming pool but turned out it were for cellars. Not many new houses nowadays built with them but that Marylands has cellars as big as the ground floor.'

'Very useful,' said Andy. 'I wish we had them. Think of the storage space.'

''Tweren't for storage. 'Twas for studios. Soundproofed they were so no noise when they were rehearsing or making records. Just as well, for little Mrs Tiffin may be blind but she's ears as sharp as a bat. Nothing much gets past her.'

'Who's Mrs Tiffin? Was she a housekeeper or something?'

'Bless you, no, boy. She do live at the end of the back drive. At least on t'other side of the road. But she'm the only one lives thereabouts and she wouldn't want rowdy music. Give 'em their due, she never had no complaints. Once the building was up and occupied the only thing she said she ever heard was them great lorries.'

'Lorries?'

'Yes. Carried all sorts of sound equipment and instruments around the country when they was doing their "gigs".' The old man cackled. 'I'd give 'em "gigs". Not but what they must 'ave been good at it, for didn' they get a contract to go to America. So they upped and left and the house was sold. That's when the new fella moved in.'

'New fella?'

'Right. That Major.'

Andy smiled. 'Yes the new fellow who's been here for ten years.'

'That's what I said, boy. Now you'm in the chair. Get 'em in and make mine a pint. I reckon you've 'ad your money's worth out of me tonight.' He grinned at Andy and handed over his empty glass.

'A pint it is, Thomas,' said Andy and walked over to the bar. No flies on you old man, he thought.

'Cellars!' cried Flick. 'Now there's a possibility. And the same size as the ground floor you said? I wonder if that's where they make the drugs? You could have a neat little production line down there. I wonder if Margaret Westcott and I will be allowed to see them? I bet we won't. There'll be some excuse, but I must tell the boss. See what he thinks.'

'Well there'd certainly be enough room for a small factory according to Thomas. He couldn't think what any one man would want such a big place for.'

'Exactly,' said Flick. 'It doesn't make sense.'

'I did remind Thomas, the Major wasn't alone and he was less than complimentary about the manservant. A queer fish, he called him and not one as Thomas would like to cross,' Andy finished in Thomas's broad Somerset accent.

Flick smiled. 'Really?' she said. 'I don't think I've ever seen him around, but no doubt we'll get a look at him next Saturday.'

On Thursday Dave Booth left for Amsterdam and on Friday he reported back to the DCI that the body of the Dutch victim was indeed ex-Inspector George Jackson. Arrangements were put under way for Booth to accompany the body back to Ridminster.

'I couldn't stand the man,' Flick said to Andy when she heard the news, 'but I never wished him dead, and in such a horrible way.'

'That makes a definite link between Tubby and your man behind the Phoenix then?' said Andy.

'Yes. It must do, but I don't see how that helps us solve anything. It just throws up more questions, and certainly doesn't give us any link with Major Carver. If we could prove he was out of the country or even just not at home on the day Tubby died we would have a starting place.'

'And was he home?'

'I don't know but intend to find out. I'll ask the boss. He knows him socially and might give me a lead.'

'What day was that, Inspector?' said DCI Westcott.

'They believe he was murdered the day after he arrived in Amsterdam, sir. They've now found the hotel where he spent just one night so the murder took place on Tuesday 15th April. We don't know what time. The body was discovered in the evening but he had booked out of his hotel that morning.

'So far none of his luggage has turned up. He could have stashed it in a Left Luggage locker at the airport or railway station. It could moulder there for months or even years before it was found.

'Rick van der Velde questioned the hotel staff. They said Inspector Jackson seemed happy, relieved was the word Rick van der Velde used. Jackson had plenty to drink, in fact treated everyone in the bar to a round. Drinking to his future. He spoke of going on, getting away from it all and, I quote, what Rick gave me as a direct quotation, "living happy ever after".'

'Well that didn't last long did it? Monday night Toc H meets in Ridminster. I know Carver is a member.

Easy enough to check and see if he was at that meeting, but he could still have made it to Amsterdam afterwards and back in time to appear at the Golf Club where I can vouch for his presence the following evening. Tuesday 15th there was a Quiz Night to raise funds for our Young Golfers Group.' He sighed. 'I wonder if the whole thing is as simple as someone in that bar seeing Tubby flash all that money around and then following him next day with intent to rob. They would have taken the passport because everyone knows a British passport is worth its weight in gold, especially near the coasts of our neighbours.'

'But that doesn't account for the strange stab wound,' objected Flick.

Westcott sighed. 'No. You're right. Back to the drawing board. What's your next move?'

'Sir, until we can get inside that house we haven't a lot to go on as far as Carver is concerned. We know the identities of Brand and Hardy. We can link them with Lenny; the van; and the garage in Swindon. I'd like to find a link between them and the bookies. The van was often seen parked down by the side of that building. I think I'll talk to my neighbour again. See if she can remember anything more about Lenny. And tomorrow afternoon, while the twins are at a party, I'm going to see Mrs Tiffin who lives by the rear entrance to Marylands. Apparently the lady has very sharp ears. It's a long shot but she may have heard something out of the ordinary.'

'I saw your car pull in,' smiled the woman who opened Mrs Tiffin's front door before Flick even had time to ring the bell. 'But Mum heard you coming along the road.

There's so little traffic except for rush hour morning and evening when folks use this road to avoid bottle necks in the town centre. She was wondering who could be passing so that's when I looked out of the window and saw you. Come in. She loves visitors.'

Flick felt quite breathless at the torrent of words directed to her before she'd drawn breath to introduce herself. She stepped into the hall of the neat bungalow and pulled out her Warrant Card.

'Ooooh a policeman, or rather woman? Whatever has Mother been up to? I'm Phyllis Tanner, Mrs Tiffin's daughter,' she wiped her hands on the skirt of her apron and shook hands with Flick. 'Handy marrying a Tanner,' she went on. 'I didn't even have to change my initials,' she laughed.

'Phyllis,' called a voice from another room, 'for Heaven's sake stop your chatter and bring the Inspector in here.'

'Coming, Mum,' said Mrs Tanner and led the way through the first door leading off the hall. This gave onto a pleasant living room which looked out over the small front garden to the road along which Flick had driven. She had looked up Mrs Tiffin's address and punched the postcode into her SatNav.

Some ornaments and photograph frames stood on a bookcase and a bureau, both placed against a wall. There was a three-piece suite, the two armchairs stood cosily on either side of a flickering false flame electric fire. On the rug in front of it lay a black Labrador. He got to his feet and walked towards Flick as she came into the room. She gave him her hand to smell and was rewarded by a wagging tail.

'That's enough now, Turner,' said the woman who sat in the chair nearest the window. 'Lie down.' The dog returned to his place on the hearthrug.

'Good afternoon, Mrs Tiffin,' Flick said and walked up to the older woman's chair. Flick reached out until she was just touching Mrs Tiffin's hand. The blind woman smiled and shook hands with her.

'Good afternoon. How nice. Do they teach you that in police college or are you just intelligent and empathetic?'

Flick laughed. 'Not the former, certainly. No matter how PC the force tries to be these days I don't think that has occurred to anyone yet.'

'Perhaps you should teach them?'

'Whatever are you two on about?' said Phyllis Tanner from the doorway. 'Now then Inspector, a nice cup of tea? I've just brought Mother her favourite lemon drizzle cake. I'm sure you'd like a piece?'

'Thank you. That sounds lovely,' said Flick. And perhaps it would take the chattering woman out of the room for a few minutes.

As if Mrs Tiffin could read Flick's mind she spoke. 'Don't mind our Phyllis. She's a good girl. Pops in most days except when her brother comes instead. I'm very blessed in my children. Do you have a family, Inspector?'

By the time Flick had told her about the twins and Andy, Phyllis was back with a laden tray. 'You won't mind if I leave you and Mum to chat, will you, Inspector? I've just got a few bits to rinse out and put on the line in this lovely sunshine. They'll be dry in a trice. Just help yourself now.'

Once Phyllis Tanner had gone out, Flick poured the tea and handed Mrs Tiffin her cup. She placed a plate with a slice of cake on the small table next to the arm of the blind woman's chair.

'Thank you, dear, 'said Mrs Tiffin. 'Isn't this nice? But what brings you to my door? You sound very young to be an Inspector.'

Flick laughed. 'Thank you - I think. I promise you I got there in the regular way, without fear or favour as they say.'

'Of course you did. But I must confess I'm bursting with curiosity. My daughter will tell you I'm a real nosy-parker.'

'I doubt that, Mrs Tiffin, but, if it is true I can tell you, you are just the kind of person a policeman loves. Particularly if you have a good memory.' Flick took a sip of her hot tea. 'Thomas Stebbins told my husband you were living here when Marylands was built,' she said.

'Little Tommy,' smiled Mrs Tiffin. 'What a young rascal he was. It was his older brother who helped in the building of Marylands – what a silly name for a house.'

'I gather the owner named it for his mother and as a sort of tribute to Elvis,' said Flick.

'I wonder if he consulted his mother first? But that's not why you're here. Is there a problem with the house?'

In spite of racking her brains on the way, Flick hadn't come up with any feasible angle to her questions, so she just plunged in. 'Thomas said you never had any trouble with the previous owners making a noise. I just wondered if the new owner was just as quiet and considerate?'

'Hmm. Just wondered did you?' said Mrs Tiffin. 'It's alright my dear, I won't tease you. The only noise I've heard from them is the van coming and going at night. And sometimes the Jag goes out at night, but not often.'

Flick could feel her eyebrows climbing her forehead. 'What van is that, Mrs Tiffin?'

'It's a Volkswagen Transporter, but I haven't heard it lately.'

Flick shook her head to clear her brain. 'Who saw the van, Mrs Tiffin?'

'I know the one you mean, Mother,' said Phyllis Tanner from the doorway. 'That white one isn't it? I've often seen it go past. More tea, Inspector? No? Then I'll just clear the things shall I?' She lifted the loaded tray. Flick got up and held the door for her. 'Thank you, Inspector. I'll be just in the kitchen if there's anything else you need.'

'So your daughter saw the van?' said Flick.

'Yes, but it never goes to Marylands while she's here. It always slows down at the same place to make the turn into the gates, but whenever Phyllis is here, or my son it speeds up again and drives on. When there's no-one here it goes into the back of Marylands.

'If no-one is here, Mrs Tiffin, how can you tell it's the same van, a Volkswagen Transporter?' Flick was puzzled.

Mrs Tiffin smiled. 'Let me explain. My father owned a garage. I think he was sad he didn't have a son, that was until he realised his little girl was as passionate about cars, and lorries and all sorts of vehicles as he was.' She smiled.

'It all started when I asked him one day why he had come home in a different motor. I suppose I must have been about four or five years old, certainly not big enough to see out of our windows. Mother was in the kitchen so he asked me how I knew. I told him it made a different noise to his usual Ford. Well, that set him off. He sat me up on the windowsill and soon he was teaching me the names of all the cars whose engines I knew.

'I never looked back. When I left school he let me work in the garage, not as a mechanic, which I would have loved, but in the office answering the telephone and keeping the books. Later I married one of his mechanics and we eventually took over the business from Dad. So you see,' finished Mrs Tiffin with a big smile, 'I've been around cars as long as I can remember. Nowadays if a new model passes on the road I get so frustrated until one of the children can tell me the make and model.'

'That's amazing,' said Flick. 'If it was the van I think, you won't be hearing it again. Which is a pity as I could have called you as an expert witness,' she smiled. 'Can you tell one car from another even if they are the same make?'

'Not always but quite often. You see engines can be adjusted differently. And if the engine needs attention small changes in the sound can occur. And they sound differently depending on who is driving. But the Jag is usually running beautifully,' said Mrs Tiffin. 'I wonder if they got the rear light mended? Of course they must have done. That was weeks ago,' she mused.

'What happened to the rear light?'

'I remember it was a very warm night for March, about the third week I think. I was sitting here reading

236

one of my Braille books. I had the window open to listen to the night sounds. You'd be amazed what goes on in the countryside at night, my dear. I heard the Jag come along and then stop. The driver got out to open the gates and that's when I heard it. The rear light smashed.'

'Wait a minute,' said Flick. 'You say the driver got out and smashed his rear light?'

'Oh, no. He walked up to open the gates. Phyllis said they are made of solid wood. I expect they're quite heavy. It was while he was opening them that the rear light smashed. The glass tinkled on the road and then there was another noise. I couldn't quite make it out – like something else fell. It was different, a sort of thud. I can't explain it because I don't know what caused it. The driver came back and walked round the car. Then he swore and banged the boot lid with his hand. Then he got into the car and drove up the drive before closing the gates again.' The blind woman frowned. 'You know, Inspector, when I tell it like that it seems such a queer thing to happen. I didn't think much of it at the time, but now I do wonder how the light broke when the car was stationary?'

Flick ran the scene through in her mind as she looked out of the window. The rear drive of Maryland was in full view on the opposite side of the road, a little nearer Ridminster. But anyone coming from Ridminster wouldn't be able to see a car parked in Mrs Tiffin's drive until they had reached the point of turning into the entrance to Marylands. That would explain the stopping and starting Mrs Tiffin described. They must have known she was blind so would only be bothered about any visitor seeing them enter the gates.

Farther along the road, Flick could see the branches of a huge tree. She must have been glancing at the SatNav when she passed it, but now she thought she recognised that tree. This was the place on the road where the mobile had been found, the mobile belonging to the missing undercover detective, Mike. Had he been in the boot of that car? Had he kicked out the rear light in an attempt to draw attention, not realising he was in the middle of the country? Was he even now a prisoner somewhere in Marylands? She turned back to Mrs Tiffin.

'Were your curtains open or closed Mrs Tiffin?'

'Open of course, dear so I could hear the nightlife.'

'And was your light on or off?'

Mrs Tiffin laughed. 'It makes no difference to me, Inspector, if the light is on or off. I certainly don't waste electricity that way. When I'm on my own in the evenings the light is never on.'

Thank goodness for that, thought Flick. 'Now, Mrs Tiffin I want you to promise me you won't tell anyone else what you have just said to me about the Jag and its light. Can you do that please?'

'Well, of course, dear, if it is important to you, but why?'

'I'm afraid I can't tell you at the moment. But one day, soon I hope, I will come and explain everything. Thank you for your help and tea and the yummy cake. I must go and pick up the twins. It has been lovely talking to you. You are a really remarkable lady.'

'The pleasure has been mine, dear. Do come again, and next time you could bring the children. Turner does love children.' The guide dog raised his head at the sound of his name. His heavy tail thumped the carpet as he wagged it. 'I'm still waiting for grandchildren, but daren't say so for fear of interfering.' Mrs Tiffin gave one of her lovely smiles again.

Flick pressed her hand and walked into the hall. She could hear a voice talking, presumably on the telephone, behind a door at the end. She tapped on it, popped her head round and mouthed "goodbye" to Phyllis Tanner then let herself out of the bungalow.

She reversed down the drive and pointed her car towards Ridminster. As she passed the end of the rear entrance to Marylands she looked across. Was the missing Mike a prisoner behind those gates? If so, what could she do to save him?

Weekend

For the rest of the weekend Flick wondered how they could find out if Mike was at Marylands, and what they could do about it? She couldn't discuss anything with DCI Westcott as he was at yet another high-powered conference. With Dave Booth still away in Holland, there was no-one she could talk to about the case except Andy. His advice was to use her time off to enjoy her family, freshen up and let her subconscious come up with some answers.

'You don't understand, Andy. We know this boss-man is a really nasty piece of work. If that Mike guy is at Marylands I shudder to think what might be happening to him. It's strange, but from what DCI Westcott has told me about Carver he doesn't strike me as the great master criminal. I mean puffing off that he was something special in the Army instead of a passed-over Major wouldn't be a very smart move for someone who would logically keep a low profile.'

'You a psychologist now, darling? Maybe it's the old double-bluff? You know, keeping something hidden in plain sight?'

'Maybe, but I don't know. Roll on next Saturday when I can actually get my eyes on the bloke. Which reminds me, I must phone Margaret Westcott and find out what one wears to a cocktail party.' Flick pulled a disgusted face.

Andy laughed. 'You look good in anything, love. I imagine it's just a case of a pretty dress. Don't forget the Chief wants you to be a bit clueless. If you go in there all sophisticated and "glammed up", he may get the wrong impression.'

'Rotter,' said his loving wife.

On Sunday morning the sun had disappeared. Depressing drizzle ran down the window panes. While the twins finished their weekend homework Flick took the opportunity to pop next door. Her useful excuse was to return a book Amanda had borrowed from her friend, Elaine. Of course Flick timed it so that Mrs Baker would offer her a cup of coffee and the two sat down for a chat.

When the subjects of the weather, the twins and who was doing what for the summer holidays had been exhausted, Flick sat back and asked Elaine to remember the time when her husband was still alive.

'You said Lenny was very good hearted when he delivered your husband's winnings?'

'Yes. Dear little Lenny. Instead of just pushing the envelopes into my hand, he used to come in and chat with my Brian.'

'What kind of things did they talk about? Do you remember?'

'Just this and that, dear. The horses, and the dogs. My Brian was never really interested in betting on football. '

'You said Brian was often lucky.'

'Oh, yes. Most weekends Lenny would be round with an envelope.' Elaine smiled.

'An envelope? You mentioned that before. What was in it? A cheque?'

Elaine laughed. 'Shows you don't bet much, dear. Strictly cash – unless you have an account with them and then I believe you have to deposit a lump sum in cash to start off.'

'So Lenny was bringing envelopes full of cash to your house?'

'Yes. That's right. But it was all open and above board. Betting is legal now, isn't it?'

Flick smiled. 'Yes, of course. Did Lenny ever say who else might be a regular winner?'

Elaine frowned. 'It was such a long time ago. Let me see. Yes. There was Mr Smith at the chemist. Being in the shop all day and not wanting to use the business telephone, he used to give Lenny his bets and Lenny delivered his winnings. And there was Major Carver, but I can't think why he couldn't put his own bets on. A real gentleman of leisure so I'm told. Perhaps he thought Lenny was a lucky charm because he won every week. And then there was Mr Fipps at the shoe shop. I expect he had the same problem as Mr Smith. But I'm sure Lenny was very discreet and after all who could complain at the delivery of a brown envelope?'

'Who indeed? Do you remember what kind of envelopes they were?'

'Very secure ones.' Elaine laughed. 'I remember saying to Lenny he didn't want to take any chances. He used to run a line of staples across the flaps top and bottom. But he shook his head and said it was the boss who packed up the money – well thinking about it, it would be, wouldn't it? Lenny just took them from his boss when he came out of the back office and delivered them to the people on the list.'

And one of them was delivered to Tubby Jackson, thought Flick. Betting winnings? No, his envelope came through the post. But if it was from the bookies, perhaps it would have to be posted now Lenny, the runner, was dead? That didn't add up. What bookies would post cash to a perfectly healthy punter able to pick up his winnings himself? Surely the same went for the Major? He or his servant could have picked up the money any time. Flick sighed in frustration.

'Everything comes back to Marylands,' she told Andy that evening. 'The white van; the Jag with the broken rear light; the mobile. Tomorrow I'm going to get a team out to fingertip search that area by the back drive. And I'll ask Forensics if they got anything off the mobile.

'Frank Pargiter plays golf. He boasted to his mates how he remembered the code for his house. I'll bet he leaves his keys in his locker when he goes out to play. Anyone could have fiddled into his locker and made an impression of his keys, put them back and he wouldn't be any the wiser.'

'You think it was the Major?'

Flick frowned. 'Perhaps, or maybe he played with Pargiter while an accomplice copied the keys. The result was the same. One of our murders was committed in that garage without anyone breaking into the house. The victim was connected to the others. And they all seem to be connected with the drug problem which was what Mike, the undercover cop, is investigating.'

'I see you've got some links but where is it leading you?'

'I wish I knew. We keep getting dead ends. Everyone we could follow up gets murdered, but by whom?'

'You're definitely linking Tubby's death with the others?'

'Absolutely. It's such an unusual way of killing. So unusual in fact even two eminent pathologists and an experienced CSI don't know exactly what caused that specific trauma.'

'Another dead end then?'

'I wouldn't say that,' smiled Flick. 'Not if I know my guys. Martin Barnes and Fred Updike won't rest until they've worked it out. I don't suppose the Dutch chap will either. They hate being beaten.'

On Monday morning DCI Westcott had returned. Flick put everything she had learned in front of him.

'I'd like to lay on a fingertip search of the side of the road where the mobile was found,' she said. 'I've been on to Forensics and they confirm there was damage to the casing of the mobile. Scratches down the sides and bigger damage to one corner. They didn't think much of it, just wear and tear, but the marks are consistent with it having been forced out of a broken tail light and falling onto the road. There were a few small traces of grass caught in the casing but that would come from where we found it.'

Westcott smiled. 'Where Kenneth found it, you mean.'

'Yes sir, Kenneth. It was probably knocked onto the grass verge by other traffic.'

Westcott's face was grave. 'But that does put Mike in the boot of the Jag.'

Flick bit her lip. 'I'm afraid so, sir. Can't we go and search the house? No, I know we just haven't got an acceptable reason for a warrant. We just don't have any hard evidence against Major Carver.'

Westcott nodded. 'We'll just have to rely on Saturday and hope the Major has been so cocky he's outsmarted himself.'

It was hard waiting. Later that day the fingertip search brought up a few tiny shards of red glass consistent with the tail light of an old Jaguar. But there should have been more. Someone had cleaned up the site of that smash before the team got there. A concerned road user? Or someone with a guilty conscience? When asked, Mrs Tiffin said she hadn't heard anything suspicious. But then she would hardly hear surreptitious sweepings made by someone anxious to avoid being seen or heard.

Permission to open Tubby Jackson's bank account arrived on Tuesday.

On Wednesday Tom Perkins reported back to Flick. The account showed irregular entries of sums other than Tubby's pay. Nothing enormous. A few hundred here and there starting from about eight years earlier.

Two years for the Major to pick out his mark, the weak link in the chain, the one who would respond to flattery, and sympathy that his abilities were not getting the merit they deserved. Bitterness is a corrosive emotion. That's what the DCI had said, thought Flick.

Over the years the sums had grown larger until they reached a peak of three thousand pounds, twice in the last year. What had happened then?

Flick looked back through past Incident records but could find nothing that stood out. Perhaps that was the point? Because Tubby had covered up, or guarded a particular building, or road, some activity hadn't been discovered. Drug movements? Or the arrival of the makings, the means to produce the drugs arriving at Marylands to disappear into the cellars there and form a production line? Flick rubbed her tired eyes and yawned. Round and round in circles. Where now? That blasted cocktail party.

'Don't worry, Flick,' laughed Margaret Westcott when Flick phoned her. 'Years ago everything was much more formal. We used to wear short frocks for cocktails. A bit dressier than an afternoon dress but certainly not long . . .nor gloves. Not in my time anyway, unless you were going on to a ball or perhaps a posh theatre party. But nowadays I think even jeans and a sparkly top would be quite acceptable.'

'Thanks, Margaret, I won't go that far the other way. I can't see your husband approving of me in trousers on Saturday, unless they were silk, perhaps.'

'I gather I'm not to look surprised to see our intelligent Felicity simpering,' said Margaret.

'Oh, Lord. Is that what he said? How does one simper? I don't think I can bring myself to do it even if I knew how. I'd feel an idiot and Andy would get the giggles and give the game away.'

'Poor you. I don't think simpering is mandatory. Just a bit fluffy. You know, wide open eyes and admiring smiles.'

'Yuk! The very thought of it puts me off my dinner.'

'I'm sure you'll play your part to perfection. See you on Saturday. We'll pick you up. William will have a driver as we shall all be expected to drink, although not too much perhaps.'

What a very nice woman Margaret Westcott is, thought Flick as she put down the telephone. With her help perhaps it wouldn't be too bad playing the part the DCI had dictated. She walked upstairs to view possible outfits for Saturday evening. Perhaps if she had a younger trendy sister it would help? With a snort of laughter, she opened her wardrobe door.

The cocktail party

William Westcott looked Flick up and down when she opened her front door to him on Saturday evening.

Her final choice of dress suited her. She had bought it for a friend's engagement party and knew she looked good in it. 'Too good.' Andy had said so Flick had applied extra make-up, especially round her eyes, back-combed her hair until her scalp was sore, and added a pair of huge hoop earrings she had worn as a fortune-teller for a fancy dress parade.

When Westcott's eyes took in the earrings and hair he smiled. 'Perfect,' he said. 'Well done, Flick. And tonight we're supposed to be off duty so its first names all round.'

'Yes, sir, er, William. Come on, Andy,' she called. 'I've said goodbye to the twins and Mum so we're ready to go.'

When they were ushered into the spacious hall of Marylands by a silent butler, Flick had no trouble pretending to be awestruck. The shine of polish on the parquet floor was echoed in the Chinese cabinets along the wall. Back-lit by unseen lamps, crystal sparkled and the rich tints of china pieces glowed. Overhead the light of a huge chandelier cast rainbow colours over the carved panelling that ran up a wide staircase to the gallery above

'Wow!' she said.

'Good evening, Manners,' said Westcott as he handed over Margaret's jacket.

So this was the perfect servant he had described to her, thought Flick. She giggled as she let Andy help her off with her short coat, and took in Manners's grey appearance. Everything about the man was grey. His suit, his hair, the tone of his skin, even his eyes. She felt a shiver as his eyes met hers, but managed a weak grin.

While the four of them took in the glory of the hall, Manners hung the coats on a row of stags' antlers set discreetly below the curve of the stairs. Then he inclined his head,

'The Major is waiting for you in the conservatory, if you will be pleased to follow me.'

Flick pulled a face at Andy as she fell in beside Margaret Westcott and they preceded the men across a large sitting room in the wake of the butler. Glancing around she saw the same type of set-up as the Pargiter's house in Ridminster and wondered if they shared an interior decorator. This looked more like retired Army than pop-star choice. The only remarkable difference in the two rooms was the complete set of bookshelves that made up the wall on the right. Only broken by a door, she presumed led into another room, they stretched from floor to ceiling and were full of volumes.

'Ah, Chief Inspector, William.' Carver came across the expanse of the conservatory with hand outstretched. The thick carpet of the sitting room had given way once again to shining parquet. The women's heels click-clacked as they stood aside for him to reach Westcott.

'And you have brought your lovely ladies. Very good. Margaret, my dear, so good to see you again. I think the last time was at that charity auction for the local hospice.' He took her hand and air-kissed her cheek.

'But this lovely young lady must be your latest acquisition, William?' he went on. He took Flick's offered hand and raised it towards his lips.

Quickly she changed her look of horror into one of charming confusion. If only she could blush. But she managed a flutter of eyelashes and a shy smile. Behind her she heard Andy choke down a snort of laughter. She knew how he felt. This party was getting weirder by the minute.

'Yes,' said Westcott. 'This is our newest inspector, Felicity Fraser. And this is her husband, Andrew. Our host, Major Edward Carver.'

Carver released Flick's hand and turned to Andy. 'What a very fortunate young man you are,' he said, but there was no warmth in his smile. 'I do hope you take good care of her. See she doesn't get into trouble. And what is it exactly that you do?'

'I sit behind a desk, sir,' said Andy.

'While wifey does all the exciting bits?' said Carver. 'Well, never mind young man. You know what they say "They also serve who only stand and wait", or sit in your case. But come and meet the others.'

Having managed to thoroughly annoy each of his four guests, Carver led them across the conservatory to meet the Mayor and Mayoress, and the Captain of the Golf club and his wife who had already arrived.

Oh, Lord, thought Flick, by the time this evening is over my reputation as a capable and level-headed police officer will be in shreds. She caught Westcott's sleeve and drew him aside. He lowered his head so she could whisper in his ear.

'Do I have to keep up the idiot role, sir? I never thought about the other people who were going to be here. I'll never live it down.'

Westcott chuckled. 'I'm sorry, Flick. Needs must. I never realised what an accomplished actress you are.' He smiled down at her and patted her shoulder. 'Keep up the good work,' he said.

Flick's jaw ached with smiling. Her eyes ached from being constantly opened to their fullest extent in awe or admiration. Inwardly she squirmed as she caught one or two puzzled looks sent in her direction by the Mayor and Mayoress, both of whom she had met on several occasions. She tried to avoid their company, also that of the Bank Manager and his wife. With the Captain of the Golf Club she was on neutral ground having never met him or his wife before. She sipped at the cocktail which, according to Carver, had been made especially for her and was called "Pretty Lady". The sickly sweet taste made Flick want to throw up. Her host made her feel the same way, she thought as he approached her. She plastered another smile on her face and the eyelashes came into play once more.

'Felicity, my dear, if I may make so bold.'

Flick tried to look arch and found she could actually simper. Yuk! 'Of course, Major Carver.' This should have been the moment when he invited her to call him Edward, but he barrelled on with his little speech. Behind the foolish look on her face Flick's brain was wondering exactly what Carver was playing at? At first glance he would seem to be flirting with her, but it didn't ring true. What was he up to?

'I thought you and your boss,' was there a slight emphasis on the word? 'You and your boss, might like to have a conducted tour of the house?'

At that moment Margaret Westcott came to Flick's rescue. 'Not William, Edward,' she laughed. 'He has no idea of decor and very little interest in architecture. But I should love a tour of this amazing house of yours.'

Flick saw a flash of irritation cross Carver's face, soon to disappear and be replaced by a beaming smile. 'Of course, my dear, Margaret. I cannot abandon my other guests, but Manners will do the honours. Please feel free to wander at will.'

Behind his bland expression Flick sensed he was enjoying some private joke.

Manners went ahead of Flick and Margaret, opening doors and answering the questions Margaret addressed to him. Beyond a few gasps of admiration and inane comments such as 'isn't it big?' 'I shouldn't like to dust this one' and 'aren't you afraid it will break?' Flick thought her role would be that of ignorant observer. But her eyes were everywhere.

Was it a waste of time? Surely Carver wouldn't allow anything on view that could connect him to the drug trade or other illegal activities? The cellars would be the place. If only she could think of an excuse to get away from Margaret and Manners, perhaps she could find them?

They had started the tour by climbing up the beautiful main staircase. From the broad landing at the top they had been shown all the rooms leading off, even a peep into Carver's bedroom; a large room dominated by a carved wooden double 'sleigh' bed. The floor to ceiling French doors gave onto a balcony overlooking the back of the house and the extensive grounds beyond.

In desperation Flick cleared her throat, 'Excuse me, Mr Manners, sir?'

Manners face showed no expression. 'Yes, Madam?'

'Er, I wonder if . . . er, where . . . I want the little girls' room,' Flick blurted out. Behind Manners she saw Margaret Westcott bite her lip to quell her amusement. But would she get the message that Flick was trying to slip away from Manners's eagle eye?

'Certainly, Madam. This way if you please.' He crossed the landing to a door they had not yet reached, opened it and stood aside for Flick to enter. 'We will await you here,' he said and closed the door on her.

Flick went through the motions in the lavishly equipped bathroom. She snooped in the cabinet to see what medication, if any, she could find. There was a shower cap still in its plastic bag, a spare tablet of soap, a brand new toothbrush, a disposable razor and a new flannel. Everything in fact an overnight guest might require. But had Mike been offered such essentials? Flick doubted it. She flushed the toilet, ran the water in the basin then as an afterthought she did wash her hands. Suppose Manners checked the soap, or the towel after she left? Everything must appear kosher. But obviously there was no chance of escape.

When Flick left the bathroom she found Margaret and Manners still on the wide landing. Margaret had managed to draw Manners to the far end by asking him about the many pictures in oils and watercolours hanging on the walls. Flick looked about her. The wall at this end was covered in photographs. Most were of men in uniform. Flick studied them closely looking for Carver's face.

Some showed men, presumably soldiers in Carver's regiment, playing football, rugby and cricket. There were one or two informal groups and it was in one of these she hit pay dirt. A group of men stood below the overhanging branches of a tree she couldn't identify. Some seemed to have lost parts of their uniforms, others had bands of bullets across their shoulders. They were all armed with knives. In his Army uniform Carver stood in the middle of the group but it was the man across whose shoulders his arm was draped that made Flick catch her breath and take a closer look. Younger, rough shaven and in one of the motley uniforms that made him look foreign to her eyes, Manners looked into the camera. Flick blinked. She had to look twice to be sure it was Manners; that grey, expressionless, totally forgettable servant who had opened the door to them this evening. The man in the photo was so different. A crooked smile showed strong white teeth; his hair was longer, wilder, and his eyes sparkled with challenge. Challenging what, she thought? The enemy? The cameraman? The war? Or fate? A rush of excitement made Flick's eyes sparkle. Had this photograph been hanging here so long it had become "part of the furniture", blending into the background so that the people who lived here didn't notice it or think of it? If so this was the first big mistake the Major had made.

'There you are, Felicity,' said Margaret, her voice carrying the length of the landing to warn Flick of Manners's approach. 'I was just remarking what a wonderful collection the Major has acquired. Apparently he has been a collector for many years.'

Flick smiled inanely. 'Not that many surely, Margaret. He's not very old is he?'

'The Major began his collection as a very young man,' said Manners.

Flick opened her eyes as wide as possible. 'And did you help him find his treasures, Mr Manners?' she said.

'Alas, no. I only came into the Major's service a few years before he came to Ridminster. That concludes the tour of the first floor, ladies. Shall we take the lift down and rejoin the party?'

'Oooh has the house got a lift?' cooed Flick. 'How posh.' Was she overdoing this act? Surely no-one in their right minds could think she had reached her present rank if she was as dim as she was putting across? Perhaps the Major thought she'd slept her way to the top? Even as the ridiculous thought crossed her mind she saw the truth.

That was exactly what he did think, or at least that she was sleeping with William Westcott now. It all fitted. His remarks to Westcott at the Golf Club, his dismissal of Andy as being of no importance, the emphasis on Westcott's ladies on their arrival and also on the word 'boss' said with meaning. He'd wanted Flick and Westcott to take the tour of the house together. Was he hoping they would disappear into one of the bedrooms after Westcott had dropped a heavy hint to Manners? Flick was sure she was right, but what now? Should she make a point of sticking by the DCI? Would it be a good idea to fuel Carver's suspicions? She rather thought it would, but how to let Margaret know what she was up to? She could hardly ask the older woman to accompany her to the toilet?

While these thoughts raced through her head, they had arrived at a discreet door exactly the same as those of the other rooms they had seen, but this gave entrance to the lift. Manners opened it, slid back the interior door and allowed the two women to precede him, then followed them in and pressed a button.

'Oooh what fun,' giggled Flick, as the lift began to descend. 'What a lot of buttons, Mr Manners. Does the lift not just go up and down?'

'It does indeed go down, Madam. Right down to the cellars'

'Cellars!' exclaimed Flick. 'I've never been in a house with cellars before. Can we see?'

'I too would be interested in seeing the cellars. Very unusual for a modern house to have them these days, more's the pity. I should enjoy the facility and storage space,' put in Margaret.

'Certainly, Madam,' assured a wooden faced Manners. As the lift came to a stop on the ground floor he pushed the bottom button of the row. The lift descended again for a short time.

When the doors opened again, even Margaret's eyes opened wide.

'Wow!' exclaimed Flick once more. She could be forgiven her reaction. The huge space in front of them was lit by overhead strip lighting. Along the far left hand side, shoulder-high walls divided the space. In one there were logs, no doubt to feed the wood-burning stoves she had seen in the sitting room and conservatory. Another held summer garden furniture awaiting better weather. In a third there were ladders, tool boxes and all the paraphernalia for interior decorating, including a heap of paint spattered materials, no doubt used to protect furniture and floors.

Flick ran into the centre of the open space and pirouetted like a little girl showing off her party frock. 'Oh this is too fantastic. What a party we could have here.' She skipped from one side of the room to the other then danced across to the opposite sides. 'Does the Major ever hold dances here, Mr Manners?' she said.

'No, Madam. We use the cellars strictly for storage.'

Flick stopped her capering in front of Manners. She stuck out her bottom lip and managed a passable pout. 'Oh, he should. It would be perfect. Now I'm not so shy of him I think I'll ask him if he'll do it. A cellar party would be such fun.'

'I don't think you should plague the Major, Felicity dear,' said Margaret in the tone of voice one uses on an overexcited child.

'I'm afraid, Madam is right,' said Manners. 'Too much vibration might disturb the wine.'

'The wine?' repeated Flick with wide-open eyes.

'Yes, Madam.' Manners led the way to a door Flick had noticed on the wall opposite the storage bays. This led into another cellar almost as big as the first. Manners indicted the large double doors on the opposite wall. 'This is how the previous occupants brought all their equipment from the grounds into the studio,' he said, 'and this room is now the Major's wine cellar.' He opened a smaller door on the right and ushered Margaret and Flick into a wine buff's idea of heaven.

Although she felt it, Flick really couldn't bring herself to say "Wow" again. All round the walls and either side of a central island were racks and racks of bottles. She and Margaret moved about bending their heads to read labels. It was clear they were organised into reds, whites and rosees. There were also sections of spirits, champagnes and liqueurs. The whole would have stocked a small shop or wine bar. Flick lingered over the different kinds of whiskies. Manners moved to her shoulder. She smiled at him.

'Aren't they lovely names? Glens and Rivers. My husband is Scottish,' she offered. 'He'd love to see these. I think they sound so romantic, but I hate the taste,' she lied, pulling a face of disgust.

'The Major is a connoisseur,' said Manners.

'Gosh,' said Flick. 'Which one is his favourite? With so many to chose from does he drink a different one each day?'

'No, Madam,' said Manners. 'He prefers the Bunnahabhain, a single malt.'

'The boonie what?' said Flick. 'What did you say?'

'Bunnahabhain, Madam. It is the Gaelic language meaning the foot of the river which is where the distillery lies on the island of Islay. One of the better Island malts.'

Good Lord, thought Flick, Manners is positively unbending. He obviously likes showing off his knowledge. But I think we'd better get back. She smiled.

'I'm sure you're right, Mr Manners, but I still don't like the taste,' she said.

Manners threw off his role of tutor and ushered the two women to the staircase leading back to the ground floor. Soon they had rejoined the party. Carver was all expansive smiles.

'My dear ladies, we thought we'd lost you. Did you enjoy my house?'

'Oh yes,' gushed Flick. 'it's perfectly super. Thank you so much for letting us see it all. But I don't know how you can drink all that whisky. I don't like the taste,' she confided.

'So Manners showed you our cellars did he?' smiled the Carver.

To Flick it seemed he was enjoying some private joke. Manners had first disappeared and then reappeared with trays of savoury nibbles which he was offering round the guests.

'Manners was very patient,' said Margaret with a meaning look at Flick, 'and very knowledgeable on your art collection. I was impressed.'

'You're so clever, Margaret,' pouted Flick. 'I'm afraid I lost interest at that point. But I loved your cellars.'

Manners appeared beside her. 'Madam wondered if you might throw a party down there, sir,' he said.

'A party in the cellars? Is that a novel idea, Manners?'

'I'm afraid I had to assure, Madam, the vibrations might upset your wine.'

Carver choked back a laugh. 'Yes, indeed, Manners. Yes, indeed.'

Soon after that the party started to break up.

'And have you any plans for the rest of the evening, William?' queried Carver.

'Margaret and I are taking Felicity and her husband out for dinner,' said Westcott, 'the girls so rarely see each other it seems like a great opportunity for the two of them to spend some time together.'

'Capital,' said Carver. 'Great idea.'

I'll give him something to ponder on, thought Flick. While Manners was fetching their coats and jackets she pulled on Westcott's sleeve, drew him away from the others and leaned up to speak quietly to him. He lowered his head so she could whisper in his ear. 'Play up to me, sir,' she said. 'I have a reason. I'll explain later.' She reached up and touched his cheek.

Westcott was neither slow nor stupid. He covered her hand with his own, let it linger there a moment then gently lowered their clasped hands and shook his head.

For a moment Flick let her head drop, her shoulders droop, then as if pulling herself together she straightened up, let go of Westcott's hand and turned towards Manners who was ready to help her on with her jacket.

'Thank you, Mr Manners. And thank you for a lovely party, Major Carver.' She gazed into the pale blue eyes of her host. 'I do hope we'll meet again soon,' she said.

Post mortems

'Sir?' said Flick once their car had pulled out of the front gates of Marylands. 'Did you mean it when you told Carver you were taking us out for dinner?'

Westcott smiled. 'Of course, I did, Flick.'

'Well, it's very kind of you but is it a place we can talk without being overheard?'

Westcott frowned. 'It's a very nice restaurant, not too crammed together but it is a public place. What are you getting at?'

'I think I know,' said Margaret, 'because I feel it too. We need to consolidate all we've learned tonight before it becomes dimmed by time. It will also be useful if we can corroborate each other's impressions.'

'Exactly, Margaret,' grinned Flick. 'I couldn't have put it better myself.'

'Why don't we cancel the reservation for dinner tonight? But we will do it another time,' said Margaret. 'Let's get a take-away on the way home and then have a pow-wow.'

Her husband laughed. 'A pow-wow?'

'Yes, it means . . .'

'I know what it means. I was a Boy Scout once. But I've never heard you use that expression in all the years we've been married.'

'I haven't been in a situation like this in all the years we've been married,' Margaret retorted. 'And I must say

I'm rather enjoying it. Not your average cocktail party. Far more stimulating,' she smiled at Flick and Andy.

'That may be true,' said Westcott. 'But we mustn't forget this is not a game. The man we are after is a vicious, cold-blooded killer and no fool. Right. Home it is.'

'By way of the Chinese,' added Margaret.

Once at the Westcotts' home, Margaret fetched a business-like pad and pen from the DCI's study. Then they settled round the large dining table, each with their own choice of meal.

'We can talk while we eat,' said Margaret. 'I'll take notes.'

Westcott smiled at the expression on Flick's face. 'You can tell who's the boss in this house,' he said. 'Right, where do we start?'

'First impressions,' said Flick. 'From the start I got the feeling Carver was enjoying some private joke.'

Margaret nodded as she wrote. 'Me, too.'

'It wasn't until we were coming down in the lift I realised what he was up to.'

'You did?' said Margaret. 'I didn't have a clue.'

Flick explained to the others how she couldn't believe anyone who had half a brain would be taken in by her act. After all she was a reasonably senior officer so surely they wouldn't buy her dim-witted behaviour. Unless of course they believed she had slept her way to the top.

'You what?' exclaimed Andy.

'What do you mean?' said Westcott.

'Once I thought of it from that angle it was so clear. When we first arrived he called Margaret and me, "your lovely ladies". Your. No mention of Andy, my husband, who was right there beside me. Then later, he put emphasis again on the word, boss, in a meaningful sort of way.

'He was put out, quite irritated, when Margaret moved in on the tour he had planned you and I, sir, should take together.'

'That's true, he was,' said Margaret.

Westcott frowned. 'You may well be right. He made some odd comment the other day about your ability, or lack of it. Apparently Tubby Jackson had been denigrating your capability; no doubt to impress Carver with his own superiority. I put him right, of course, so he may have thought I was leaping to your defence for quite other reasons. But if that's the case is it useful or should we put him right?'

'It could be useful, sir. If he thinks I'm the village idiot he may not be so careful next time we meet. Manners wasn't.'

'What do you mean?'

'I was acting the fool down in the cellars.'

'You certainly were,' laughed Margaret. 'I thought you'd lost the plot for a minute. As for Manners, his pained expression when you were dancing around was worth seeing.'

'Dancing around?' Andy was puzzled. 'Whatever for?'

'She was all over the place like a teenager. "Ooo what a lovely place for a party, Mr Manners",' mimicked Margaret.

Flick grinned. 'Very useful dancing as it happens. There's nothing of interest in the big cellar – well that's not true but I'll come back to it later. But in the outer one there is a discrepancy. We saw where the big loads came in, in the old days. Manners even showed us the wine cellar. But both of those together don't add up to the floor space of the rest of the house. We need to see the original plans. If the cellar area does match that of the rest of the floors then we have a hidden room, one we weren't shown.'

'How do you know?' said Andy.

'It was a very rough measurement, but my dancing around covered the dimensions of both cellars. They were not as aimless as I hope they appeared,' Flick said to Margaret.

'Well I was fooled,' smiled the older woman. 'I just thought you were playing your part amazingly well.'

'Good. Let's hope Manners didn't twig what I was doing either. We know the house was built by pop musicians who recorded down in the cellar, so where is the sound-proofing? Mrs Tiffin, whose ears are as sharp as a bat's, never heard them playing. Would Carver have gone to the bother and expense of ripping out sound-proofing? I don't think so. Why would he? So I believe it is in the hidden room which by my rough calculations should be under that library or study, whichever he calls it.'

'Thomas Stebbins told me the cellars were as big as the house and they were sound-proofed,' said Andy. 'He might know where we can lay our hands on a copy of the plans without alerting Carver. I'll ask him, discreetly, on Monday.'

'Good man,' said Westcott. 'That's a really good night's work, Flick. Well done.'

'I haven't finished. On my pirouetting round the cellar I saw a store of decorating stuff, paint, brushes etc. Also a heap of paint-spotted old material. I suppose it's used for covering floors and furniture. In that heap was the identical curtain we found stuffed into the car to keep in the fumes when the so-called suicide was murdered. It's possible there's no connection. There could have been countless curtains made in that material, but I believe it is the other half of the pair. Particularly as the whisky bottle found in the car was Bunnahabhain, the Major's favourite tipple. Was he in a hurry and snatched up the first empty bottle he had to hand? I guess this stuff, this single malt, is quite pricey so he wouldn't want to pour away the contents to provide an empty bottle. And the lab told us there were no prints at all on the whisky bottle.'

'If we had his prints on the bottle that would clinch it,' said the DCI. 'Lack of prints points to murder. What suicide would bother to wipe the bottle clean? But without them you can't connect the whisky bottle to Carver. As to the curtain it may be possible to match it up with the one we have by analysing the fade patterns; the stitching; the dust content and other tests the lab would try. It's worth a go, when and if we get our hands on it. Well I think that calls for a drink. We've had a very successful evening.'

'But there's more,' said Flick. 'While Margaret was stunning Manners with her knowledge of fine art,' she grinned across at Westcott's wife, 'I was studying the photos on the other wall. Most of them were fairly innocuous snaps of Regimental sports occasions. But there was one of interest. When I asked Manners how long he had been with Carver he said he had only been employed for a few years before they came to Ridminster. That may be so but they knew each other long before that. Carver was standing with his arm across Manners's shoulders in a picture dating from the Balkan war. Carver was in regular uniform but Manners looked more like one of the locals with bits and bobs of uniform and a bandolier of ammunition slung across his chest. I think he was a mercenary. Perhaps that's where they met?'

'Well done, Flick,' said Westcott. 'Are you sure it was the Balkan war?'

'It said Kosovo 1999 underneath, so that would be right wouldn't it, sir?'

He nodded. 'Yes, the Racak massacre took place in January of that year forcing the international intervention for peace. I wonder why my contact didn't mention Carver's posting to Kosovo? He intimated the Major hadn't served outside Britain. Perhaps he really did do some secret work as he implied to me.'

'Leave that with me,' said Margaret. 'I'll trawl the internet and contact a few people. See what I can learn. I wish we had a copy of the photo.'

'I haven't got one of those,' said Andy. 'But I do have a picture of Carver and Manners. They were so busy talking over by the door I don't think they realised I had my phone out. The camera on it is quite good. I just took a few shots of the conservatory really to send to my Mum. She'll be tickled pink when I tell her we've been to a posh cocktail party. I thought I'd send her the photos too.'

'Brilliant,' said Margaret. 'May I have your camera, Andy? I'll download them and let you have it back before you go home. Now, William, I think we really do deserve that drink. A very satisfactory night's work.'

'A very satisfactory night's work,' said Major Carver. 'We've consolidated our position with the Bank and the Golf Club.'

'Very Army, sir,' grinned Manners. 'Shades of the good old days.'

'Except we're not getting shot at, and that's how I prefer it. Nothing wrong with a bit of Army strategy. Know your enemy, his strengths and weaknesses.'

'We certainly know the latter after tonight. It was a very good idea to invite that particular mix.'

Carver smiled, satisfied. 'Yes. I thought it would be and I was right. You couldn't see, because they were behind you, but as you lead them into the conservatory Westcott and his bit on the side fell back. She pulled at his sleeve to draw him closer, he bent down so she could whisper in his ear. Maybe sweet nothings or a plea to get him on his own? Anyway he smiled down at her and patted her shoulder comfortingly. Clear as clear there's something going on there.'

'I don't think his wife is stupid,' said Manners.

'Margaret? No. She's always struck me as a sensible woman, but when a man has his eye on a younger, prettier female his brain is in his trousers.'

'Do you think she suspects something?'

'Why do you say that?'

'She was very quick to push into the tour of the house wasn't she? Said hubby wouldn't enjoy it before he had a chance to speak for himself.'

Carver was thoughtful for a moment. 'Yes. She did. That might be true, but I wanted to laugh when Little Miss Big Eyes had to pretend to be pleased to have wifey's company instead of her lover's.'

'Yes and this business of taking the younger pair out for dinner. Your Chief Inspector is obviously trying to pull the wool over the wife's eyes.'

'Not a bad idea,' said Carver. 'Take the husband along as camouflage and that let's him play footsie with the girl all night. No problems on the tour?'

Manners shook his head. 'The wife knows her art, I'll give her that. Made some quite interesting remarks while we were waiting for the other one to come out of the bathroom.'

Carver was alert. 'Which bathroom?'

'The blue one of course. Don't worry, sir, everything's under control. We've verified our suspicions and they're none the wiser. As you say, sir, a very good evening's work.'

'I think that deserves a snifter. You can join me, Manners.'

Manners inclined is head. 'Thank you, sir,' he smiled.

Monday

'Have we got the registration number of Carver's Jag?'
Flick asked at the Monday morning briefing.

Around the room heads were shaken. People looked
at each other but no-one had the information.

'Right,' went on Flick. 'Tonight Carver will, if he
follows his usual pattern, be attending a meeting of Toc
H. You, DC Spence will be in the vicinity of the hall . . .
no, better still I will ask Mrs Tiffin if you can keep watch
from her house. We don't know at what time he will be
leaving and returning or which entrance he will use. You
can't hang about in the street for hours. See me after
lunch and I'll have fixed it then. While you are watching
the rear, DC Jarvis can keep an eye on the front entrance.
I'm interested too in any visitors the Major may have.
Car reg. and, if possible, names of occupants, certainly
number and sex.

'DC Nisbet. I want you to start looking for the garage
where the Jag had its tail light replaced. Until we have
the registration you can just make general enquiries about
any red Jag and take the number if you find one.
Remember it's the old type with glass lights, not the new
plastic kind.

'DC Whiteman I want you to revisit the pub, the
Crown and Sceptre and find out what was the favourite
tipple of Lawrence Hardy, our so-called suicide. Was he

269

left-handed? Did anyone hear any of the conversations he and Brand might have had?'

'Right up your street, Harry,' called a voice and there was general laughter. What DC Harry Whiteman didn't know about every pub within a radius of twenty miles was not worth knowing.

He grinned. 'Specialist knowledge always pays dividends,' he said.

'DS Booth is accompanying ex-Inspector Jackson's body home today,' said Flick. At once the mood in the room sobered. Tubby Jackson was never the most popular of men but he was one of their own and to die just as his retirement began made it seem worse somehow. No-one but Flick in that room knew of Tubby's extracurricular activities. 'I'll let you know details for the funeral as soon as I have them. Now has anyone got anything else to offer or ask?' Again heads were shaken around the room. 'Right, see you back here this evening and please have something for me. This case is meandering along like a country lane, going nowhere, slowly.'

Flick stomped out of the room. Shouldn't take it out on the troops. They were doing their best but every advance meant another load of questions and dead ends.

Flick was well into the pile in her In Tray when Martin Barnes telephoned.

'Hello, Martin, what's new with you?'

'Can you come over, Flick?' the pathologist asked. 'I've got something for you.'

Flick looked at the papers that covered the top of her desk. 'Can't you tell me over the phone? I'm up to my eyes here.'

'It's not something I'd like to discuss this way. If you could manage to come over some time today I think you'll believe it was worth the journey.'

'Very cryptic,' said Flick. She looked at the clock. 'Okay. Will you be in your den this afternoon?'

'Unless we get another suspicious death, the answer is yes. I'll be here all day.'

'Fine. I'll see you about three then.' After she'd hung up Flick stared at the phone wondering what Martin Barnes may have for her. Surely Tubby Jackson's body couldn't have arrived yet? And even if it had Martin wouldn't have had time to examine it. She pushed speculation out of her mind and lifted the receiver again.

'Mrs Tiffin? It's Felicity Fraser, Inspector Fraser from the Police Station. I have a favour to ask you.'

Mrs Tiffin was quite excited at the thought of entertaining a police officer on duty. Of course he could sit with his binoculars in her front room. He'd be great company and she promised him lemon drizzle cake and as many cups of tea as he needed.

Flick laughed. 'Save some cake for me,' she said. 'And please don't give my officer so much tea he might miss the car we want to see when he's on a bathroom break.'

Mrs Tiffin chuckled and promised to be sparing with the liquid refreshment.

Flick's next interruption came from Harry Whiteman. He put his head round her door after a perfunctory knock. Flick looked up.

'Yes, Harry, what is it?'

'Lawrence Hardy's favourite tipple was vodka. Never drank anything else and couldn't abide the smell of whisky. The landlord of the Crown and Sceptre said a lot of drivers stick to vodka because it doesn't smell on their breath. Even if they're under the limit, any employer or even member of the public would be put off if they stank of gin or whisky. And he was right-handed. At least the landlord never saw him using his left hand for anything other than to scratch his ear,' explained Harry.

'That's fine. Thank you, Harry,' said Flick and made a note. Little things but together they added up to a solid case of murder.

She managed to snatch a quick sandwich in the canteen and then paid a visit to the local florist. When Barry Spence arrived for his personal briefing she warned him against drinking too much tea and then handed over the sweet-smelling bunch of flowers. 'Give these to Mrs Tiffin this evening please, Barry.' His eyebrows rose in surprise. 'Don't look like that. By the time Mrs Tiffin has entertained you this evening you'll probably want to buy her some flowers yourself.'

'Flowers, for a blind woman, boss?'

'It's her eyes that are blind. There's nothing the matter with her nose. She'll enjoy them. Tell her they are from me with grateful thanks and I will bring the twins to see her someday soon.'

'Ah! Friend of yours is she, boss?'

Flick thought for a moment, then smiled. 'I hope she will be, yes. She's a remarkable lady. And as soon as you have that vehicle reg, you phone it in. Alright?'

'Right you are, boss.'

Having dealt with DC Spence and cleared as much as she could of her desk, Flick put on her coat, tidied her hair at the small mirror behind the door of her office and picked up her handbag. The phone rang. She sighed but lifted the receiver.

'Felicity?' she heard Margaret Westcott's voice and frowned. What on earth could Margaret want? She wouldn't ring the station to gossip or rehash Saturday's cocktail party. They'd had a fairly thorough going over that ground the other night.

'Margaret. What can I do for you?' she said.

'The other way round I hope,' said Margaret Westcott. 'I think I've got some information that will be very useful for you.'

'Really?' What on earth could Margaret know that would help this investigation along?'

'Can you come and see me? It's not something I really want to talk about over the phone.'

That seems to be the order of the day. 'I'm just on my way out to the morgue,' Flick said.

'Poor you. Not I imagine one of the pleasanter parts of your job. Do you think you could call in here on your way home? I've been doing some digging and I think you'll be pleased with the results, but it's far too complicated to tell you like this.'

'Yes. I'll do that, but I have no idea what time it will be. I'll give you a ring when I'm ready to leave Flax

Bourton. It could take me a good hour from there to Ridminster.'

Flick hung up the phone and looked at her watch. An hour, if she was lucky, to reach Martin at Flax Bourton, the public mortuary where nearly all autopsies were performed. How long he would keep her she had no idea but then a visit to Margaret, and she wouldn't be home in time for the kids' tea. Quickly she dialled her home number.

'Mum? I think I'm going to be late this evening. I've no real idea when I'll get back so probably best if I just have an omelette or something when I get in. You go ahead and eat . . . okay then, if you've got chops they won't take too long. Save mine from the ravening hordes . . . Right, Mum. Give them my love, Bye bye.'

She managed the journey in just under the hour and greeted Martin Barnes with the news she was in a hurry.

'What can you have for me that is so secret you couldn't tell me over the phone?'

'Something very nasty indeed,' said Barnes. He lead her into his office. Flick kept her coat on. Martin Barnes didn't seem to feel the cold. His office was always freezing but that wouldn't bother his guests next door of course. 'I'm a keen swimmer and have done some diving,' he began.

What on earth have Martin's hobbies to do with the job in hand?

'This weekend I was invited to do some wreck diving. The group I went with are serious divers. They've been all over the world and have the most amazing kit.'

Flick glanced at her watch.

Martin went on. 'I promise I haven't dragged you here on false pretences. One guy had what he called a "wasp knife". A very nasty weapon it was too.'

'A weapon? I thought these dives were for fun. Were you playing war games?'

'No way. This is for defence against anything from shark attack to giant squid getting hold of you. Hunters use them too against bears or other wild creatures that might attack them.'

'A knife against a bear? That doesn't sound like very good odds,' said Flick.

Barnes was serious. 'You haven't seen the knife,' he said. 'Here, look at this website on my computer. I wanted to talk you through it because I believe this is the weapon that killed our victim in Ridminster and, once I get a look at him, I think we'll find the same one did for Tubby Jackson.'

Flick looked at the screen where there was a drawing of a vicious knife. It had a pointed blade and chunky handle but seemed no different from a score she had seen, confiscated from the youth of the county.

'Look at the cross-section drawing of the handle,' said Barnes. 'It holds a small canister that can propel a ball of compressed gas through the tip into the victim. The gas instantly expands to the size of a football bringing about death and freezing every part it touches so, in the case of a shark attack by one lone beast, its blood in the water wouldn't attract others to the scene. This is definitely the type of thing that could cause the trauma in our victim and, from what your Dutch friend says, in Tubby too.'

'My God!' Flick was horrified. 'What will they think of next? But if the victim was frozen internally why didn't we pick it up before?'

'From the information I have, the Ridminster victim probably lay undiscovered for eight or nine hours. The same with Tubby. Time enough for thawing but of course, negligible blood loss as death had already occurred.'

Flick nodded. 'Yes. I see. Heaven help us if these get onto the streets.'

'Absolutely. Of course they started out as life-savers and man in his unwisdom has turned them into life-takers. It says here they are used in the States by hunters and divers but it wouldn't surprise me to find the "sneaky beaky" parts of the Army have them too.'

'You think they're used by the military?'

'Maybe not in our country but if you're fighting a dirty war, you use dirty weapons. So was your journey wasted?'

'Absolutely not. And you were right to bring me over. A great deal of this case is on a "need to know" basis. I certainly don't want any loose talk about this. In fact I'm on my way to the DCI's house now. I think I'll brief him on this there rather than at the nick.' And I can think of a dirty war where this might have been used she thought.

The phone on Barnes's desk rang. He picked it up.

Flick gathered her handbag and car keys ready to leave but was stayed by Barnes's hand.

'Right you are,' he said. 'DI Fraser's with me now. It'll be quicker if she comes along. Yes, sir. I believe she was coming to see you at home on her way back . . . Will do, sir. Thank you.'

Flick frowned. 'Was that the boss? My boss? What's up?'

'Another body apparently.'

'What? I don't believe it. It's an epidemic. We never have this much murder in a whole year. Now look at us.'

'We don't know yet if it is a murder.'

'Of course not. Sorry, Martin. I tell you all these interlinked bodies are getting to me. It's like trying to extricate yourself from a bramble bush. The more you try the more it grabs hold of you. I'll take my own car and follow your wagon. I shall want to go home straight from the scene. What have we got? A farming accident?'

'I wish, although they can be pretty gory. No. A farmer was clearing out his drainage ditches and scooped up more than he bargained for. The copper who first attended the scene was an older guy who'd served in Northern Ireland as a youngster. He wasn't too squeamish to have a look and reckons the body has been lying in water for some time, so not a fresh one. I'll see you there.'

Flick swung her car into place behind Barnes's vehicle and wondered how much later this diversion would make her. And why had Westcott asked she go with Barnes on this one? Hadn't they got enough on their hands? And what about that lethal knife? Was it possible Carver had brought it back from Sarajevo?

As she followed Martin Barnes Flick's mind was racing with possibilities for the advancement of her case. She hoped this body could quickly be identified, perhaps as a drunken farm labourer staggering home from the pub and losing his footing. He could have hit his head or just been too drunk to get out of the ditch and so drowned. Nasty!

Monday

The place the body had been found was much nearer Ridminster than Bristol, so perhaps it wasn't surprising DCI Westcott had asked Flick to attend. By the time they arrived the usual police tape was in place preserving the scene and they were assured the CSI team were on their way.

'Although there can't be much to preserve after tractors have been running all over it,' remarked Flick.

'You're right,' said Barnes, 'and of course we don't know if the body died here or elsewhere. And if it's been here a long time dear knows what animals or small fish have been at it while it was in the water.'

Flick's vivid imagination made her swallow rather hard. 'I don't think there's much I can do here,' she said. 'I'll have a peek at the body for form's sake and a look round the site, then wait for your report.'

The country road was muddy from the wheels of the large tractor that sat beside the ditch. An arm attached to the front had a grab mechanism on the end of it. This now rested on the ground, holding its grisly burden. Flick put on the wellies she always carried in the boot of her car and together she and Barnes walked up the road from where they had parked outside the tape barrier.

As they neared the tractor Flick felt a weird sensation. She just didn't want to go any nearer. This had never happened before and she had seen some very horrid sights in her time with the Force. More familiar was that tingle between her shoulder blades. It was not often she felt it but it usually spelled danger. This was different. But what harm could there be in an unknown dead body? The dead cannot hurt you. She repeated these words in her head as she moved forward beside Barnes, but the feeling of dread persisted. She really didn't want to be here.

'Now then what have we got?' said Barnes.

A large man with a very white face was leaning against the tractor, talking to the policeman guarding the scene. He straightened up as they approached.

'I started a bit back, like,' he said. 'Couldn't make out why the drain weren't running at this time of year. No leaves falling to block 'un, so I started in to clear 'un. First couple of drags were fine, bits of twigs and mud and that. Then the grab were heavy and when I pulled 'un up I thought first t'were a sheep had maybe fallen in and drowned. But that ain't no sheep.' He nodded towards the grab lowered to the verge of the road. 'Been dead some time I reckon. No sight for a woman,' he said severely to Barnes.

'This is Inspector Fraser from Ridminster,' said Barnes.

'Even so,' said the man, 'T'aint right.'

'And you are?' queried Flick.

'Herbert Corbin. I farm's all the land round here. My family's been in these parts for four generations and never had no trouble.'

'How do you do, Mr Corbin. Thank you for reporting this so promptly. I hope it won't cause you trouble.

We'll remove the body as soon as we can. Over to you, Martin.'

'I don't suppose it will matter moving him as he's been shifted already,' said Barnes and bent over the corpse.

'Him?' said Flick. 'It's definitely a man then?'

'Yes.' Barnes cleared some of the mud from the body's face and frowned. 'Well, I don't think he drowned.'

'How can you tell with the state he's in?'

'I know. I wouldn't swear to it in court yet but you get a feeling for these things and he just doesn't look right for a drowning. Of course there's been bloating and he's waterlogged but . . . I can't put my finger on it. There's just something. I'll be able to tell you more when I get him back to the morgue, but I'd say he's around thirtyish. For more than that you'll have to wait.'

Flick opened her mouth to speak, then thought better of it. Martin Barnes would let her know his findings as soon as possible. The fact she had a bad feeling about this body, together with the knowledge there was one missing person who fitted the brief description Martin had given her, she kept to herself.

She looked all around the area, noting access from an adjacent field, made a brief sketch of the exact location in which the body was found and, from Mr Corbin, got the postcode and the address of the farm buildings. Then she looked at her watch.

'Martin, I'm off. I think I've done all I can here. I see the cavalry's arriving,' she said as the vehicles of the CSI team pulled up.

'I won't be far behind you,' said Barnes. 'I have formally declared the body is deceased. As soon as those guys have finished their photography, they'll let me take him away. I'll be in touch, Flick. Bye,' he said as he turned away to greet the CSI.

Flick hesitated. Should she or shouldn't she? 'Martin,' she called after him.

Barnes turned back. 'Yes? Have you forgotten something?'

'I know you're always busy,' said Flick. 'But do you think you could make this a priority?'

Barnes's eyebrows went up in surprise. 'A priority? Why? Do you know who it is?'

'No,' said Flick. 'I hope not. But there is someone whose whereabouts I'm not sure of just now. I'd like to be able to reassure myself our new body isn't him.'

Martin Barnes levelled a questioning look at Flick, then realised he wasn't going to get any more out of her. 'Right. Just for you, Inspector, I'll do it,' he grinned.

'Thanks, Martin, you're a star,' she said and walked back to her car.

'So that's the situation, sir,' said Flick to DCI Westcott in the sitting room of his home later that evening. She had hit the rush hour traffic on her way back and it was now past seven o'clock.

'Have you eaten, Felicity?' queried Margaret Westcott.

Flick smiled. 'No. I came straight here from the station once I had checked on my messages, but Mum's promised to save me a chop. It won't take long to cook.'

'A cup of tea and a sandwich at least,' said Margaret. 'I've saved my news to tell you both together, which is why I stayed to hear your report. Normally as you know I would leave you two alone to deal with police business, but I feel quite involved this time. It will only take me a minute, but you must eat.' She hurried out of the room and Westcott smiled at Flick.

'Orders is orders. She won't let you starve and in the meantime what is it that's bothering you?'

Flick shivered. 'Call me stupid if you like, but I have a horrible feeling this new body is our undercover copper.'

'I would never call you stupid, Flick, but what makes you think that? There wouldn't seem to be any connection between a body found in a drainage ditch out in the middle of the countryside and the deaths we have had in Ridminster.'

'And Amsterdam,' Flick reminded him.

'Yes, and Amsterdam. You're saying there are no boundaries to this business?'

'Yes, sir. We know it's already taken in Priors Parveneau and Swindon.'

'Speaking of Amsterdam. Is young Booth back yet?'

'Yes, sir. There was a message on my mobile. He went with the body to Flax Bourton and then back to the nick. Obviously I wasn't there so I'll see him in the morning.'

'Here we are,' said Margaret Westcott as she carried a tray into the room. 'I'll put it on this little table beside you and you can eat and drink while I tell you my news.'

'Thank you,' said Flick as just at that moment her tummy rumbled loud enough for everyone to hear.

Margaret laughed. 'That's what happens when you don't eat properly. Tuck in. Now then, you remember I said I'd see what I could find out about Carver and Manners in Sarajevo. I don't suppose you know, Flick, that before I married William I was in the Army?'

Flick's mouth was full of a delicious chicken and salad sandwich so she just shook her head.

'I resigned my commission when I got married but I still keep in contact with several of my old mates, some of whom are quite high up these days, important wheelers and dealers. With a bit of judicious blackmail from days gone by,' Margaret smiled at the memory of past high jinks enjoyed by junior officers, 'I managed to persuade some information from the archives of the Ministry of Defence. I e:mailed them a copy of the photo Andy took of Manners and Carver and struck gold. Manners wasn't Manners then but ex- Paratroop Corporal Frank Donnelly. You were quite right, Felicity. He was a mercenary. He had been discharged from the Army under a cloud no-one will talk about, and then he went out to the Balkans freelance.'

Flick swallowed the last mouthful of her sandwich and took a mouthful of coffee. 'So what was Carver doing there?'

'From what I can gather, he was loosely liaising with the mercenaries. Their intelligence of what was going on was often better and faster than ours so of course we made use of it. When the wheels came off Carver was detailed to bring Donnelly in, but he was long gone. Or so Carver said at the time.'

'What wheels came off, Maggie?' said Westcott.

'There was a nasty business in one of the villages. The whole community wiped out; men, women and even the children, butchered and burned. Certainly bad enough to rate as an atrocity even in all the horror of those days and Donnelly's name was right in the middle of it. He was wanted for questioning, but disappeared before he could be apprehended. When time passed and there was no sign of him it was believed he had been killed, either by the opposition or by his own side who found him an embarrassment. In any event there was no long term search for him. So many dreadful things were happening then. But here we have him under a new name working for his old commander.'

'Commander?' queried Westcott.

'Apparently that's what they called him in the field. I suppose he gave them some kind of orders or suggested battle tactics, although I hardly think mercenaries would need that kind of thing from the Brits.'

'So what exactly was he doing out there?' said Flick.

Margaret shrugged. 'Supposedly the same thing as usual, providing necessary supplies to the international troops. Although now I think he might have been involved in the Road as well.'

'The Road?' Both listeners spoke at once.

'Sorry. I left that bit out. You've heard of the Silk Road from the far coast of China to ancient Rome ? Spices and other goods used these routes as well. While Donnelly was in the Balkans he became involved in a Drug Road running from Russia down to Afghanistan and then back into Europe. The authorities knew he and others were probably involved but, apart from having no jurisdiction over mercenaries, there were other   more pressing matters to take care of – like the vicious bloodshed from different parties trying to wipe each other out.'

'Well done, Margaret,' said Flick. 'You've established a link between drugs and Carver. I must say that makes me feel a lot better.'

'It does?' queried Margaret.

'Yes. You've seen the Major. At first glance I would have thought him rather an ineffectual leader. It bothered me we were thinking of him for these crimes. But now I believe his whole character is just a big act. If he was out in the Balkans mixing with the mercenaries and perhaps dabbling in the drugs there, it tells us he is a much harder type than we gave him credit for. If he had the respect of mercenaries he was no pushover. I've read they're usually a lawless bunch answerable to no-one but the paymaster of the moment.'

Westcott frowned. 'Yes. That's true and I wonder if we've now found how these murders could have been done when Carver had an alibi? If Donnelly, who is now Manners, was recognised by Carver in civvy street, it would mean Carver had a hold over him. He employs Donnelly as his manservant, gives him a new name and job, somewhere safe to live, and in return Donnelly/Manners gives him loyalty strong enough to kill for him. He was a Para so would know how to go about it even without this new knife Flick was telling us about.'

'But where do the drugs come in?' said Margaret.

'I think Carver was probably in on the Drugs Road in the Balkans,' said Flick

Westcott nodded. 'Just what I was going to say. He had the opportunity. He made friends with the mercenaries, especially Donnelly, if that photo can be trusted, and he seems to have plenty of money. We must dig deeper into his finances, Flick.'

'Yes, sir. I've got DS Tom Perkins on it, but he says it is like one of those Chinese puzzles. You get inside one and there are two or three more to discover. But I've never known Tom fail.'

At that moment her mobile rang.

Margaret smiled. 'I expect that's your Mum wondering when you'll be home,' she said. 'It doesn't matter how old you are, Mum's still do the same thing.'

But it wasn't Amanda on the other end. It was Martin Barnes.

'Flick? I thought you'd like to know about the body.'

'Yes, Martin, go on.'

'As you seemed so keen, I gave him a preliminary clean up as soon as we got him back to the morgue. Of course there's still the full autopsy to do and I suppose you'll attend, but I can tell you now, this was no accident.'

'You're sure?'

'Absolutely. Even from first brief examination I can tell you this man was systematically tortured before he died.'

Monday Tuesday

Flick's face was white as she disconnected the call. The lovely sandwich she had eaten threatened to leave her. She swallowed hard and turned to the others.

'That was Martin Barnes. He's had a quick look at the body from the ditch. A man, about thirtyish, who was tortured before death.'

She heard Margaret's quick indrawn breath.

'Who do we know, sir, who might fit that description? Especially after what we've just learned about Sarajevo. Merciless men - mercenaries. It's said they grow hardened to the atrocities they see. A spot of torture on the side would mean nothing to someone like Manners.' She bit her lip. 'If only we'd been able to go in there when we found the mobile,' she burst out. 'We may have been able to save him.'

Margaret moved as though to comfort Flick, but Westcott stayed her with his hand.

'Guessing won't do us any good, Inspector,' he said. 'We don't know for certain Mike was at Marylands. We don't know where he was tortured. We don't even know for certain at this moment that it is his body in the morgue. Facts, Inspector, facts and proof are what we need.'

Flick gulped and cleared her throat. 'Yes, sir,' she said. As he had know it would, Westcott's business-like tone had helped her far more than sympathy and a hug from Margaret could have done. 'I'll be at the autopsy tomorrow morning and let you know as soon as possible what Martin's findings are. We must have Mike's fingerprints on file, but is there any possibility his DNA is stored anywhere? It's just - from what I saw, it might be difficult to get a decent set of prints off the hands.'

'Good thinking. Paddy Murphy will know where Mike was staying undercover. There may be hairs in his comb or hairbrush; something he sweated on or spat into. I'll get onto that right away. If it isn't Mike – dammit, I don't even know if that's his real name, or what his surname is – if it isn't him there'll be nothing lost as, after all this time without checking in, I'm very afraid he's dead. Go home now, Flick. You deserve a stiff drink. If you weren't driving and needing your car in the morning I'd pour you one now.' He smiled. 'You certainly deserve it.'

That night when the house was quiet and everyone was in bed, Flick turned to Andy. 'Hold me tight, And. I've had a hell of a day.'

With his good arm Andy pulled her close and laid her head on his shoulder. 'I knew there was something,' he said. 'But obviously nothing you could discuss in front of the kids or even Amanda.'

Flick told him all they had learned about Manners and Carver.

'Wow!' said Andy quietly. 'Well done. That's really moved you on, hasn't it? But there's something else. A step forward like that wouldn't upset you, pet, so what is it?'

Flick told him their theory that the new corpse was probably the undercover policeman and that he had been tortured by Manners and, or, Carver.

'Bastards!' hissed Andy. 'Bastards! You've got to get them, lass. Even if it's not this Mike guy, it's some other poor sod who probably didn't deserve to die like that. Who would?'

'Don't worry, love. We'll get them. And I shall take great delight in wiping that smarmy look off Major Edward Carver's face.'

In the darkness, Andy smiled. 'That's my lass,' he said. ' I almost feel sorry for him, but not quite. Go for it girl – tomorrow. But in the meantime, forget about them and just think of me.' He pulled her closer into his arms and very satisfactorily emptied her mind of all thoughts of wrongdoers.

Next morning Flick was at her desk early as usual. Andy's love had strengthened her inner defences against the horrors men can do to their fellows. Dave Booth knocked on her door.

'Got a minute, boss?' he said.

'Sure. Come in, Dave. Sit down. Just let me sign this off and I'll be with you.' She finished with the papers on which she'd been working and shoved them into her Out tray. 'Now, how did it go? You, okay? No problems with Customs either end?'

'I'm fine. No problems once I'd got all the right paperwork. I had to hang about over the weekend. It's a bit like here. All the government offices seem to be closed from four o'clock Friday until Monday morning. But your pal, Brigadier van der Velde, Rudi, was great.

When I first heard his rank I thought he was in the Army.'

'No,' said Flick. 'It's just the way Dutch police ranks go. Did he look after you, then?'

'Yes. He steered me to a cheap but decent hotel and then took me out to his house on Sunday. I met his wife and kids – lovely family. They were very kind to me.'

Flick smiled. 'Yes, they're a great bunch.'

'He gave me something for you, and something for Andy.'

'Really? What? Come on, give.'

With a big grin, Booth lifted up the carrier bag he'd placed on the floor and drew out a bottle.

Flick laughed. 'Oh, no! Not the dreaded firewater he brought last time?' She took the bottle and read the label. 'My, my. Andy will be pleased. This is a very superior brandy. So where's my present?'

With a very straight face Dave Booth fished out another parcel and handed it over. A label was attached by a piece of string.

Flick tilted her head to read it aloud. 'To my dear greedy friend,' she read. 'Cheek! Oh, now I know what it is. It's *Boeren Leidsen* my favourite Dutch cheese. The van der Veldes introduced me to it when we stayed with them. It's cheese with a cumin flavour which I love, and yes, I was a greedy pig the first time I had it in Rudi's house. I think I finished the whole thing. Thanks, Dave, I must give Rudi a ring.'

'About Tubby,' said Booth. 'Martin Barnes said he would go through the Dutch autopsy notes today. He spoke as if he thought I would be there.'

'You will,' said Flick and put away Rudi's gifts. 'We both will. I hope you've had a good breakfast, Dave. It's going to be a long day.'

A knock on her door stopped her telling Booth about the new body. It was DS Tom Perkins.

'Before we go into Briefing, boss, I'd like to show you these,' he waved a sheaf of papers in his hand. 'These are copies of what I've dug up. Fascinating trail.' His eyes sparkled with the joy of the chase. 'Quite a challenge.'

'But it didn't defeat you, Tom,' said Flick. 'Alright, come on in and spill the beans.'

Perkins came round her desk and spread the papers in front of her. 'You see it's a matter of hiding the truth behind other truths. A bit like those Russian dolls. You open one and there's another one inside.

'Here we have Speedy Drive and Raymond Hill Motors. Two separate companies, but both are subsidiaries of Traktion Express; as are Green Lane Carriers, which has a warehouse in Putney, and Carriers4U which has a building in Bristol with warehouse and office space. Speedy Drive is registered as a non-trading company, as is Green Lane Carriers. Carriers4U is registered as trading but hasn't shown any trading figures for two years. The building is empty but I managed to find out that mail is still sent there and presumably uplifted as our friendly local bobbies checked for me there is nothing lying on the floor at the entrance.' Tom Perkins beamed at Flick. 'Inter force co-operation is a marvellous thing. And it depends on who you know,' he added.

'All this is very good, Tom,' said Flick, 'but how does it affect our case?'

'I haven't finished. Traktion Express is a subsidiary of Global Unique UK which in turn is a subsidiary of Global Unique International. That seems to be a legitimate importing business, quite low key and bringing in goods for various respectable companies. But they do some trade with South America, some with Afghanistan and some with Russia. Small shipments of different items picked up along the way as makeweight for a complete cargo. But the thing is, with the size of these shipments it wouldn't pay the company to detour to uplift them – unless they were more valuable than it says on the ship's manifest.

'As to the interest it has for us, guess whose name appears on the Board of Global Unique International?'

Flick almost guessed correctly, but then decided to let Tom have his moment of glory. 'Tell me,' she said.

'One Edward Carver, Major, retired' said Perkins.

'Gotcha!' said Booth.

'Well, well,' said Flick. 'Does his name appear on any other company Boards?'

'Yes. He's listed as a shareholder in Raymond Hill Motors. Most of the companies are Limited with only one or two shareholders who are also directors. But I've saved the best 'til last. The aforementioned Major Carver is the major – no pun intended – shareholder in Global Unique International and one of its subsidiaries is none other than Global our neighbourhood bookmakers.'

'Global, of course!' said Flick'

'Yes. The only difference here seems to be that Stan Hatcher, the guy who runs the shop is also a part-owner.

At least he has shares, quite a wodge, and he is named as a director.'

'Now that is interesting,' said Flick. 'He's the only person apart from Manners, and we know his position, who we can trace as having any connection to Carver. Good work, Tom. I bet we'll find he's in on the drugs too. All we have to do now, is to prove it.'

At the morning briefing Flick detailed off her squad to follow up on any sightings of Manners and Carver on the days and at the times when, so far as they knew, the three murders had been committed. 'But try and be discreet,' she urged to general amusement.

'What about Lenny?' called a voice from the back of the room.

'I believe we have firmly established Lenny was killed by Jake Brand and Lawrence Hardy, run down by the white Volkswagen Transporter van. It hardly matters which of them was driving as they are both dead now. So we move on. I want a written and signed statement from Mrs Pargiter as to her husband discussing his security code in Major Carver's presence. DC Short, you'd better take that one. I imagine Frank Pargiter is less likely to bite your head off if he's at home.' There was another ripple of laughter around the room.

Louise Short shrugged and shook her head. She was an exceedingly pretty girl, never taken for a copper and used to her Inspector sending her on jobs where susceptible older men were involved.

'But try and catch Mrs P when hubby's at the golf club.' Flick continued. 'If she's sticky, remind her she has already told me that story and I will not be a happy bunny if she makes me come back and see her again.

'The rest of you have plenty to get on with, I know, so that's it until this evening.'

Tuesday

'You can drive, Dave,' said Flick. 'I want to think.'

There was silence in the car as Booth pulled out of the Police Station car park and made his way through the town, taking the road to the M5.

Once on the motorway Flick decided to share her thoughts. Dave Booth had been working with her for just a year now and she had learned to trust the young Sergeant. He may be a little surprised at confidences like these coming from his boss but he would respect them. Of that she was sure, and it would be no bad thing if he opened up as well and they learned more of each other. Past experience had taught her she needed to know her colleagues well, their strengths and their weaknesses.

'This is a weird case for me,' she began. 'Usually I'm in on a case from the beginning; view the crime scene or at least where the body was found, like yesterday. But with Lenny, Brand and Hardy it was all tidied away before I even knew they had existed.'

'That was down to Tubby,' said Booth.

'Yes, drat him. What was he thinking of, brushing those murders under the carpet?'

'Who knows? And we never will now, of course,' said Booth.

'No. Because of him I feel I haven't got a proper handle on these killings. You know I was with the Met for some years before I came here?' She didn't wait for an answer. It was just a reminder for him. 'I saw some pretty gruesome sights and sometimes one could have said the victims, who were the worst type of baddie, deserved what they got. But I always felt some kind of, not necessarily pity, but a sadness that the human race could do such inhuman things to their species. I felt a connection. Often it spurred me on to bring the perpetrator to justice.

'But with this lot I feel as if I'm a spectator, looking in from the outside. For me it is a very uncomfortable feeling. I'm not used to working this way and I don't like it.'

'I thought we were taught never to get personally involved?' said Booth.

'True when you are talking about *personality* involvement. You can't take sides, as the twins would say,' Flick smiled. 'You have to play fair, not bend the rules because you feel an affinity with someone involved. And I don't mean you should always take your work home with you. It's a good thing to be able to switch off. But not to get *personally* involved would intimate that you didn't care much what the outcome of the investigation was. And that's nonsense. Every good copper should care intensely that wrongdoers are brought to justice and victims are protected.' Flick was quite vehement.

Booth glanced sideways at her. 'Okay, boss. Don't get your knickers in a twist.'

'Wrong answer, Sergeant,' said Flick. 'Just because I may occasionally lighten the mood during an investigation does not mean I don't care passionately about the outcome.

'If you gaze at one object for too long you get tears in your eyes. Your vision is blurred. You need to look at something else and blink your eyes a bit before returning to the original object, then your vision is sharper and you can see clearly. That's what a leaven of humour can do when times are grim or you seem bogged down.'

Booth was quiet for a minute then said. 'You're right. But I've never thought it out. Before you came here, Tubby always sat on any comment or suggestion that didn't come from him or wasn't directly connected to a case. You couldn't say he inspired us. Most of the time we resented him, especially as he was such an idle sod.'

Flick grinned. 'You don't subscribe to '*de mortuis nil nisi bonum*' then?'

Booth shrugged. 'I know that one. Don't speak ill of the dead. But why not if it's true? I'd say it if he was still alive so what difference does it make that he's dead?'

'You have a point.'

'By the way, boss, I tried to trace the broken glass found on the road outside Marylands. The lab had already established it was from the tail light of an old model Jag. Major Carver has an XJ6 1997 model. None of the local garages replaced a tail light for the Major. It would have to have been ordered specially. Modern tail lights aren't made of glass. After I'd drawn a blank as far as Bristol I suddenly remembered the garage in Swindon.'

'Oh, hell,' said Flick. 'You didn't ask them did you?'

'Yes, but what's wrong? Why shouldn't I have got in touch with them?'

Flick sighed. 'It's not your fault. You couldn't have known but we've just discovered the Major is part owner, certainly a shareholder, in that garage. I really hope you haven't spooked him.'

'I don't think so, boss. I can't believe the young girl I spoke to on the telephone is in on anything shady and of course I didn't come right out and ask if they'd mended Major Carver's car. I said I had a Jaguar XK6 and was having difficulty getting parts. Could they help? She said what a coincidence because they never had old Jags in as a rule and here they were dealing with two in the space of a month. Of course I asked her what she meant and we took it from there,' he grinned.

'She thinks it ever such a pretty car,' he said mimicking the kind of voice he'd heard on the telephone. 'She was a very helpful kid and as I spent a bit of time chatting her up afterwards, I don't think she'll remember to tell her boss I even rang. She said I'd get her the sack, so I told her what the eye don't see the heart won't grieve over. She giggled so I guess she got the message.'

Flick smiled. 'Very unscrupulous Sergeant Booth. But you're quite sure it was Carver's Jag? If it is his, you must let Nisbet know he's off the hook. I had him chasing it up.'

'Right. It is Carver's. I got the registration number. Wondered if it was my mate's car, from the same Jag club, don't you know.'

'You were born to be hanged.'

'I've got just one word for you, boss. No it's two actually. Louise Short.'

They both laughed then but it was the last time either of them felt like laughing for the rest of the day.

Booted, gowned and masked, Flick stood beside Booth in the autopsy room of the mortuary at Flax Bourton. He was similarly dressed, a must for attendance at autopsies. Martin Barnes was just about to begin his examination of the body on the steel table in front of them. He had already told them that, after queue-jumping the items recovered from Mike's room, the lab had confirmed the body found in the ditch was that of the brave undercover officer. Overhead harsh neon lights made every tool and surface shine. To Flick it seemed a cruel light. Nothing could hide from it. The poor corpse on the table could keep nothing secret from Martin. Vulnerable was the word in her mind. She shook her head to chase away fanciful thoughts and as she did so caught a movement at the corner of her eye. She half turned to see what it was and realised two more figures had entered the room behind where she and Dave Booth stood. Her eyes widened as, in spite of the enveloping gown, she recognised her boss, DCI Westcott. How long ago, she wondered, was it since he had attended just such an event? It took a moment before she realised his companion was Paddy Murphy, the Drug Squad liaison officer. So they had both believed this victim was the missing under-cover cop, Mike. That was the only reason that could explain their presence here today. And now it had been confirmed.

She turned back to watch as Martin Barnes addressed the microphone that hung just above his head. It would relay his findings and opinions to the machine in the office next door. From it a secretary would type up a report for the files. Flick clenched her teeth, swallowed hard and concentrated on Martin's hands and voice. Beside her she felt Dave Booth stiffen as though standing to attention. People dealt with what they had come to witness in different ways.

As time passed Flick rolled her head from side to side to ease her aching shoulders, bent and straightened her legs and moved her feet to keep the blood flowing. Beside and behind her she was vaguely aware of the others going through the same motions. But nothing could detract from the scene in front of her.

Martin Barnes had established the body was male, about thirty years of age. From head to toe, surface examination revealed some probable animal and marine life damage, post mortem, and multiple abrasions suffered ante mortem. It was Barnes's opinion the victim had been dead for four to six weeks and had been tortured before death.

Behind Flick DCI Westcott interrupted Martin Barnes's monologue. 'Tortured, Mr Barnes? Not beaten up?'

Barnes turned towards the speaker. 'Of course he was beaten as well, hence the abrasions and evidence of heavy bruising. But the torture was specific.' He was standing at the end of the table and lifted a naked foot in each hand. 'There are twenty six bones in each human adult foot. Every single one of them in each of these feet is broken.'

Flick heard her own gasp of horror echoed by those around her as Barnes's words sank in. How? Flick thought the question, but DCI Westcott asked it.

'I believe something like The Boot was used on him,' answered Martin Barnes. 'It was popular in the Middle Ages and I believe frequently used by the Spanish Inquisition. An adjustable iron clamp consisting of two plates roughly in the shape of a shoe or boot enclosed the foot. It could be slowly tightened until, as in this case, the flesh was lacerated and every bone was shattered. You can imagine how painful that was. Pain could be increased by slackening the boot from time to time to allow blood to flow more freely, then tightening it again.'

Flick felt sick. Her vivid imagination could see only too well how this man on the table might have suffered. Beside her the others stayed quiet. There were no more questions.

Martin Barnes gently lowered the broken feet to the table and moved back to the middle of the side opposite his audience. The body lay with its head to his right and its feet to his left.

'Torture was developed into a quite exact science in the Middle Ages,' Barnes went on. 'After all, the object was usually to gain information, not to kill the victim outright.

'In modern times when torture is mentioned, people possibly think of the period of gang warfare when the Kray twins ruthlessly ran the East End of London, or perhaps the sufferings of prisoners of war in the Japanese camps. Like words that cannot be unsaid, so human knowledge is rarely lost. Horrors resurface generation after generation.

'I don't know what this man knew, but whatever it was, someone was determined he should share that knowledge. From the state of his feet, if he eventually succumbed it was not until he had suffered more than most people could ever bear. But it didn't kill him.'

He must have had a heart as strong as an ox, thought Flick. Surely constant agonising pain would eventually be enough to make your heart fail? But apparently not.

Barnes had resumed his minute inspection of the body. She saw him stop, look up, blink several times and then bend over to look more closely at whatever he had noticed on the side of the body away from the watchers. Whatever it was, he wasn't about to share it just now and somehow no-one felt like questioning him.

Barnes moved nearer to the head of the table and reached to the tray of instruments beside him. Flick watched as he opened up the chest and stomach region with the Y shaped cut usual for investigation of the inner body. She watched him nod his head as if satisfied with what he saw. Then he raised his head. Above his mask his eyes moved until they rested on Flick.

'Like buses, Inspector,' he said. 'I'd never seen this kind of damage until a body arrived from Ridminster a month ago, and now we have the same method. A small incision to the side of the torso, just below the ribcage, producing devastating trauma and instant death. From what we have discovered lately I believe I can positively say this man died in the same way as the body from behind the nightclub in Ridminster and, if our friends in Amsterdam are to be believed, I will find the same damage to the body of ex-Inspector Jackson. We are now just about certain the weapon that caused all three deaths is known as a Wasp knife. If you can find me the knife I should be able to prove our theory. It was designed to be used by divers and huntsmen for defence. It has now progressed to being someone's favoured method of execution.'

Tuesday

'The only way we can find out what happened where is to get into Marylands,' said Flick. 'We must get a search warrant, sir, and go in before Manners or Carver gets rid of the knife.'

'There you have the root of the problem,' said Westcott. He was sitting behind the desk in his office at Ridminster station. Flick, Dave Booth and Paddy Murphy were in the room with him. 'And for all we know they will have disposed of all incriminating evidence as well as Mike's body.'

'No, sir,' said Paddy Murphy.

'No?' queried Westcott.

'No, sir,' said Paddy again. 'You're thinking, under torture, Mike told them all we knew about their operation.'

'Well I think we must admit it is a distinct possibility. The man must have been in unimaginable agony for hours on end.'

'But he didn't crack, sir. I know he didn't.'

'I know he was a friend of yours and no-one is denying his bravery, Inspector, but how can you be so sure?'

'Quite simple really, sir. If Mike had spilled the beans there would have been mighty ripples going out to all corners of their operation. But everything is carrying on as normal. The guys we have under observation show no signs of panic or dismay.'

'I see. Yes. I think you're right. There would certainly have been mutterings in the ranks if not downright mutiny with every man jack of them trying to save their own skins. But it's all quiet you say?'

'Absolutely. It's the kind of thing we are always on the watch for in case we have to swoop earlier than planned. So I'm certain, sir, that Mike kept the faith.'

'A good man,' said Westcott.

Once Martin Barnes had completed his autopsy on the undercover police officer, they had had to go through the ritual again with Tubby Jackson's body while Barnes verified the findings of the Amsterdam pathologist. There were no surprises. The small entry wound and massive internal trauma were exactly the same as those found on Mike and also on Jake Brand, the assault victim.

All four police officers were glad to leave the mortuary and took great gulps of fresh air in the car park. Then it was back to Ridminster and the meeting in DCI Westcott's spacious office.

'I don't understand, sir,' said Flick.

'You said Manners or Carver. Who do you want to arrest?

'Both of them,' said Flick with conviction. 'They're in it together up to their necks.'

'I tend to agree with you but, before we can apply for a search warrant for their home, we must have some facts to put before the judge. We have suspicions, but based on what evidence?'

'I saw the matching curtain material used to block up the car window of the supposed suicide,' said Flick.

'And how many other pairs of curtains have been made out of that material?'

'The smashed Jag tail light glass was found at the rear entrance to Marylands, near where Mike's phone was found,' offered Booth. 'I checked and it is possible if you are in the boot of that model to kick out the rear light and push out a mobile phone.'

'And Mrs Tiffin is a very good witness,' added Flick. 'Even though she is blind I would be prepared to call her as an expert in court.'

Westcott raised his eyebrows. 'She obviously impressed you, Inspector. But let's hope it doesn't come to that.'

'Didn't you say Carver mentioned 'F's' to you one morning when he shouldn't have known anything about them?' queried Flick.

'True, but he could have heard it on the street. It had by then been verified those were the drugs the teenagers had taken at their rave, or gig, whatever they called it. Although it was not supposed to be generally known, you can't legislate for idle tongues. It's the "I know something you don't know" syndrome. Even police officers suffer from it.'

'But he also knew the Pargiter's security code. He could have got into the house and the garage to stage the suicide and left undetected,' went on Flick. 'That's another connection with these Wasp knife deaths.'

'How do you work that one out?' said Westcott.

'The Wasp knife victim behind the Phoenix was the driver of the van that ran Lenny down, and the partner of the man dead in the Pargiters' garage,' said Flick. 'Carver had the means to enter the Pargiters' home and it all connects.

'The van belonged to a company in which Carver has an interest and the garage where it was kept is also part owned by him. That was where the Jag taillight was replaced,' she explained.

'Doesn't that smack of guilt?' put in Dave Booth. 'There are plenty of garages nearer that could have ordered a replacement light for him. Swindon's a hell of a long way to go for a tail light.'

'True, but he could always say he preferred to deal with his own people,' said Westcott. He frowned. 'Do we know if the transaction went through the books?'

'Not for definite, sir. But the receptionist knew it had been dealt with. She probably wouldn't have anything to do with the paperwork however so it might have been done on the QT.'

'Indeed, but that's not a hanging offence. Have we anything, anything at all concrete that we can put forward to warrant a search?'

'Manners actually said your wife and I had seen the lot after he showed us the wine cellar at Marylands. But we know that's not true. He was laughing at us, being smug because he was so clever.'

'Do we know for certain he was hiding something?'

'We will soon, sir. Through his contact in the Darts Team Andy is getting a copy of the plans of Marylands without going through any official channels. We should be able to have a look at them tomorrow without alerting Carver,' said Flick.

'Do I want to know how these were obtained?' said Westcott. 'No, I don't think I'll ask,' he answered himself. 'I just want to be sure they will be returned and that no-one will be banging on my door asking what the hell I'm playing at.'

Flick grinned. 'Promise, sir. My Andy's not daft. I'm sure it will be all kosher.'

Until now DI Paddy Murphy had kept quiet. Now he spoke up. 'If Mike was tortured in this place, Marylands, there must have been a hell of a lot of blood, not to mention noise.'

'The cellars were soundproofed originally to use as recording studios,' Westcott explained. 'That accounts for the noise element.'

'Blood isn't that easy to get rid of,' said Murphy. 'No matter what type of cleaner you use there's usually some trace left behind. When we go in, sir, I'd suggest we take a dog. If there's been blood, the dog will tell us and we can take it from there with the lab boys.'

'I note you say "when", Inspector, and not "if",' said Westcott.

'Absolutely, sir. I knew Mike Corbett. He was a brave man and a good friend. I believe you have enough suspicion for a warrant and I know my guv'nor will back you all the way.'

'Good,' said Westcott. It now only remains for us to examine the plans of Marylands. It would be useful if we could find the entrance and make sure there isn't another one through which Carver, or Manners could escape.

Once I am sure they have a concealed room there DS Booth can write up the application form for the magistrate's clerk. I don't want anything to go outside the people in this room. As we'll be looking for proofs of both drugs and murder, we'll go in under a Section 8, Serious Crime Warrant. And, please God, we'll find what we need,' he added.

It was late by the time Flick got home. Amanda and the twins were in bed. Andy sat at the kitchen table, a glass of beer at his side and his head bent over a large sheet of paper spread out in front of him. He looked up as Flick came in.

'Hello, pet. Had a bad day? You look washed out.'

Flick smiled. 'Thank you, kind sir,' she said. 'You really know how to make a girl feel good.' She put a hand on his shoulder, kissed the top of his head and leaned over the table. 'What have you got there?'

Andy got up and gave her his chair. 'Here, you sit down and I'll fetch you something to eat. Amanda left a casserole in the oven on low. While I dish some up for you, cast your eyes over this plan of Marylands' cellars. See what you think.'

'You got it already. Well done, And.' In spite of her tiredness Flick felt a surge of energy at the thought of being able to prove her conviction there was a hidden room at Marylands. 'Thanks,' she said as Andy put a glass of wine beside her hand.

'Now then, let's see. Here's the lift Margaret and I came down in. And this large area is the internal cellar with the divisions for storage. They held the wood and the summer garden furniture and the decorating stuff.

The curtain was with that lot in this bay here, I think,' Flick pointed with her finger, but Andy was busy serving up a delicious smelling stew. As she was really talking to herself, Flick didn't wait for a response.

'They're actually marked here so must have been built of brick, then plastered over and painted when the house was complete. It's all white down there now.

'Here's the dividing wall and opposite is the big outside door where Manners said the original owners brought in their large equipment. So far, so good. But that's set nearer the outside wall on what must be the front of the house. So this area to the left where we went into the wine cellar, should take up the whole of the rest of the floor space, equal to the internal cellar, but it doesn't. According to this plan there should be two rooms there with a connecting door. I wonder how we missed that?'

'Well try wondering after you've got your laughing gear round this little lot,' said Andy. He pushed the plans aside and laid a mouth-watering plate of food in front of Flick. She realised she was starving and tried to remember when she had last eaten. She and Dave Booth had each grabbed a wrapped sandwich from a garage forecourt shop on the way back from Flax Bourton. They'd eaten on the journey and that was all she'd had since breakfast. No wonder she felt so empty.

Andy busied himself tidying up while Flick demolished the plateful of stew. Then he put a dish of apple pie and custard in its place and refilled her wine glass. 'You'll think better with that lot inside you,' he said. 'I have the plans until next Monday evening when I have to return

311

them. So you'd better make copies if you want your boss to study them. Feeling better?' he added as Flick pushed her empty dish way.

'Great. Thanks. I hadn't realised how hungry I was. How did you get hold of the plans? Westcott doesn't want to know in case it's illegal,' she grinned.

Andy laughed. 'No I don't think it's illegal. It may possibly be unethical but I don't really see why. You know Tommy Stebbins's brother helped to build Marylands? Well, Tommy asked him about plans and it appears the brother is a pal of the architect who obviously kept a copy of the plans on file. He agreed to let Tommy have a look at them and show his granddaughter, who is a big fan of the original owners, the pop stars.'

'You devious lot. And Tommy was OK with all this?'

'Tickled pink to be helping the rozzers for a change – and without asking any awkward questions. I think Tommy may have been a bit of a poacher in his younger days but, like him, I'm asking no questions. Now let's see what you've got.'

As they poured over the large sheets spread out in front of them Flick traced the route she, Margaret, and Manners had taken on the night of the cocktail party. 'This one is the first floor. Here's the bathroom I used, and at this end are the paintings. The photo of Carver with Manners is just on this wall not far from the bathroom. From there we took the lift down to the basement to see the cellars. But let's have a look at the ground floor.'

Andy folded the sheet they had just been looking at and spread out another one. 'Here we are.' He twisted it round on the table. 'I think that's the front door, isn't it? The conservatory should be jutting out from this wall, but there's nothing there.'

'So does that mean it was added on by Major Carver, I wonder,' said Flick. 'Or was it an afterthought by the original owners? You might ask Tommy to find out from his brother, Andy.'

'Right, but it really doesn't matter for our purposes. If it's jutting out then it won't be above the cellars.'

'You're right, but I'd still like to know. Now we'll concentrate on the ground floor plan and try to marry it with the cellars. We came in through the front door and crossed the hall. That's right,' Flick pointed to the plan, 'because here is the staircase that goes up to the first landing. And before that on the right there is a cloakroom and small room for whatever. We didn't actually see that one. On the left of the front door this must be the dining room. I do remember seeing the corner of a sideboard in there as we passed.'

'Yes and behind that must be the kitchen and store rooms, utility room here, and then a door leading into the dining room and another into the sitting room. That was the one with the carpet on the floor,' said Andy.

'So far so good,' said Flick. 'Now we know the conservatory doesn't lead anywhere but to the garden so what's on the other side of the sitting room from the kitchen?'

'Hang on, we've missed a door here, but it only seems to go into a cupboard, too big for coats I would think and no access except from the hall.'

'Where? Oh, I see. It's between the dining room and the kitchen. I know what it is, And. It's the lift,' said Flick, her eyes shining. 'We walked up the stairs, took the lift to the cellars and then walked back up to the hall, so I never realised the lift door on the ground floor was there. That's great. It will give us a marker for comparing the cellars to the ground floor plan.'

'Here it is,' said Andy. 'If we lay them side by side the right way up we can compare. Here's the lift so this must be the front.' He aligned the two sheets. 'Now you can see those big doors are next to the side of the house. The land must slope down there or else it's been cut away to give access by the road that leads out through the grounds to the rear.'

'How come we didn't see that from the conservatory on Saturday? I looked out of the windows.'

'Well think back. What was growing in the garden to the left hand side?'

Flick frowned. 'There was a lawn and then a sort of shrubbery, all green.' She frowned. 'I didn't see any coloured flowers at all. How odd. Then behind the shrubs there were trees, so I suppose they hid the access road to the cellars.'

'That'd be right. After all you don't want to sit in your sitting room or conservatory and watch the coal being delivered, do you?'

Flick smiled. 'Logs in their case. Nice log-burning fire in the sitting room. So where are we? Out of the lift into the inner cellar. Okay. There are the divisions for the stores. Then across to the communicating door here and you see the outer doors are almost in front of you across this empty space. But that gives you a huge area to the right.   On the ground floor that would equal some of the sitting room and that other room next to it which is quite big.   I think I heard Carver talk about his study looking out onto the garden, so I bet that's what it is. His little sanctum. What's in the cellars here, Andy?'

'Quite a wide room leading off the main area.'

'That'll be the wine store we saw.'

'But it doesn't take up half of the space left. There's an entrance here to the rest of the space which seems to be divided into four. Not enormous rooms but I imagine big enough for practising in and then they recorded back in the bigger room in what is now the wine cellar.'

'I think you're right. I couldn't tell if it was sound proofed or not as the shelves reached right up to the ceiling on all sides except the door where we came in,' said Flick. 'Okay, so there's a door from the wine cellar into the part that's divided.   But we didn't see one so does that mean it's closed up and sealed behind the wine racks so they don't use it?   Or do you think the wine racks are moveable so they could swing out a section to give access to a door?'

'In theory, why not?' said Andy. 'But I don't think it would do the wine much good to be shoogled about every time anyone wanted to go into the other cellar. And as Carver is supposed to be a real wine snob I can't see them going for that option.'

'No,' agreed Flick. 'I think you're right. Is there anything else marked on the plan?' She peered at the drawing, her forehead wrinkled with concentration. 'What do these small marks here mean, Andy?'

'Where? Let's see.' He looked where Flick was pointing then laughed. 'She's done it. By Jove, she's done it,' he quoted.

'What are you on about?' demanded his loving wife.

'It's from a show,' said Andy.

'I know where it's from, but what have I done?'

'You've found the entrance to the hidden room.'

'How? Where?'

'Those marks you looked at mean there's a staircase there. Look at the first floor plan. You see? It's much bigger there and they are properly drawn, but it means the same thing. And they can only lead to one place. Carver's study. Have you ever been in there?'

'No. It wasn't included in our tour. But the adjoining wall in the sitting room is covered with bookcases so if the same thing is on the study side you could fit a small staircase in the depth provided by the two lots of shelving. Tomorrow morning, as soon as the library opens, I'll make copies of these plans for Westcott and then return them to you. What shift are you on?'

Flick went to bed that night happier than she had been for a long time. At last there was an end in sight. Carver and his henchman would be brought to book. A drug ring could be smashed and a brave undercover officer avenged.

Thursday

On Thursday morning the same team assembled in DCI Westcott's office.

The previous day had passed in frantic activity. Westcott had studied the copied plans and agreed there was a hidden room. Booth had written up the warrant application; got it signed off by an inspector and delivered it to the magistrate's clerk. The clerk would decide to which magistrate he would present it. Meanwhile Flick, and Dave Booth, had completed the tedious but necessary job of filling in the paperwork on all they had found so far. Paddy Murphy had gone to lay all the facts in front of his boss in the Drugs Squad. Now they were assembled to sort out their plan of attack.

'I'll have the warrant for Marylands by noon,' Westcott said. 'Simultaneous raids will take place at the Swindon Garage; the warehouse and office in Putney; the warehouse in Bristol; and the Global bookies here. HM Customs will seize the latest shipment for GUI on board their vessel due to dock at 1230 hours in Liverpool. Hopefully with everything happening at once there will be no time for one site to warn another of the raids. From the undercover surveillance DI Murphy and his team have been conducting over the last few months we know most of the main players. The various buildings are being watched as we speak. If any person of interest is not on the premises when Zero hour comes then his, or

317

her, home and usual haunts will also be visited. We've worked through the night on this one to ensure everyone is clued up.' Westcott's piercing gaze moved from one to the other around the room. 'I don't want any cock-ups,' he said. 'Is that understood?'

There was a murmured 'Yes, sir,' as everyone acknowledged the seriousness of the situation.

Westcott beckoned them to come closer to his desk on which the copied plans of Marylands were spread out. 'Inspector Fraser, you will accompany uniformed officers to Marylands.'

Flick's eyes opened wide. 'But don't you want to be in at the death, sir? I thought you would be the officer in charge.'

Westcott smiled briefly. 'And dearly I would enjoy it, Inspector, but I hardly feel it is appropriate as I am on first name terms with one of the accused and have played golf with him on several occasions. I shall accompany the team that will visit the bookie's, but will be in touch by radio at all times.'

'Yes, sir,' said Flick and tried to hide her elation at being in charge of the raid at Marylands. What a stroke of luck the boss was a member of the same golf club as Carver.

Westcott continued. 'With you will go a sniffer dog. The uniforms will be stationed at the front and rear gates of Marylands; also at the back door of the house and the French windows from the conservatory. A uniform will wait at the front door with the dog and its handler until the warrant has been delivered. DS Booth and a further uniform will accompany you into the house initially. No firearms have been authorised but I want everyone to remember this man has been responsible for five deaths that we know of so far. It may be from our findings and the forensics there will be others also. We are dealing with a very dangerous man and let no-one forget it.' He looked round the assembled company again. 'Watch out for yourselves and each other at all times.'

Flick frowned. What was the matter with her? Why didn't she feel elated over the coming action? Something was niggling at her mind. What had she heard recently? "If something doesn't feel right, it probably isn't." Yes. That was it. But why didn't this feel right? They had all the info and some of the proofs. This raid was the chance to knit them all together, but . . .

'So we'll have a briefing of all concerned in thirty minutes.' Westcott's voice broke into Flick's thoughts. 'Any questions?' he concluded, and receiving no answer dismissed them with a nod. 'Right then, off you go.'

Promptly at twelve thirty Flick rang the bell of Marylands's front door. It was opened of course by Manners. His bland face gave nothing away even though the two uniformed officers and the dog with his handler were standing on the drive behind Flick and Dave Booth.

'Please take us to Major Carver,' said Flick.

Manners frowned slightly. A movement of his facial arrangement that passed so quickly Flick might have thought she imagined it. But inwardly she exulted in the knowledge the man in front of her had been surprised at the firm tone of her voice and her impressive back-up. Prior to today he had only heard her being a fluffy-headed lightweight. Time for the real Inspector Fraser to step up to the mark.

Manners inclined his head. 'Please follow me, Inspector,' he said.

Flick fell in behind Manners with Booth behind her and a uniform bringing up the rear. The other officer stayed at the front door. They crossed the polished floor of the impressive hall. The grey form of Manners seemed almost invisible against the sparkle and beauty all around them. His feet made no sound on the parquet while those who followed him sounded rough and out of place in such a gracious setting. In single file they traversed the thick carpet of the sitting room and halted momentarily at the door let into the solid wall of bookshelves to their right.

Manners tapped lightly on the panels, waited a moment then opened it and gestured for Flick to precede him into the room. She smiled. 'No. After you, Manners, if you please.'

One moment he hesitated. Flick tensed, ready to bar his way to freedom, but he inclined his head again – picture of the demure servant who knows his place – and moved to stand inside the room just beyond the door. Something made Flick hand the Warrant to Booth as she moved to Manners's side. She nodded to Dave to go ahead. He stepped forward to stand nearer to Carver. Manners moved forward too, as did Flick. The uniform stayed in the doorway.

As Booth announced the formal search warrant and held it out to Carver, Flick watched the Major's face. His eyes flickered. He looked puzzled, then annoyed and finally disbelieving as he took in its meaning. He turned to his servant, 'Manners?' he said.

The truth came to Flick in one second. It explained everything. Mike hadn't said "lined the drone" but "behind the throne". He was trying to leave a last message that Manners was the power behind the throne and Carver was his front man. Was that why Mike had kicked out the rear light of the Jag and pushed out the phone? He must have realised he'd never get out of Manners's clutches alive, but was determined to complete his mission and bring Manners to justice. As these thoughts flashed through Flick's mind Manners stepped forward.

'It's alright, sir. Don't worry,' he said as he stood beside Edward Carver. He put his left hand up to the Major's cheek. 'Everything's going to be alright, my love. I promise,' he said; pulled Carver's face towards him and kissed him full on the mouth.

Flick had not been expecting that, but some intuition made her dart forward even as Manners right arm, hidden until now, moved just once. The Major's body sagged. Flick reached to support him as Booth sprang forward to grapple with Manners. The man giggled as he withdrew the knife from Carver's body. At the manic sound the hairs on the back of Flick's neck crisped. In a freeze-frame moment she looked up into Manners's eyes. They were blank, an empty void, no expression no soul. She shivered and the spell was broken. Frantically Flick laid Carver down, felt for a pulse and prepared to administer CPR.

Manners shook his head. 'A waste of time. My dear Edward is gone. I'm afraid he would have been unable to stand up to you, Inspector. And he would have hated prison. So you see it's better this way.'

Flick stood up.

'Clive Manners, I am arresting you for the murder of Edward Carver.' She completed the words used to charge a suspect, but as she heard her own voice reciting the well-know formula she was uneasy. Something wasn't right. The man gave no trouble, no sign, but stood quietly looking at the body of his former lover.

'Do you understand the charge?' she finished.

'Of course, Inspector, you must arrest me,' said Manners. He looked at her as he spoke and now there was a gleam of mockery in his eyes.

'And as an accomplice in the distribution of drugs in this area.'

'Of course, with us being so close,' he smirked, 'you would think I was an accomplice. Dear me. If I'd only known earlier, perhaps I could have stopped him.'

Flick frowned. What was the man playing at?

'You're in it up to your neck,' she said.

'Prove it, Inspector. I'm sure you can't find anyone who can link me with whatever dear Edward was doing.'

He's probably right, thought Flick, because he's murdered them all. This was what had bothered her all along. She couldn't see Carver as a cold-blooded killer, but Manners? Yes, indeed. And surely there must be some way to make it stick?

'And that is just the beginning,' she went on. 'Once this search has unearthed the evidence, as I know it will,' she emphasised, 'there will be additional charges.'

'Really, Inspector? But I only learned about the dreadful things Edward had done this morning.'

'And I suppose you didn't think about phoning the police?' Flick's sarcasm was wasted on the man in front of her.

'We were in bed at the time, Inspector. Together,' Manners explained. The gleam of malicious amusement in his eyes was more pronounced.

The bastard is actually enjoying this, thought Flick. What the hell is going on?

'I couldn't believe what I was hearing,' continued Manners, 'and so I searched for the weapon. I'd only just found it when you so fortuitously arrived.'

Flick couldn't believe her ears. 'And that's your defence?' she said.

Manners opened his eyes wide. 'Don't you think it will work, Inspector? Me, the heartbroken lover, appalled at Edward's actions but unable to let my soul mate suffer in prison. A sympathetic jury and a good Brief – and I assure you, Inspector, my Brief will be very, very good.' He shrugged. 'A few years at Her Majesty's pleasure in a cosy cell with all mod cons. And then, of course, when I get out the tabloids will be begging for my story and perhaps a book? What do you think, Inspector? Is that a bit too tacky in memory of my beloved Edward?'

Flick wanted to hit him. The monster she was sure had murdered four people, one of them right in front of her, was actually boasting about how he intended to get away with it. And the trouble was he might just do it.

Flick called to the uniform at the door to take Manners away.

As he passed her he smiled at her again. 'Don't take it to heart, Inspector. You played your part well, but dear

Edward was never any good at keeping secrets and I have so many. Of course, perhaps you didn't know I used to be a Boy Scout?'

Flick clenched her fists determined not to give him the satisfaction of a reaction.

Once Manners had been accompanied out of the room she relaxed. What had that meant? Manners, a Boy Scout? If it wasn't a sickening thought it would be laughable. Boy Scout? Their motto was "Be Prepared". Did that mean Manners had all along realised this day could come and had planned to sacrifice his lover to secure his own future? She thought of the torture of Mike Corbett. Would a man who could do that flinch from betraying his nearest and dearest? Had Carver known he was expendable? Surely not? But imagining something and the reality were so far apart he may have colluded in the preparation of Manners's protection without actually believing it would ever come to anything? They would never know now – unless, of course, Manners put it all in his book.

Loose ends

'Could he get away with it, sir?' Flick asked DCI Westcott in his office. It was a week to the day from Manners's arrest.

Westcott was disgusted. 'From what I've heard,' he said, 'he will probably only be tried for Carver's death. There were very few traces of Manners in the hidden cellar where the blood was located - Mike Corbett's blood. Manners can claim whatever was found of him was there from the times he had entered the room on his usual duties. After all they have lived there for ten years.

'He'll give it mitigating circumstances and plenty of sob stuff – the man's a consummate actor. He must be to have kept the persona of Manners all these years when we know his true character. Then all he'll need is an ultra PC judge and I doubt he'll get much more than a virtual slap on the wrist.' Westcott shook his head. 'He'll do his sentence in a cushy prison with his own room, his own TV, access to a gym and a library, three good meals a day and the best of medical attention. I bet some of our pensioners would like such a life of comfort and security. With time off for good behaviour he'll be out in a few years.'

'But we know he did it,' protested Flick. 'All those people dead, sir.'

'Yes. We do. But there's no link to him anywhere. His name doesn't appear in connection with any of the companies, not even a note in his handwriting. Everything is Carver, Carver, Carver.' Westcott thrust his hand through his hair in frustration.

'DI Murphy reported all the Drug Squad raids were successfully completed. Very little in paperwork in any place except the offices of Global Unique International and that covered the legitimate transactions. The stock certificates, deeds for the various companies etc. found at Marylands were all in Carver's name. There was money in the safe. One £50 note was torn and the serial number I was given matches the scrap found in Tubby's envelope.' Westcott paused for a moment and gazed out of the window.

Was he seeing a younger, happier, cleaner Tubby there? Flick wondered.

'Of course it still doesn't prove Manners went to Amsterdam to kill Tubby Jackson and recover the money,' Westcott went on. 'It could have been Carver, even though we found another passport with Manners's photograph in it over a different name. That's hardly a hanging offence. We can't prove he has ever used it. But HM Customs are very hopeful of the seizure at the docks of GUI's latest shipment from Afghanistan. And in the Green Lane warehouse in Putney there is definite evidence of drug manufacture as well as drug trace in Marylands' cellars. Our own Stan Hatcher from the bookie's is apparently singing like the proverbial. He'll own up to receiving shipments of drugs and passing them on, but it's all about Carver. We know the white van distributed all over the South and West of England. Everything he tells us will be followed up. I think we can deserve a pat on the back for our part in smashing a well organised drugs ring. We just can't pin anything on Manners.'

Flick considered for a moment. 'Manners, who is actually former Para Corporal Frank Donnelly.' Slowly she started to smile. 'May I borrow your computer a minute, sir?' she said.

Westcott frowned. 'What for? Don't bother, just go ahead if you think it will help.'

Flick sat at his desk and quickly Googled the information she wanted. 'Did you know, sir, that according to the United Nations Convention of 1968 there is no statute of limitations on war crimes? The international courts have been convicting war criminals since the Second World War. For his actions in the Bosnian conflict Milosevic was finally sentenced to 29 years imprisonment.'

Westcott shook his head. 'Where are you going with all this, Flick?'

She smiled. 'The best is yet to come, sir. Milosevic is serving his sentence in Estonia. Now do you think their prisons are as comfy as ours?'

Westcott gazed at her. 'You're a miracle, girl,' he said, 'a bloody, brilliant miracle.'

Flick laughed, then looked thoughtful. 'Manners would do a runner if he got half a chance, sir. We know how canny he is. He could just disappear and assume a new persona. And I wouldn't put it past some sympathetic judge to give the grieving lover a break. Just like Manners said. No apparent danger to the general public. A short sentence with time off for good behaviour. Do you know anyone we could feed our information to sharpish so he doesn't wriggle out of custody before the War Crimes people can pick him up?'

'No, I don't,' he said. 'But I know a woman who does.' He reached for his telephone and dialled. 'We'll get the bastard yet, Flick.'

As the telephone was answered at the other end he grinned. 'Now then, Margaret?' he said. 'About these influential pals of yours at the Ministry of Defence . . .'

Finale

Clive Manners gazed up at the clear blue sky. He was as free as the birds soaring above him. He had waited a long time in the courthouse until finally all the reporters and gawping passers-by had gone. The street was virtually empty.

He allowed his mouth to twitch in a smug smile. He'd done it. He had never doubted he would. He had played the grief-stricken lover to perfection. One woman on the jury had even dabbed her eyes as he allowed his voice to hitch on a half-sob when he told how betrayed he felt by his erstwhile love – how appalled he had been to discover to what depths the upright Major had sunk. Silly bitch!

He would miss dear Edward. They had been good together. But Edward could never have withstood interrogation, even by the gentle methods of a British Police Force. It had always been on the cards that, as the weakest link, he would have to go in such a situation. That was why all roads led to Edward. Some over-zealous 'plod' had even traced Edward's involvement in obtaining Manners's false passports. But even there they couldn't unpick Manners's careful planning. Thinking ahead. That was the answer. He'd always done it and the proof of success was his present freedom.

Now all he had to do was disappear. All plans had been made while he was awaiting the start of the trial.

No sense in going away before he had cleared the Manners name. He didn't want to start a man-hunt unnecessarily.

He smiled, went down the courthouse steps to the pavement, turned right and headed for the railway station. What was that pop song about? A ticket to ride? Well he was going to buy a ticket to hide. Goodbye Manners. Hello . . .

His pleasant thoughts were interrupted by a hand on his upper arm.

'Excuse me, sir,' said a man on his left.

As Manners turned to speak to the stranger his other arm was taken.

'Let us just keep walking,' said the newcomer quietly. His accent was not English. The two men fell into step with Manners. He tensed to make a break for it. Their grips on his biceps tightened. A short way ahead of him a man stepped out from a doorway. He stood facing the oncoming trio. Like the other two he was inconspicuously dressed in a neat suit, sober tie, and lightweight, unbuttoned, three-quarter length overcoat. Manners twisted his head to look behind. The fourth man followed them a few paces away. The trap was sprung.

'Just keep walking please, Corporal Donnelly, sir,' said the first man. 'It won't be long now.'

For the first time in his life Manners was afraid. He was very afraid.

Acknowledgements

I should like to thank Detective Chief Inspector Richard Kelvey of Avon and Somerset Police and his staff for technical assistance in the writing of Murders like Pyramids. Truly special thanks go to Detective Constable Darren Lipscomb for his tireless patience in answering so many questions and for reading the finished proof. I thank my friends and colleagues in Ulverston Writers for useful criticism and again Dr Peggy Savage for following the construction of this story, pointing out my errors and proof reading. Grateful thanks to Graham Troth for his technical expertise and of course as always my thanks to Alick for his constant faith and support.

www.lulu.com/spotlight/4booklovers